one more wish

by ROBIN JONES GUNN

Christy & Todd

THE MARRIED YEARS

BOOK 3

ISBN 978-0-9828772-7-2

Scripture quoted from THE HOLY BIBLE, NEW INTERNATIONAL VERSION®, NIV®. Copyright © 1973, 1978, 1984, 2011 by Biblica, Inc.™ Used by permission of Zondervan. All rights reserved worldwide. www.zondervan.com. The "NIV"and "New International Version" are trademarks registered in the United States Patent and Trademark Office by Biblica, Inc.™ Also quoted is the ESV® Bible (The Holy Bible, English Standard Version®), copyright © 2001 by Crossway, a publishing ministry of Good News Publishers. Used by permission. All rights reserved.

Brief excerpt from *Peter Pan* by J. M. Barrie. Copyright © 1911

Published by Robin's Nest Productions, Inc.
P.O. Box 2092, Kahului, HI 96733

Edited by Janet Kobobel Grant and Julee Schwarburg
Cover Images by Jenna Michelle Photography
Cover and interior design by Taylor Smith, Ringger Design, Nicolas Ace Wiinikka, and Ken Raney

Printed in the United States of America by Believers Press
Bloomington, Minnesota 55438

*"I will wait for the LORD, my whole being waits,
and in his word I put my hope."*

~ Psalm 130:5, NLT

one

*C*hristy closed her eyes.

"Go ahead," Todd said. "Make a wish."

Maui. I wish Todd and I could go to Maui.

Returning to Maui had been a secret hope ever since Todd and she had gone there for their honeymoon more than four years ago. Now that her aunt and uncle were planning a trip for the fall, Maui had been on her mind.

Christy opened her eyes, took a quick breath, and victoriously blew out all the candles. The circle of friends gathered around the kitchen counter cheered.

"Wait till you taste this carrot cake." Doug pulled out the tiny candles so his wife could cut slices for everyone. "It's gotta be Tracy's best recipe so far. Not that I want her to stop experimenting, since I'm her official taste tester."

Todd slipped his arm around Christy's waist and leaned close to murmur into her long nutmeg-brown hair, "So, what did you wish for?"

"I can't tell you," she said playfully. "If I do, it won't come true."

"I think we can all guess what she wished for." Tracy put

down the cake knife and used both hands to shape an invisible bubble in front of her belly.

A baby. Christy's heart did a little flutter. *Oh yes, please. May this be the year!*

"Light the candles again," Christy said. "I need to make one more wish."

"Too late," Doug said. "The cake has already been cut. Guess we have to eat it. You first, Christy. Go for it."

"If you didn't wish for a baby," Tracy said, "then what did you wish for? Now I want to know, too."

A nervous twinge made Christy's stomach tighten. *I'm not ready to have a baby. Why did I just say that I wanted to make one more wish?*

She dodged her petite friend's question and pulled a gallon of milk from the refrigerator. "Todd, could you grab some more paper cups?"

The teens gathered in her kitchen were local beach kids who showed up each week for the Friday Night God Lovers Gathering. Christy was eager to move the focus off of any possible discussion about when Todd and she should start having babies. She was glad when Tracy held out the first slice of birthday cake.

"Mmm." Christy nodded her approval. "Doug's right. This is your best cake ever."

One of the girls stuck forks into the slices as quickly as Tracy plated them. The gang helped themselves and headed back into the living room or out onto the front deck.

Sidling up to Christy, Todd gave her a familiar chin-up nod. She read the signal and offered her beach-boy husband a bite of her cake. His grown-out, sun-bleached hair fell across his forehead as he leaned in closer for a second bite.

"Hey, Mr. Moocher," Christy teased, pulling her plate away from him. "You better get your own piece. I have plans for the rest of this one."

"Here you go." Tracy held out a big slice for Todd. "Mooch no more."

Doug eyed Todd's piece of cake. "If you have another piece that size, I'll find a good home for it."

"I bet you will." Tracy grinned and elbowed her husband's stomach. She cut him a large slice, and he leaned over and kissed her on the side of her head.

"You should be the one getting the bonus piece," Doug said. "Now that you're eating for two."

Christy paused in midbite. "What did you just say?"

Doug stuck his fork in his mouth, but it might as well have been his foot by the look of exasperation Tracy gave him.

"You didn't tell Christy already?"

No one else from the group was still in the kitchen so it was unlikely anyone besides Christy and Todd had heard Doug's comment. That didn't seem to bring much comfort to Tracy.

"No, remember? I told you I wanted to wait. Tonight was supposed to be all about Christy and her birthday."

"Sorry, Trace. I thought you had told her."

Christy scooted around to the other side of the counter and wrapped her arms around her friend. "I'll share my birthday celebration with you and your good news anytime. Congratulations!"

Todd joined Christy's expression of cheer by giving Doug a shoulder-bump sort of handshake and hug while both men were balancing their cake plates in their free hands. "That's great news, man. Happy for you guys."

"I think it's pretty awesome." Doug wrapped his arm around his blushing wife.

"I just want to be sure before we tell people. We haven't been to the doctor yet. I'll feel better about announcing it after we see him." Tracy lowered her voice and looked at Christy. "But if I am pregnant, I hope you get pregnant soon, too. It would be so fun to have babies close together."

Christy smiled and felt the nervous clenching sensation return. She glanced at Todd to see his response to the thought of their having a baby in the near future.

"I wouldn't mind that," he said. "Couple more little grommets around here would be great."

One of the teen girls came into the kitchen and tossed a stack of emptied plates into the trash. "Did you just say we need more grommets here?"

Todd nodded and took another bite of cake.

"No! We need more older guys. Not more young surfer boys who can't even drive yet. Don't you know any college guys you could invite?"

"College guys?" Tracy questioned. "Lindee, aren't you going to be a sophomore this year?"

"Yes, but I like older guys. That's normal, right?" Broad-shouldered Lindee towered over petite Tracy. Her dark, thick eyebrows were her most noticeable feature and seemed to cave in at the top of her long nose, which caused her to appear angry much of the time.

"So, are you saying you think our dating service skills are lacking here on Friday nights?" Doug's good-natured personality served him well when it came to being around teens like Lindee. Secretly, Christy felt intimidated by her.

Lindee put her hand on her hip. "Since you put it that way, yes. I mean, seriously. Come on, you guys. Don't you remember what it was like when you were our age? You've gotta help us out here."

Doug gave her a look of fake shock. "And here I thought all this time that you were coming because of the great Bible teaching and awesome worship."

"Well, yeah, I know that's the main thing. But ever since Rick and Nicole got married and moved to New York none of Rick's friends has been coming anymore."

Todd gave a shrug. "We go with what we've got. This is what we've got. At least for now."

"It could change," Tracy said. "Start praying that more quality guys start coming."

Lindee looked doubtful.

"Better than that," Tracy added. "Start praying for your future husband. Christy and I did."

Lindee studied Todd and then turned her focus on Doug as if deciding whether they represented a worthwhile answer to prayer. She seemed undecided. "Neither of you guys have tattoos, do you? I want to find a nice guy who has tattoos and a motorcycle and likes cats."

"In that case," Doug said, "we should all start praying for the poor guy right now."

Christy wanted to laugh. Instead she licked the last bit of cream cheese frosting from her fork so her expression wouldn't give away her thoughts.

"You guys are making fun of me."

"No," Doug said. "I just use every opportunity I can to make fun of cats."

"You're mean." She gave Doug a scowl, turned, and walked away with an awkward thumping of her feet.

The four friends exchanged bemused glances.

"You know, she has a valid point about how this group has changed," Tracy said. "It feels different now that we don't have other people here that are our ages. We started with mostly twenty-somethings and now it's all teens."

Todd repeated his line about going with what they had, and Doug continued his teasing mode by adding, "Are you saying the three of us aren't fun enough for you on a Friday night?"

"I love you guys. You know that. I guess I just miss the conversations I used to have with other peers here on Friday nights." Tracy blinked behind her glasses. "It's the Mommy Syndrome, I think. There's too much toddler time going on in my life right now."

"Why don't we meet up this week at Julia Ann's?" Christy suggested.

"Yeah, for one of your girly tea parties." Doug straightened up and squared his broad shoulders so that he stood taller than the rest of them. "Weren't you just saying the other day how much you missed doing that with Christy?"

Christy wasn't sure when she could fit in a leisurely morning sipping tea lattes with Tracy. But it seemed like a good idea to suggest it, and Doug certainly supported the idea.

"Yes. I'd love that," Tracy said. "Maybe we could go on Tuesday since that's your official birthday."

"Sure, Tuesday would be great."

"Do you think they'll invite us?" Doug raised his pinky finger and pretended to be sipping tea.

"Not a chance," Todd said. "And I'm thinkin' it's better that way."

"Definitely," Tracy chirped.

The guys tossed their empty cake plates in the trash and headed out to the front deck. Typically they sat around the fire pit to play guitars with a few other guys for an hour or so while the rest of the teens dispersed.

Tracy cleared the counter. "I think I'm going to go. I'm really tired. I'll make sure my mom can watch Daniel on Tuesday so we can meet at Julie Ann's. What time works for you?"

"We would have to meet at seven when it opens. And I'll have to leave at eight forty-five to get to work. I hope that gives us enough time to catch up, but it's better than waiting until we have more open space on our calendars."

"I don't know how you've kept up with your work schedule this summer now that you're working Saturdays at the spa. Are you still glad you took on a second job?"

Christy nodded, hoping she looked convincing. "I like the spa a lot more than I like working at the Balboa Treasure Chest. I think I'm burned out on working retail in book shops and gift shops."

"I'd be burned out on working six days a week."

"It's not that bad. And, as you know, we need the money."

"I understand that, believe me."

"Did Doug hear anything yet about his raise?"

Tracy shook her head. "Does Todd have another construction job lined up when this one ends?"

"No, not yet."

The two friends exchanged mutually sympathetic glances. They had shared plenty of heart-to-heart conversations over the past few years about the challenges of being a young married couple living in expensive Newport Beach, California. The financial pressure was like a hungry bulldog on a frayed leash.

"I'll be praying for Todd and his job situation."

"And I'll be praying about Doug's raise."

"Thanks." Tracy reached for her purse and pulled out her car keys. "Could you let Doug know I went on home?"

"Sure. I hope you get some good rest tonight." Christy gave Tracy a hug and whispered in her ear, "I'm really happy for you, little mama. Congratulations."

"Thanks." Tracy pulled back and started to leak a stream of tears.

"Are you okay?"

"Yes. Sorry. My emotions are all over the place. Must be evidence that I am pregnant, right?"

"Could be." Christy gave Tracy another hug.

"It will good to catch up on Tuesday," Tracy said.

"Yes, it will. I'll see you then."

Tracy slipped out the back door, and Christy headed upstairs to put on a sweatshirt so she could join Todd on the deck. This had become one of her favorite things to do at the end of their Friday Night Gatherings. It brought back memories of the summers during her teen years when Todd, Christy, and the rest of the God Lovers group gathered at the fire pits on the beach to sing under the stars. They had different problems and pressures back then. Somehow those teen worries seemed like nothing compared to the cumbersome issues all of them were working through in this season of life. Sitting by a fire and singing always made Christy feel young and reminded her of when the days ahead seemed to hold endless possibilities.

At the top of the stairs Christy heard voices coming from

her bedroom. She yanked open the door and found Lindee and a young guy sitting on the edge of her bed.

"What are you guys doing in here? You need to be downstairs or out on the deck."

The guy hopped up and mumbled, "Sorry" as he brushed past Christy.

Lindee stayed where she was, arms crossed, giving Christy a defiant look. "We were just talking. That's all. You don't have to be so bossy."

Christy was fuming. She bit her lip to keep from saying what was on her mind. Instead she stretched out her arm like a traffic officer and motioned for Lindee to make her exit.

Lindee stood and glared at Christy before heading out the door. "I thought you and Todd wanted to help us and be there for us and show us God's love and all that other stuff he was saying tonight."

"We do." Christy's words were calm and evenly paced even though her adrenaline spiked. "All that love and other stuff happens downstairs. Not here. Downstairs."

Lindee stomped past Christy. "You're just like my mother."

Christy stepped into the bedroom and closed the door behind her, pressing her back against it. Her heart pounded. *What was that? I was not ready for a confrontation.*

She circled the room as if trying to reclaim the space. Her space. None of the students had ever ventured upstairs before. Why did Lindee think she had the right to do that? Christy went to the closet for her hoodie and drew in a deep breath. *This is our home. She needs to respect our space.*

With firm steps Christy went back downstairs, ready to confront Lindee with stronger words if necessary. However, both Lindee and the young guy had left. Only two high school guys were sitting out on the deck with Todd and Doug.

Christy joined them and pulled up one of the folding beach chairs. She could feel her riled spirit calming as she warmed her feet by the metal fire pit and settled in to listen to the talented guys as they jammed.

I hope I handled that the right way. I don't want to drive Lindee away. She needs to be here. But I don't want to be disrespected in my own home either.

The two teen guys were perched on "Narangus," the bench Todd had made out of the backseat of his old VW van, "Gus," and his old orange surfboard, "Naranja." The unique seat had finally been relegated to the deck last year when Christy's Aunt Marti had donated her cast-off sofa and loveseat to Christy and Todd.

Christy much preferred the comfort of the low, reclining beach chair. She leaned back and took in the night sky. The summer stars looked like silver freckles on the dark face of the cosmos. She erased all thoughts of the encounter in her bedroom and listened to the words of the song the guys were playing.

In You, O God, will I put my trust.
On You alone will I rely.

Christy thought about Tracy and how distraught she seemed over the possibility of having another baby. She knew that Tracy had been resistant to getting pregnant again because their toddler, Daniel, was such an active and fussy little guy. He had become her full-time job.

Have I let Tracy's fears influence me? Is that part of the reason I'm so hesitant for us to have a baby? Or is it because our lives don't feel stable yet?

Christy thought again of their financial situation, and a submerged anger arose.

We can't afford to have a child until Todd gets a steady job with benefits. That's the bottom line. If he wants his own little grommet around here, then he needs to take on the full financial responsibility for our family.

The song ended, and the two guys packed up their guitars and said they had to get going. Doug caught a ride with them, leaving Christy and Todd alone on the deck as the coals in the fire pit turned a dusty rose color. A medley of lovely notes from the vibrating chords lingered in the air as Todd plucked the strings of the guitar he was given when they were in the Canary Islands. He played a rapid succession of notes and patted the palm of his hand on the body of the guitar, keeping time with the song he seemed to be composing.

Todd looked over at Christy and grinned. His face glowed with the look of a man who had everything in the world he ever wanted right there in front of him.

That look right there, Todd Spencer, that is why we can't have a baby yet. You think this is all we need.

But I know we need more.

two

$\mathcal{A}$t nearly midnight Christy and Todd headed for bed. She had put aside all thoughts of babies and finances and had let Todd's music lull her to a place of being half-asleep in the reclined beach chair under the canopy of summer stars.

As they made their way upstairs and got ready for bed, Christy told Todd about finding Lindee with a young guy in their bedroom.

"You did the right thing," Todd assured her. "That's how I would have handled it, too. It's our home. Anyone who comes into our home needs to respect our space and our rules."

"I'm glad you agree. I thought you might say that I scared her off."

"No, not at all. You didn't scare Lindee away. She'll be back next week."

"How do you know?" Christy slipped into her summer pj's, aware that her husband was watching her as he leaned against the door frame of the master bathroom.

"Trust me," Todd said. "She'll be back. She was just testing you. She's starved for attention." He went to the bed and crawled under the covers, adjusting the bedding the way he liked, with one foot sticking outside.

Christy climbed in and rested her head on the pillow.

Todd gazed at her with his penetrating silver-blue eyes, as if trying to read her thoughts. "When you made your wish tonight, was it really for a baby?"

"No. Well, sort of no. My first wish was that you and I could go someplace that both of us, shall we say, have a lot of *aloha* for."

"Maui?"

"Oh, you guessed it," Christy said playfully. "I'm so surprised you figured it out."

Todd grinned.

"I always wish for a return trip to Maui," Christy said. "You know that. Maui is my go-to wish."

"Mine, too." Todd stroked her hair. "I used to always wish for this."

"Me, too," Christy whispered.

They lay quietly looking into each other's eyes. The ceiling fan above their bed gently stirred the air. Her earlier frustrations with Todd not feeling the weight of their financial situation seemed to have evaporated.

"Come here." Todd put his arms around Christy and drew her close. He kissed her with a lingering tenderness.

She returned her investment with added interest.

From outside their open window came the slow, rhythmic sound of the rolling ocean waves a few blocks away. All the dreams of love they had denied themselves the first few summers they were together had been reserved for future summer nights like this one. In the intimate moments that followed, the patience of their teen years was well rewarded.

They fell asleep holding hands. Christy dreamed of sitting on the lanai of Uncle Bob's Maui condo and watching a white sailboat languidly skim across an aqua-blue sea.

As wonderfully alive and young as Christy felt in Todd's

embrace during the night, by the next morning when the alarm went off, she felt old. Old and tired and grumpy.

She missed her routine of sleeping in on Saturday mornings while Todd rose at dawn to go surfing. She could hear him downstairs, bumping around, closing the cupboards, making his latest favorite breakfast of peanut butter and honey on an English muffin. Christy thought it would be a sweet gesture for her to shuffle downstairs and give him a big kiss before he hit the waves.

Grogginess overtook her romantic intentions, though, and she heard the back door close before she could pull herself out of bed. She lingered under the covers another five minutes before finally rising and scurrying to get ready for work.

The only thing Christy didn't like about her receptionist job at the White Orchid Spa was that on a gorgeous July morning such as this, she had to wear a uniform of black pants and a black tunic top. Her shoes had to be closed toe and comfortable to stand on all day. She had to wear her hair back and very little makeup, which wasn't a problem because she had never been one who spent a lot of time getting her makeup just right. The image she was to portray, according to her manager, was an "ongoing sense of calm, natural loveliness, and professionalism."

Christy wasn't sure she had met any of those criteria in the past eight Saturdays since she had worked at the spa. But she had received only positive feedback from the spa manager so Christy guessed she was doing something right.

The White Orchid Spa was located inside one of the high-end resorts in Newport Beach. Driving into the employee parking lot made her feel somehow important and part of the upper class even though she was just a uniformed receptionist. She parked her car and thought about how wonderful last night had been and how much she loved Todd.

We do have to talk about the realities of our finances, though. Hopefully soon.

She strode through the grand lobby of the hotel and into

the fragrant spa. A scheduled bridal party arrived only moments after Christy took her position at the reception desk. She pressed the button to start the soothing instrumental music that floated through the spa.

The women were all ages and the older ones commented on everything as Christy checked them in and led them to their private room. They loved the plush robes and the tray of fancy glasses filled with iced water and floating cucumber slices.

"I feel like a movie star," one of the larger women said as she reached for a handful of diced, dried papaya and pineapple from the assortment of snacks prepared for them. "We don't have anything like this in Willow Springs."

Christy smiled at the ladies and delivered her well-rehearsed welcome speech. "After you've changed into your robes and slippers, you can make your way back to the Serenity Room. Your massage therapists will meet you there. If there's anything at all we can do to make your time with us more pleasant, please don't hesitate to let us know. Welcome to the White Orchid, and enjoy your treatments."

"You have such pretty eyes," one of the women said. "They match all the aqua blue colors around here. Are you wearing contacts?"

"No." Christy could feel herself blushing. She'd often been complimented on the blue/green shade of her eyes but never by a woman who was old enough to be her mother.

"I thought maybe they made the staff wear color coordinated lenses to go with the spa colors."

"That's silly," the bride-to-be said.

"Not according to the magazine I read on the plane. This is California. They do things like that here."

Christy quickly made an exit. She could hear the enthusiastic women chattering as she returned to the reception area. It was fun to think about the bride being pampered and surrounded by the women in her life on the morning of her special day, even if some of the relatives were quirky. Groups like this reminded Christy of when her father-in-law had gotten married two and a half years ago in the Canary Islands. Christy had joined his new bride, Carolyn, as she and her aunts enjoyed a spa day at one of the resorts on the island of Gran Canaria. The luxurious experience made Christy want to work at a spa someday. She was thrilled when this one-day-a-week opportunity showed up on an online posting, and she was hired the same week.

If she could resign from the Balboa Treasure Chest Gift Shop and work at the spa full-time, she would. Unfortunately the other employees at the White Orchid Spa seemed to feel the same way, and none of them seemed in a hurry to resign.

The rest of Christy's workday continued with a steady flow of guests. Most of them were staying at the resort, but several were local women who booked regular appointments. One of the women greeted Christy by name. Christy assumed it was because she was wearing a name badge, but then the woman asked Christy how her aunt was doing.

"We missed Marti at our last meeting. Is she in town?"

"Yes, she is. My husband and I are having dinner with them on Tuesday."

"Tell her hello for me. And please let her know that she was missed."

"I'll tell her."

After the woman had gone down the hallway to the Serenity Room, Christy checked the schedule to find out her name. Pulling out her phone, Christy made a note because she knew she would forget.

She noticed that she had two text messages. One was from Tracy asking if they could meet at Julie Ann's on Thursday instead of Tuesday. Christy tapped out a quick reply.

SURE. THURS WOULD BE GREAT. SEE YOU THERE AT 7:00.

The other was from Aunt Marti, reminding Christy about her birthday dinner on Tuesday.

BE HERE AT 6:30 SHARP. YOUR UNCLE AND I HAVE

A TROPICAL SURPRISE FOR YOU.

Christy felt her heart flutter. *Tropical surprise? That has to mean what I think it means. They're going to invite us to go with them to Maui!*

Christy hoisted her imagination sails and let the "happily Mauied" thoughts merrily sail around in her head for the next few days. By the time her birthday arrived on Tuesday, she was convinced that Todd and she would be winging their way across the Pacific that fall. She even put in a tentative vacation request at the gift shop and said she would fill in the preferred dates later that week.

When she arrived home after a tiring day of work, Christy opened up the windows and welcomed in the soothing ocean breeze to air out the stuffy space. She loved their home. This was her haven. She loved having the quiet space all to herself after a day that was filled with summer tourists at the gift shop. Todd and his dad had lived here for well over a decade so this house was Todd's haven, too.

Todd had done a major renovation of the three-bedroom beach house after a horrible rental experience several years ago. The disastrous rental experience convinced Bryan that he needed to sell the house at a time when Christy and Todd were in a meager financial position. Christy's Aunt Marti surprised all of them when she bought the house and rented it back to Christy and Todd at a rate that was way below the current rental market.

That huge blessing of low rent was a foundational part of their lives. They would be wiped out if it were taken away. Todd seemed to have more confidence in Marti than Christy did. Or maybe Todd's unswerving confidence was rooted in God's provision for them, and Marti was only part of the bigger plan.

Either way, Christy felt apprehensive about assuming this was their permanent home. As she got ready for her birthday dinner at Bob and Marti's, she realized that if she was uneasy about Marti's continued benevolence with the house, she should be more apprehensive about the gift of a trip to Maui being offered tonight at her birthday dinner.

Christy put her hair up in a twist and spent a little extra time with her makeup. She chose to wear her favorite summer dress and added a cropped sweater that matched the coral colors in the dress. She managed to squeeze out the last few squirts of coconut-lime hand lotion that had been a Christmas gift and was smoothing it over her bare legs when she heard Todd come in.

He clomped upstairs and greeted her with a kiss that smelled like paint and wood shavings from his construction job. While he jumped in the shower, Christy went downstairs to start a load of clothes in the washer. She emptied the dishwasher and organized the stack of mail and other clutter on the end of the counter. When her house was in order, she always felt more relaxed.

"Hey, it's your birthday," Todd said when he came downstairs wearing a button-down shirt with his shorts. "You shouldn't be doing dishes."

"I don't mind. It's the neatnik in me. You know that."

"Are you ready to go?" Todd glanced at the clock.

"Yup, I'm all set."

"Do you want to walk over to Bob and Marti's? We have enough time."

"Sure. Or we can ride our bikes." Christy liked that idea even more. Nothing reminded her of her youthful summer promises more than riding bikes with Todd on a perfect July evening. She also wanted to make sure they showed up at six thirty sharp.

"Are you able to ride a bike in your dress? And by the way, you look good. Really good."

"Thanks." Christy held out the sides of her dress and gave a little curtsy, demonstrating that her dress wasn't a problem because it was long enough and full enough for her to pedal easily.

"Let's go then."

They took off on their beach cruisers and rode down the wide cement walkway that ran the full length of the beach, separating the sand from the houses. Christy loved the way the evening breeze cooled her face. A familiar tinge of sea salt clung to the corner of Christy's lips and spiced up her lip gloss. She kept glancing to the left to watch the Southern California sun perform its daily magic show. The sun turned the light around them to a rosy, amber hue and gave the lifeguard station long, spindly shadow-legs in the sand.

"It's such a beautiful night," she called over her shoulder.

"God's birthday gift just for you."

His words made Christy smile.

They slowed down as they approached Bob and Marti's beachfront home and then pulled their bikes alongside the front patio. Todd secured them in an open spot next to the outdoor shower. Everything felt so familiar. For a moment, Christy found it hard to believe that her teen years had been filled with so many leisurely hours. When she visited her aunt and uncle during high school, she had enjoyed unlimited moments like this of riding bikes and spending the day on the beach.

I didn't appreciate what I had. Todd and I rarely have moments like this, even though we live here.

Slipping her arm through Todd's, Christy said, "Let's do this more often."

"Sounds good to me."

"I feel like I need to get outside more. I'm so pale." She compared the fair skin on her arm to his beefy, bronzed arm.

"Christy?" The voice that called to her from the patio was her aunt's what-in-the-world-are-you-doing? voice.

"We had to put up our bikes, Aunt Marti. We rode over here."

Christy and Todd made their way from the side of the house to the front patio and stopped to take in the beautifully decorated table. Small orange candles lined the deep-blue table runner. The white dinner plates complimented the etched stemware and matched the dozens of bleached-white starfish that were sprinkled across the table like large confetti.

"This is beautiful, Aunt Marti. So festive."

"Well, we are celebrating, you know." Marti went to Christy and gave her what Todd called one of her "drive-by" kisses where she would get close enough so her smooching sound could be heard but not an inch of her meticulously made-up person touched the other person. "Happy birthday, Christina."

"Thanks, Aunt Marti."

Ever-stylish Marti wore a flowing ivory jacket over an ivory silk top and wide black silk pants. The long string of black pearls around her neck was tied in a cluster in the middle of her abdomen. She eyed Christy's outfit, and with a pleased expression she said, "You look lovely this evening. Those are very good colors on you."

"Thanks."

Todd, in an un-Todd-like manner, pulled out a chair for Christy. "I take it the birthday princess sits here."

That's when Christy noticed a lei draped over the back of her chair. Her heart picked up its pace. *Could this mean what I hope it means? A lei means a trip to Maui, right?*

Uncle Bob stepped out onto the patio just then. He was carrying a tray laden with several bowls of scrumptious-smelling Chinese food. "Here, Todd. Put these on the table for me, will you? Oh, good. You didn't give the birthday girl her special gift yet. Allow me."

Uncle Bob lifted the fragrant lei made of purple orchids and small, fragrant, white tuberose. He placed it over Christy's head, kissing her soundly on both cheeks. "Happy birthday, Bright Eyes."

"Thank you so much." She lifted the flowers to her nose and drew in the heady scent of the tuberose. "Or should I say, *mahalo*?"

"I knew you liked those little white flowers," Uncle Bob said. "You had those in the wreath you wore around your head in your wedding, didn't you?"

"Yes. Good memory."

"I'm the one who remembered," Marti said. "You have no idea the challenge it was to find a place where we could order just the right tropical flowers for your wedding. So when your uncle said he wanted to surprise you with a lei for your birthday, I remembered the florist your mother used and ordered this one for you specifically with tuberose."

"Thank you, Aunt Marti. I love it. Thank you both so much."

"You're welcome. Happy birthday. Now, everyone have a seat, please." Marti nodded at Todd to sit down. "We decided to serve fresh Chinese food from our favorite new restaurant, as you can see. Everything should be hot and ready to eat. Todd, why don't you start with the bowl of Szechwan chicken in front of you? Christy, could you pass the brown rice this way?"

"Mind if we pray first?" Bob asked.

Marti waved her hand at Bob, dismissing his suggestion. "I think God knows we're grateful. The food won't be nearly as good if it cools."

Bob seemed to evaluate whether he was going to let Marti call the shots on this one.

"We can pray after we've eaten," she said with a firm tone. "Some of us might even be more grateful then. Please. Everyone, start eating."

Marti's eagerness to dive in set the pace for their dinner. They ate quickly with little conversation. While Christy didn't agree with Marti's preference of letting the cuisine take center stage over dialogue around the table, the food was good, and she enjoyed the view immensely. The sun appeared to be as round as a beach ball and as orange as a pumpkin as it melted into the blue Pacific.

She thought of how that morning when Todd woke her, the sun was just making its appearance and had sent a handful of sunbeams to squeeze through the window and brighten up their bedroom. Her lovingly prepared breakfast in bed included scrambled eggs and an English muffin with her favorite apricot jam. It was the first time Todd had ever done anything like that for her, and she loved it. She also loved his morning kisses and his birthday card that came with a gift certificate for Julie Ann's Café.

Marti pushed away her half-emptied plate and gazed at the sherbet-colored clouds that lingered on the far horizon. "What a pretty sky we have tonight."

"Lovely sunset." Bob leaned back in his chair and rested his folded hands on his slightly rounded stomach. He looked content and ready to set a more leisurely pace.

"I told Christy on the way over that the sky was God's birthday card for her."

"Indeed it is," Bob said. "Reminds me of the year we celebrated your birthday here on the patio with all your beach friends. If I recall, the volleyball game that evening was pretty cutthroat. What year was that?"

"That was my seventeenth birthday." Christy remembered every detail of that fun night. She had just returned from being a summer camp counselor, and she and Todd were starting to get serious about each other.

"No, that can't be right," Marti protested. "It had to have been your sixteenth birthday. You were still quite young."

"No, it was my seventeenth. Remember? My sixteenth birthday was spent with you on Maui."

"Oh, yes. I suppose you're right."

"Speaking of Maui." Bob leaned forward.

Christy glanced at Todd to see if he was anticipating the same big announcement she was hoping for. Todd was finishing off the last of the Mongolian beef and seemed unaffected by Bob's baited line.

"You know we're planning to go to Maui for Christmas this year, don't you?"

Christy nodded, her eyes fixed on her uncle. She hoped

her expression didn't appear too eager. She wanted to look grateful and humble and surprised after he delivered his next line.

Marti picked up his dangling comment and said, "Your uncle and I have decided it's time to sell one of the condos. Did we tell you that already?"

"No." Christy looked at Todd again. "I don't think we knew that."

"Well, that's what we're doing," Marti said.

"We're keeping the one on the end of the building," Bob said. "It's a larger unit and has two lanais, as you probably remember. Our best guess is that it will take us three weeks to settle the arrangements on the unit we're selling so we're going to Maui from December 14 to . . . what is it, Marti? January 6?"

"January 8."

"Right. January 8. The point is, before we sell the second condo, we wanted to make good use of it one more time by inviting another couple to join us for a week."

Todd looked up from his plate and glanced at Christy with a slight grin that revealed his dimple just enough to let Christy know he was paying attention after all.

"So, this is where you two come in," Uncle Bob said.

Christy held her breath and waited for her uncle to speak the words she had dreamed of. With the sweet fragrance of the islands looped around her neck and the view of the gorgeous sunset exuding romantic thoughts of tropical nights, Christy's mind had already set sail for the beautiful islands across the sea.

three

"Do get to the point, Robert," Marti said. "Ask them the question."

"Right. So, as you may have already figured out, we would like to invite your parents to come with us."

My parents?

Christy didn't blink. Her swiftly sailing, halfway-to-Maui dreams capsized into the deep blue.

"It was Marti's idea," Bob added. "And I'm all for it. You know it's your folks thirty-fifth anniversary this fall. They've never been to Hawaii, and we were thinking this would be a nice way for them to celebrate."

Todd reached over and gave Christy's arm a squeeze. "Don't you think your parents will like going to Maui?"

"Yes. Yes, of course. They'll love it. Who wouldn't? I mean, what a nice thing for you to do for them." She quickly added, "I'm embarrassed because I didn't realize it was their thirty-fifth anniversary."

"What we wanted to ask the two of you is if you think we should tell them ahead of time so they can pick the dates they want to come. Or should we book the flights and surprise them with the tickets?" Bob looked at Christy first and then at Todd.

"I don't think Norm is big on surprises," Todd said. "Seems best to invite them and then let them make their own plans."

"That's what Robert thinks, too," Marti said. "But I think doing it that way will diminish the surprise. I want them to be surprised."

"They'll be surprised." Christy tried to keep the wobble out of her voice. "I'm sure of it."

"Okay, then. It's settled. We'll give them a call tomorrow." Bob's focus returned to the sunset. The hues of pale pink and tangerine had faded to a silky shade of lavender.

"Glad we could help break the tie for you," Todd said.

Christy wasn't feeling very glad that their role had been as referees between her aunt and uncle. Marti didn't seem too happy either. She looked flustered, as if she was still trying to figure out a way to convince them that her way would be better. Marti's dark eyes narrowed. She'd recently changed her hair style to a short, modern cut that took on an edgy silhouette as the evening turned to dusk around them. What stood out were the strategically placed highlights in Marti's dark hair. It looked as if she'd had expensive silver tinsel woven between the strands on only one side.

Before Marti could say anything, Uncle Bob drew in a deep breath and prayed aloud.

Christy lowered her head and felt humbled by what had just happened. Her spirit started to settle, and she thought of all the ways her generous aunt and uncle had surprised her over the years. She had had her chance to go to Maui. Twice. It was her parents' turn now. If anything, they should have gone long ago.

Bob's prayer started off thanking God for His goodness to all of them over the years. He thanked God for Christy, for her life, gentle spirit, and deep love for others. Then he added, "And thanks for the good food we devoured, the beautiful sunset, and the birthday cake we're about to enjoy."

Bob had barely said, "Amen" before Marti rose from the table and corrected her husband. "It's cupcakes. Not birthday cake. I didn't know what flavor you would like, Christy, so we bought an assortment of mini-cupcakes from Cheri's, my favorite bakery."

Bob followed Marti into the house with the cleared plates, leaving Christy and Todd at the table with the flickering orange candles glowing like miniature sunsets. The sky had darkened, and the starfish decorations on the table took on an amber glow from the candles.

Todd covered Christy's hand and intertwined his fingers with hers. He leaned close. "You okay?"

She nudged her lips up in a smile and nodded.

"I know you were hoping they were going to invite us. I was hoping, too."

She felt ridiculous that a cluster of tears had formed in the corner of her eyes.

"It's great that your parents are going with them," Todd said.

"I know. I feel like a spoiled brat," Christy whispered. "Look at us. Look at this. It's a perfect night. We live in Newport Beach. I'm having birthday dinner on the beach and wearing this beautiful lei." That's when she realized that the lei must have been the tropical surprise Marti had alluded to in her text.

"And you are loved very much by many people." Todd lifted her hand and kissed it.

"I know. Todd, we've been given so much. I have no right to wish for anything more. I feel ashamed of myself for secretly wanting them to invite us to go."

"No shame in wishing, *Kilikina*." As Todd looked at Christy, she could see in his silver-blue eyes a hint of disappointment that they weren't making plans to head to Maui right now.

His words calmed her and helped snuff out the tears as she blinked and reached for a napkin. "It's not just that we're not going to Maui. I know this is going to sound ridiculous, but I feel old all of a sudden. When Uncle Bob was talking about my seventeenth birthday, I realized that was nine years ago. Nine! How did I get so old?"

Todd grinned. "Welcome to being twenty-six."

"Don't say that number aloud." Christy gave him a woeful look. "Please."

He leaned over and kissed her tenderly. With his forehead to hers he whispered, "Twenty-six looks great on you. You're more beautiful now than you were when you were seventeen. Especially tonight. You are so beautiful, Kilikina."

Christy kissed him, and Todd kissed her back. He straightened his posture and leaned back but kept a hold of her hand.

"What matters most is that we keep on trusting God in every season, and at every age. He's always taken very good care of us."

"I know."

Todd's expression remained serious. "Whenever God has said no to us, it's always been for His good purpose. His timing is flawless. And you know, sometimes when we think God is saying, no, as in, 'no, you can't go to Maui,' He's really just saying, 'not yet.'"

Christy nodded her agreement. "I think that's why I feel so spoiled. God has given us lots of 'yeses.' I hardly know what to do with a 'no' or a 'not yet.'"

"We wait. And we keep trusting Him. That's all we can do."

Christy felt as if they had had this same sort of conversation many years ago. Was it during their later teen years when they were waiting to see if their friendship would blossom into something more? Or was it when Todd came to see her in Switzerland the year she studied abroad? They were apart for many painfully long stretches when both of them were pretty sure they were going to spend the rest of their lives together, and yet they had to wait.

Waiting was what they had done in the past when they wanted God's best.

Christy shook off the melancholy that was trying to settle on her. From inside the house came Bob's deep voice as he stepped out onto the patio and sang out, *"Happy birthday to you . . ."*

Todd joined in along with Marti, who was right behind Bob with the plates and forks. They ended their eclectic rendition of the birthday song with Bob holding a plate in front of Christy that contained an assortment of the smallest, most elegant cupcakes she had ever seen.

"Make a wish," Bob said.

On the heels of everything she and Todd had just whispered about in the candlelight, Christy felt as if she was all out of wishes. She wasn't sure what to hope for. Gazing at the single, tall taper candle rising from the center of the plate, Christy closed her eyes and did what was expected. She blew out the candle.

But she did so without making a wish.

The next day, Christy wavered between feeling melancholy and feeling grateful for all that God had blessed her with. Turning twenty-six was a surprisingly difficult adjustment, and she was eager to meet with Tracy so she could process some of the intense emotions she had been feeling.

As Christy drove to Julie Ann's on Thursday morning, she realized it had been far too long since she and Tracy had shared a deep, heart-to-heart conversation. Christy always benefited from Tracy's kindness and wisdom. Tracy had often said that she received the same benefits from her talks with Christy.

When Christy arrived, she found Tracy already seated at a table in the café, having ordered for both of them.

"I've concluded that I'm definitely pregnant because what I've experienced this week could only be morning sickness." Tracy made a grimace at the raisin bagel on the plate in front of her. "It's all yours, Christy. Nothing looks good to me. I've barely kept anything down. Don't be surprised if I make a sudden dash to the restroom."

"I know you can't feel enthusiastic about being pregnant right now, but I am thrilled for you and Doug." Christy tried to sound upbeat and yet sympathetic at the same time, even though she felt queasy just looking at Tracy. "I wish you weren't getting hit so hard by the morning sickness, though."

"I know. Thanks. I was hoping I'd feel better once I got going this morning. There's so much I need to talk to you about. But first, happy birthday." Tracy slid a small gift box tied with a blue-and-white polka-dotted ribbon over to Christy's side of the table.

"Tracy, you didn't have to get me anything. The carrot cake was my special birthday request. That's all I wanted. Really."

"It's just a little something. You can open it later." Tracy's attempt at a festive expression slid into a frown. "Did Todd tell you about my parents?"

"No. What about them?"

"They are seriously talking about moving."

"Why would they move?"

"Ever since my dad retired a few months ago, all they've talked about are finances. They're worried about the high property taxes here and don't think they can keep renting their Balboa bungalow to us at the rate we've been paying. They want to sell their house and move to Oregon." Tracy teared up.

"Oregon?"

"Yes, Oregon."

"I thought you were going to say they were moving to somewhere else in the LA area like Irvine or Tustin. Not Oregon."

"My mom's sister lives there now and loves it. My parents went to visit last week, and all they can talk about is moving." Tracy reached for a napkin and wiped her nose. "Doug and I moved into their bungalow two years ago so we could be close to them while our children are little. Now they're talking about moving a thousand miles away. I don't understand it."

"Are they thinking you guys will move to Oregon, too?"

"I don't know what they're thinking. I don't want to move to Oregon. Doug says they're having a midlife crisis. He's frustrated because the only reason he took the job at the insurance company was that my dad worked there, and it meant we could live near my parents." Tracy took off her glasses and rubbed her eyes. She looked awfully pale.

"Are you okay?" Christy reached for Tracy's hand, which felt cold and clammy.

"No. Sorry. I'll be right back." Tracy scooted through the tiny café to the restroom.

Christy frowned. She knew how much Tracy depended on her mom. This distressing news couldn't be good for Tracy's emotional condition right now. Christy waited a few minutes, nibbling on the bagel and wondering if she should check on Tracy to make sure she was all right.

Tracy returned and pulled some money from her wallet. "I'm sorry, but I have to go home. I am not doing well at all."

"Don't worry about the bill. I've got this. You just go. I'm so sorry, Trace."

"Thanks for understanding." She stopped and turned back to Christy. "Oh, and Doug and I decided we're not going to Santa Barbara with you guys this weekend for Sierra's wedding. I'm working on a gift for her. I'll have Doug drop it off." Tracy drew in a slow breath and looked like she might be sick again.

"Okay. Take care, all right?" Christy watched her friend weave her way to the exit and hoped she would be okay driving home. The bungalow was only a few blocks away, which was a good thing.

Alone at the small table with her jarred thoughts and a soup-bowl-sized tea latte, Christy hoped that Tracy and Doug wouldn't move. Their lives had been so woven together over the past few years, she couldn't imagine what it would be like if they were no longer around.

Christy pulled the polka-dotted ribbon from the gift box and peeked inside. Tracy had placed a handwritten note on top.

I have loved our girly tea parties ever since our first one together in England. Happy birthday, Christy. I look forward to celebrating many more with you and even more tea parties. Your Forever Friend, Tracy.

Christy felt a sweet sadness. She wanted them to share many tea parties in the years to come as well. Doug and Tracy couldn't move to Oregon. They just couldn't.

Under the note Christy found a pack of tea-party-sized napkins and two teaspoons decorated with scallop seashells on the ends. The napkins had a starfish in the top corner with the words *Wish Upon a Star* written in flowing script. Christy loved the little gift. It was so like Tracy to make the effort to put together a sweet remembrance for Christy even though Tracy didn't feel well.

Christy finished her latte, paid the check, and added a nice tip.

As she had done many times before, she left her car in the public parking lot down the block from Julie Ann's Café and walked the short distance to the Balboa Island ferry. It was a perfect summer morning, and she was wearing her most comfortable pair of sandals so she didn't mind the walk. She paid the pedestrian fare to the attendant and sat on one of the splintered wooden benches as the small ferry chugged across the water and docked a few minutes later on Balboa Island.

The greatest disadvantage of the job she had held for more than a year at the gift shop on Balboa Island was that parking was a problem. Sometimes Todd dropped her off and picked her up. A couple of times she rode her bike. Most of the time she did what she was doing today, parking near the ferry and riding it across the short channel to Balboa Island.

The charm of working at a gift shop that catered mostly to tourists had worn off after the first few months. It wasn't difficult work. Christy liked the older women she worked with. They reminded her of some of the sweet ladies who worked at The Ark Bookstore with her when she and Todd were first married. The salary wasn't great, which was why she had taken on the Saturday job at the White Orchid Spa.

What would it be like to only work part-time or be an at-home wife and mom like Tracy?

Christy looked out at the water and thought back to when she and Todd were in Amsterdam during their college years. They stayed in an efficiently run hostel where Christy felt an immediate warmth for the couple who served as their hosts. A small dream began growing inside her there. The dream was that one day she and Todd would serve side by side in ministry and have a house where people would always feel welcome to come and stay.

That wish was only partially being realized with the Friday Night Gathering. The rest of the week Christy was barely home. If she didn't have to work so much and could stay home, she could do things like watch Daniel for the afternoon so Tracy could rest. She could start making decorative throw pillows again like she did when they first moved to Newport Beach. Their guestroom would be used as a sweet haven for weary guests instead of as a place for storing excessively large bundles of paper towels from the big box store.

It's the stupid money issue. It's always the money issue. We need every penny I make. I don't know when I'll ever have the luxury of staying home or expanding my dream of using our home as a place of ongoing hospitality.

The ferry docked, and Christy walked the last few blocks to work feeling like the Winnie the Pooh character, Eeyore, who had lost his tail.

Oh, well. Never mind. Thanks for botherin' to notice.

She paused to look in the window of a children's clothing

shop that had put up a new display. A dozen silver stars hung from the ceiling on thin wires and floated above an old-fashioned infant's cradle. The cradle was filled with books: *Peter Pan, Alice in Wonderland, The Cat in the Hat, The Very Hungry Caterpillar,* and *Winnie the Pooh.* Seeing the *Winnie the Pooh* book made her almost smile. She felt like God was playing a little joke on her. If she was going to identify with Eeyore, God might as well let her know that He had noticed.

Okay, so why would You put such a dream in my heart, but then I end up spending the first four years of marriage working in shops? It doesn't make sense.

Once she arrived at work, her prayers and ponderings had to be put aside. She knew that the best thing to do was wait, as Todd had said at her birthday dinner at Bob and Marti's. Like the wish to go back to Maui, maybe the dream to run a sort of B&B was another prayer that God had answered but His answer was "not yet."

On her lunch break Christy returned to the children's shop and impulsively bought a copy of *Peter Pan.* She never had read the classic book by J. M. Barrie, and she wasn't sure she would read it all the way through anytime soon. But she loved the cover and wanted to add another classic to her collection of hardbacks. The other reason she purchased it was because Todd had often seemed like a Peter Pan to her. He was the boy who never wanted to grow up.

He was also the boy who taught her how to fly.

That evening, while Todd was at a surfboard reshaping shop, Christy made a cup of tea and curled up in her favorite chair by the window in their bedroom. She opened up her new book and felt content.

Todd came home when she was only twelve pages into *Peter Pan.*

"That was quick."

"Yeah. Zane had another guy at his shop that he needed to talk to, but he said I should come back early next week. He's backed up on an order for a bunch of boards this month.

He said he would welcome my help."

Christy bit her lower lip. Zane was a friend of Todd's dad. His shop was a warehouse where he shaped surfboards and welded things like bike stands. Todd had done lots of trades with him in the past but had never committed to working on a big project with him.

"Would it be a paying project for the boards? Or just a trade sort of deal?"

"Paid."

"Are you sure? I mean, did he say how much it would pay?"

Todd looked irritated that she was questioning him.

"Like I said, another guy was there he was helping out so it wasn't the right time for us to talk about payment. I told him I'd come in Monday."

"Okay." Christy could tell it would be better to drop the subject for now.

The good news, she supposed, was that he had some work lined up. Over the past few years that he had been working from project to project in construction, painting, and renovations, one job always seemed to lead to the next one based on whom Todd met along the way. She didn't want to start an intense conversation late at night, especially when Todd didn't appear to be in an objective mood. They needed to sit down and thoroughly discuss their financial situation, but not tonight.

"What are you reading?"

Christy held up the book so he could see the cover and the title.

He didn't have much of a response. Christy didn't know if he was unfamiliar with the classic tale or if the book didn't interest him. He leaned against the dresser. "We should talk about this weekend."

"Okay."

"Do you think you could take Monday off of work? I was thinking that since Doug and Tracy decided to not go to the wedding with us, you and I could drive Gussie up the coast and stay overnight on the beach somewhere. What do you think? I thought we could stay for two nights."

Christy immediately recognized the Peter Pan expression on his face, and she knew that having a small adventure like this meant a lot to him.

"Sure. I'll ask for Monday off. I've already arranged it so I can leave the spa at two o'clock on Saturday so we can get to the wedding on time. We'll have to have everything ready ahead of time, though. Can you pick me up at the spa?"

"Of course. I'll pull all the stuff together and load up Gussie and be there to pick you up at two o'clock."

"Sounds good."

Now Todd was the one who seemed to be questioning her answer. "So, you're good with going camping then? Two nights on the beach, sleeping in Gussie?"

"Yes."

Todd stepped over and planted a kiss on her upturned lips. "You're the best."

Christy smiled and received a second kiss from Todd before he headed for the bathroom. She leaned back in her snuggle chair and imagined what their campsite on the beach would look like. Shabby chic came to mind, a bohemian beachcomber-style setup with folding beach chairs, Moroccan lanterns strung over the picnic table, and a colorful print tablecloth covering the ice chest where they had a game of checkers ready for their evening entertainment.

Christy decided she would bring lots of her puffy pillows and several hefty blankets to brace them against the night air. She wished she had an ankle-length, flowing seashore kind of skirt to wear. And a long, embroidered linen top with a luxuriously thick vest made of something warm like alpaca. She would wear her hair in one loose braid pulled over her shoulder and complete the outfit with her new birthday bracelet she had bought at work with the gift certificate her mom gave her. The bracelet had dangling seashells and turquoise-blue beads.

They would drink cucumber- and strawberry-infused water from her Mason jars that had the hole in the lid for a straw. And for dinner she would make a Caesar salad with big croutons and a sprinkling of dried cranberries. It would go perfectly with the lemon and dill salmon that Todd would cook for them on the campsite grill.

Christy's Pinterest-style daydream came to a screeching halt when Todd returned to the bedroom wearing his favorite pair of well-worn gym shorts and a very old T-shirt that had three holes in it.

If my husband looks like a homeless person when we're at home, why do I think we're going to look like a magazine cover when we're camping?

"What?" Todd asked when he noticed the bemused way Christy was staring at him.

"Nothing. I love you."

four

At exactly two o'clock on Saturday afternoon, Christy left the White Orchid Spa and scurried out to the parking lot. She was relieved when she saw Gussie the Bussie was waiting at the front entrance with the engine running.

Todd was behind the wheel, grinning like a monkey. He had put tons of money and effort into fixing up their vintage Volkswagen van over the last few years. Gussie's engine hummed contentedly. Her pale-yellow paint shone in the August afternoon sunlight. Todd's new orange surfboard was strapped to the roof.

Christy was excited that they were headed out on their getaway. It had been a long time since they had done something like this. She was determined to have a fun, lighthearted time and enjoy every free minute they had with each other. That morning she had made herself promise not to bring up jobs and finances on their surfin' safari. They could work through all that when they got home.

"Do you have everything?" Christy asked as she jumped in.

"I think so. Your clothes for the wedding are there on the

backseat like you asked. I stopped at the grocery store deli for sandwiches and some snacks."

"Thanks." Christy reached into the bag between their seats. "Does it matter which sandwich I take?"

"No, they're both the same. Turkey, avocado, bacon, and pesto on sourdough. With extra tomatoes."

Christy didn't want to calculate how many calories were in Todd's choice of a "healthy" sandwich.

He probably thought the extra tomatoes were what I meant when I suggested he pick up a healthy lunch for us to eat on the road.

Christy took a bite of the slightly soggy but definitely tasty sandwich.

Todd pulled onto the 405 freeway. "I hope this is a good sign. There's not much traffic." He fiddled with his iPod and got the new sound system in Gussie to play one of Christy's favorite songs.

"Are you kidding me? I haven't heard this song in so long. I used to love this song. I think I listened to it a thousand times during my senior year of high school." Christy opened the bottle of iced green tea Todd had bought her and took a drink.

"I put together a mix for us." Todd looked pleased with himself. "It's labeled on my playlist as 'Summer Hits for my Mrs.' Get it? Hits for my Mrs."

Christy swallowed a cough. She could feel a bubble of green tea trying to go out her nose. She swallowed and coughed again before giving him the lighthearted laugh he seemed to be waiting for. Todd kept looking straight ahead, grinning broadly.

"You liked that, huh?"

"You are in a rare mood, Todd Spencer."

"You know it. We should have gotten together a trip like this a long time ago. We always talked about it but never loaded up Gussie and hit the road."

"I'm glad it worked out." Christy leaned back and let the

contentment of the moment surround her.

They puttered along as the traffic began to build, neither speaking for several minutes. Todd turned up the music and tapped his fingers on the steering wheel.

"I'm excited to see Sierra and meet Jordan," Christy said. "You know he's a photographer, right? One of his photos made the cover of *Surfer* magazine."

"I know. I kept that issue. I'm looking forward to meeting him, too." The song changed and Todd sang along.

Christy smiled. The tune was another random blast from the past, one she hadn't heard for years. High school memories rushed in, and she couldn't help but sing along with Todd on the chorus.

This is exactly what both of us needed. I'm so glad we decided to take this trip.

They arrived in Santa Barbara only half an hour before the wedding. The ceremony was held in a park, and from the first glance of the hanging lanterns and bunches of wildflowers tied to the white folding chairs, Christy thought the setting fit Sierra perfectly.

Sierra, with her unruly, long, curly blonde hair had always reminded Christy of an earthy nature lover who could be found on an average day dancing in a forest with flowers in her hair. It followed that Sierra's wedding would reflect those elements.

Christy changed into her wedding outfit in the park restroom. It wasn't ideal, but the nice thing about having come from work at the spa was that she still carried the fragrance of the calming oils and lotions that surrounded her at the front desk. She emerged with her hair down and brushed smooth over her bare shoulders. Her simple blue dress was a little looser than she remembered it being the last time she wore it. Looser was much better than tighter. She had learned that at Todd's dad's wedding when she had crossed her legs and pulled out the side seam of the little black dress she borrowed.

Christy felt pretty, and she could tell by the look on Todd's face when she exited the restroom that he had the same thought. He always liked it when she wore her hair down.

Todd had changed into a Hawaiian print aloha shirt and khaki slacks. He had planned on wearing shorts, but Christy convinced him to go with the slacks. His wavy hair was tousled in its usual surfer-boy fashion. Christy gave him an approving grin and let him take her straw beach bag when he reached for it.

"Anything else you want me to put back in the car?" Todd asked.

"Wait. Let me grab my sweater out of there before you put it in the van. Do you want me to wait for you or go find seats for us?"

"Go ahead. It looks like it's filling up fast. I'll come find you."

Christy signed in at the guest-book table and left their wedding card with a gift card in the basket. She had included Doug and Tracy's names on the card since Tracy hadn't been able to work on a gift for Sierra the way she had wanted to.

Cheerful music played through the hanging speakers as the ushers helped the guests to their seats. Christy slid into an open seat near the back on the left side and put her sweater on the empty seat beside her, saving it for Todd.

"Such a nice evening for a wedding, don't you think?" the older woman next to Christy asked.

"Yes. This is a beautiful setting."

"And how do you know the couple?"

"My husband and I met Sierra when we were on a mission trip in England. It was quite a few years ago. I haven't seen her since she went to Brazil."

"I remember when she went to England. How wonderful that you could come to her wedding."

"I was looking forward to it very much. What about you? How do you know Sierra?"

"She worked at my bakery when she was in high school.

She was always one of my favorites."

"I remember hearing about the bakery Sierra worked at in Portland." Christy tried to recall the name. When it blitzed into her mind she blurted out, "Oh, Mama Bear's. Are you Mama Bear?"

The woman chuckled. "Yes. Yes, I am. And this is Papa Bear." The man beside her gave Christy a nod.

Mama Bear leaned closer. "Did you know that instead of a wedding cake, Sierra and Jordan are having cinnamon rolls? My cinnamon rolls. We brought them with us on the plane this morning. It was quite a production packing them just right. We only had two or three that were too squashed to serve. I'm so pleased."

"I can see how you would be. Cinnamon rolls sound like what Sierra would have at her wedding." Christy smiled. "I can't wait to have one."

Todd arrived and slid into his chair just minutes before the music changed to a more stately and solemn song. The pastor took his place, facing the guests that had filled all the chairs. As the significant relatives were ushered down the center aisle to their seats, Christy thought back on how her best friend, Katie, had hit it off with Sierra the first day in their shared room in the castle in Northern England that served as the headquarters for the mission organization. Doug and Tracy had been there, too, but they hadn't spent as much time with Sierra as Katie and Christy had.

When Sierra ended up going to Rancho Corona University the year Christy and Katie were roommates, the three of them shared many late-night talks about guys, life, and their dreams for the future.

Christy slipped her arm through Todd's and rested her head on his shoulder. It was a wonderful thing that they could be here. This beautiful wedding on this perfect August evening made everything around them seem sacred. All she wanted to think about was this present moment. This beautiful, sacred, present moment. The past had laid the stepping stones to this moment. The future didn't frighten her when she felt this content.

It is the joy of the sacred "now." I don't have enough of these moments in my life.

The sweet and solemn feeling all around them made Christy even more convinced of something Todd had said a long time ago. The Holy Spirit loved to attend the weddings of believers because every such union was marked by a covenant relationship being sealed before God. It was a glimpse of the wedding feast of the Lamb talked about in Revelation. One day all of God's children would gather at His feast and celebrate being united with Him for eternity.

The bridesmaids finished their trek down the aisle. The music changed to a triumphant swell. Sierra's mother stood, and all the guests rose. They turned to gaze on the bride, who came down the white runner with her arm linked through her father's arm. His expression made it clear that he was trying to hold it together while he gave away his little girl to the man who had won her heart.

Sierra was radiant. She looked elegant in her simple gown with her bouquet of colorful wildflowers. Christy hadn't seen her in so long. It seemed Sierra was more mature but still in every way the carefree, winsome, and woodsy young woman Christy remembered from their first meeting.

Christy looked toward the front where the groom stood waiting. She loved catching a glimpse of Jordan's expression as Sierra came down the aisle toward him. He clearly was smitten with her, and that made Christy very happy. She needed to remember to tell Katie about the look on Jordan's face. It reminded Christy of the way Eli looked when Katie went to him to become his bride.

The vows were exchanged with a continuing solemnity, and even the couple's triumphant exit down the center aisle seemed covered by a calm sort of maturity and finality. They linked their arms in a natural way and came down the aisle, beaming.

Christy teared up as the newlyweds slid past them. She reached for Todd's hand and he gave her three squeezes, their secret signal for *I-love-you.*

During the casual, picnic-style reception under a canopy of strung café lights, Christy and Todd stayed close together. They met lots of Sierra's relatives and one of Jordan's surfer friends. But they didn't get a chance to say hi to Sierra or to meet Jordan.

The DJ started the music for the first dance with the father and the bride and the groom and his mom. The song was "What a Wonderful World." With Todd's arm around her shoulders, Christy watched them dance. She choked up on the line, *"I hear babies cryin'. I watch them grow . . ."*

Christy turned her face up to Todd's with a wistful smile. He kissed her on the tip of her nose. She wished they already had figured out their finances so she felt free enough inside to start wishing about one day having a baby and watching it grow. She knew that they weren't there yet.

After this weekend Todd and I have to talk. No, actually we have to do more than talk. We need to resolve the imbalance in our jobs, figure out our finances, and put together a plan for the future. We have to do it.

The dance ended, and the parents handed off Sierra and Jordan to each other. They looked comfortable in each other's arms. Neither of them was an especially suave dancer, but they moved in sync and with confidence as their song played and all the guests took in the heartwarming image of this traditional celebration of love.

"We should go," Todd said.

"We haven't said hello to them yet."

"I know, but you remember what it was like at our wedding. It's hard to make the rounds to see everyone."

Christy glanced at Sierra and Jordan one more time. They were locked into their own bubble of bliss. Maybe Todd was right. They still had to drive another half hour and try to set up their campsite in the dark. But she hated to leave just yet.

"Are you just trying to get out of the possibility of having to dance with me?" Before he could answer, Christy added, "And we haven't had a cinnamon roll yet."

"Cinnamon rolls?" Now she had his attention.

"They came from Mama Bear's in Portland where Sierra used to work." Christy walked Todd over to the side table where the iced cinnamon rolls were displayed on several tiered stands. Each roll was tucked into a white paper wrapper that made it look like a fancy pastry in an upscale coffee shop.

"You're welcome to take one if you like." The young woman behind the table motioned for Todd and Christy to help themselves.

"I heard about these cinnamon rolls," Christy said. "Do you work at Mama Bear's?"

"No, I'm a friend of Sierra's. My name is Kaitelynn."

"I'm Todd. This is Christy. We're friends of Sierra's, too."

"I hope you guys will help out here. You see, Sierra and Jordan aren't doing a special cake cutting or anything. They wanted people to just come and pick up a cinnamon roll. Only nobody thinks it's okay to take one yet since it's not in keeping with the usual wedding cake-cutting tradition, I guess."

Christy hesitated. The cinnamon rolls looked perfectly balanced the way they were displayed on the table. She sided with the other hesitant guests. It didn't seem right to take one.

"Please," Kaitelynn said. "I'd be so grateful if you guys would just take one and walk around, then other people will get the idea that they should help themselves, too."

"Anything to help," Todd said with a grin.

Kaitelynn looked relieved. "Oh, good. Thank you. Now I feel like I'm finally doing my job."

Todd and Christy made their way back toward the dance floor, cinnamon rolls in hand. The looks they got from the other guests were unnerving.

"We were told to dig in," Todd said to people who stared.

"You can go get a cinnamon roll over there. Ask Kaitelynn. She's trying to give them away. Honest."

As soon as two of the younger boys in the wedding party found out that Todd wasn't kidding, they took off, and a steady stream of guests followed their lead.

"These are good," Christy said after the first bite. She wished she had picked up a napkin because the icing was sticking to the side of her mouth.

"Christy!"

She was startled to hear her name called out and nearly dropped her cinnamon roll. Sierra had spotted her and was coming toward them with a wide grin on her face. Her arm was linked through Jordan's, and even though several other people tried to get them to stop and chat, Sierra had her sights fixed on Christy.

The two friends hugged, and when Christy pulled back, she realized that the cinnamon roll had come out of the paper wrapper and stuck to Sierra's long, curly blonde hair.

"Don't move," Christy said. "Sierra, I am so sorry!"

"Why? What happened?"

Jordan calmly reached over as Sierra stood still, her eyes opened wide. He removed the cinnamon roll from her tresses and showed her the culprit. With a good-natured grin, Jordan said, "My wife gives exuberant hugs. It's not the first time her hair has tried to pick-pocket a souvenir in the process."

Sierra laughed and smoothed her hand down the back of her mane. "It's like living with an octopus on my head sometimes."

"I hope your hair isn't sticky from the frosting," Christy said.

"Doesn't matter." Sierra reached for Christy's hands and gave them a squeeze. "I'm just so glad you guys came."

"You look stunning," Christy said. "Your ceremony was beautiful, and this is such a fun reception. We're so happy for you both."

"Thank you." Sierra looked over at her husband and said,

"Jordan, this is Todd and Christy, the friends I told you about who live in Newport Beach."

Jordan shook hands with Todd. "I hear you surf."

"I do."

"Hey, that's my line," Sierra said playfully. "You can't come to a wedding and start going around saying 'I do.' Especially since you already 'did.' They're married," she said to Jordan. "But you already figured that out, didn't you?"

Bending in closer, Sierra confided, "Sorry. I'm starting to get a little spacey. I just introduced Jordan's dad to someone as his grandpa. And his grandpa isn't even here."

"Don't worry about it," Jordan said. "You're doing better than I am at remembering names."

Sierra turned her face toward her husband with a glowing look of admiration. He gave her a quick kiss.

Christy grinned. It was good to see that under the elegant wedding dress, Sierra was still the flighty person everyone knew and loved. From the look on Jordan's face, he liked her just the way she was.

Sierra turned back to Christy. "Let's get together sometime, you guys. We're only a couple of hours away from each other now. We could go down there, or you guys could come up and spend a weekend with us here in Santa Barbara."

"We would love it," Christy said. "We have a guestroom, and you would be welcome to stay with us anytime."

"Thanks," Jordan said. "My parents live in Irvine, so we probably wouldn't need a place to stay. But, Todd, if you or any other surfers in Newport need some shots, let me know. I'd be happy to fit in a session or two in Newport when we come down."

"I'm not a competitor," Todd said. "Tried it for a season when I was in college. Had a good run. Good enough to let me know I'm more at home on the summer swells at Newport than on the North Shore at high season."

"You surfed the North Shore on Oahu?" Jordan asked.

Todd nodded. "Spent a winter at Sunset Beach. It was

pretty epic."

"Sunset Beach is where we met," Sierra said excitedly. "Well, we first saw each other when we were at a wedding on Maui, but then we ended up trapped in a house during a winter storm at Sunset Beach. We're going there for our honeymoon. Not the rickety old house at Sunset. We're going back to Maui."

"Nice," Todd said. "That's where we went on our honeymoon."

"We loved it," Christy added. "I'm sure you guys will have a great time."

"Do you have any recommendations for places to eat?" Jordan pulled his phone from his tux pocket and took notes as Christy and Todd tried to remember some of the restaurants they had gone to.

They chatted a few more minutes before another couple came up to congratulate Jordan and Sierra. Christy gave Sierra another hug and quickly added a hello from Doug and Tracy and then told Sierra that Katie wished she could be here.

Sierra pouted exaggeratedly. "I wish Katie could have been here, too. I'm so glad you guys came. Really. Thank you so much."

As Christy and Todd left the reception hand in hand, Christy said, "Thanks for waiting until we had a chance to talk with them."

"Yeah. That was a good call. The cinnamon rolls were good, too."

"You know, with some people it doesn't matter, does it? You can be apart for years, but the moment you're together again it's like no time has passed."

"Forever Friends," Todd said. "They're golden."

Christy gave his hand a squeeze. "So are you. You're my golden Forever Friend."

"And you are my ninja wife who attacks unsuspecting brides with sticky cinnamon rolls."

Christy laughed.

They climbed back into Gussie and puttered out of the parking lot. Todd put the music back on, and they teased each other and sang off-key all the way to the campground. Christy felt as if they had fallen into a sweet, blessed, and un-expectedly sacred pocket of time. She recognized the distinct specialness of it and couldn't stop smiling. This was a time for love.

Nothing but love.

five

The first thing Christy noticed when they pulled into their reserved spot at Refugio State Beach, and she got out of Gussie was how loud the waves sounded. The night air felt chilly, and tinged with the faint scent of salt and seaweed.

"Eee! It's freezing. Where's my jacket?"

Todd opened the sliding side door of their renovated VW van and pulled a blanket off the raised bed in the back. He had removed both the bench seats and designed a comfy sleeping area.

Christy reached for Todd's hoodie. "Can I wear this until I find mine?"

"Sure. Let's go down to the beach."

"Now?"

"Yeah. Come on." He grabbed a flashlight and wrapped the thick blanket around both of them so she had little choice in the matter.

Christy laughed as they tried to find their way by the bouncing illumination from Todd's flashlight. He had his other arm around her shoulder under the blanket, and she

had her arm around his waist. She felt like they were sharing a horse costume, both going in different directions when
they were trying to move as a cohesive unit. Christy couldn't
stop laughing.

"It's this way." Todd confidently pulled her closer and directed them toward a row of palm trees. In the glow of his
flashlight the trees looked like sentinels, lined up and guard-
ing the beach.

Christy was still wearing the dainty shoes she had worn
to the wedding. They were better suited for the grass at the
park than for the damp sand that came in the sides as soon as
she and Todd hit the beach. She suppressed a small squeal at
the chilling sensation and picked her way toward the water in
sync with Todd in their push-me, pull-you-style blanket walk.

Todd stopped and did a quick scan of the water with his
flashlight. "Two to three is my guess. Not like the swells that
can come through here in the winter. Still, it might be enough
for a decent sesh in the morning."

Even though Christy had become accustomed to Todd's
surfing terms, she didn't fully appreciate how the waves at
one beach along the California coast could be more desirable
than at another beach. Todd had been talking about the offshore swells ever since they decided to camp along the cen-
tral coast. He had brought his wetsuit, and she could tell he
was planning an early morning.

"Are you ready to go? Because I sure am." Christy shiv-
ered and rubbed her bare legs together to try to fend off the
goosebumps.

"First we have to look up." Todd turned off the flashlight.
They tilted their heads back to the darkened night sky that
was blistered with a thousand vibrant stars.

"Wow," Christy whispered. "Look at that one. Do you see
it? Straight up. It looks like it's winking at us."

A warm, contented sound of agreement rumbled in
Todd's chest. "Tonight the stars are wishing on us."

As much as she loved the majestic beauty above them and

as much as she adored Todd's poetic comment, she couldn't get her bare legs to stop their burst of goosebumps. "Come on. Let's go get cozy."

Cozy was a good way to describe the interior of Gussie once the two of them were in the van's belly, trying to arrange their bedding. Nothing about their caravan camper setup was remotely close to the visions of the bohemian oasis Christy had conjured up. Except for the stack of colorful blankets and pillows she had brought along in hopes of staying warm through the night.

Once the bed had been haphazardly prepared and the plastic bins containing their food and clothes were moved around to provide a little more wiggle room, Christy reluctantly ventured back outside to the brightly lit campground bathroom. She washed her face with the cold water that poured from the corroded tap and quickly brushed her teeth. Pulling up her hair into a twisted bun on the top of her head, she put up the hood on her Rancho Corona sweatshirt and scampered back to Gussie. All she wanted to do was cuddle with her surfer boy and get warm.

Todd had more amorous ideas about how to warm up, and Christy decided after several ardent kisses that she agreed with his idea.

Nothing but love.

When the morning light shimmied through the open spaces under the curtains Christy had made for Gussie's windows, Todd kissed her on the cheek and whispered, "Dawn patrol. Gotta go."

Christy rolled to the side so he could crawl over her. She squinted in the faintly lit space and said, "Have fun stormin' the castle."

Todd didn't seem to catch her clever farewell because he was opening the side door. He did it slowly, but it still made a lot of noise. He had to stand inside the van to undo the binding that held his surfboard to the roof. With the noise and slight rocking of the van as he unleashed his surfboard came a great whoosh of ocean air.

Christy pulled the blankets over her head and curled up. She knew it would be impossible to fall back asleep now. What she really wanted was a warm shower, but after testing the hot water spigots in the bathroom last night and finding they produced nothing but cold water, she doubted her morning wish would come true.

"Later," Todd said as he slid the side door closed.

Christy pulled back the curtain and watched as Todd ventured into the morning coastal fog with his wetsuit in one hand and his orange surfboard under his other arm. His wild, wooly blond hair was the last thing she could see as he passed the sentinel palms and answered the call of the sea.

In that moment, Christy felt that even if she had never decided before that she loved that man, the mental image of him striding barefooted into the mist was enough to seal him in her heart forever.

The part of camping that Christy liked best, once she was warm enough not to be miserable, was making breakfast. She liked using the camping gear they had packed and setting up a makeshift kitchen on the picnic table that sat under the scruffy tree at the end of their campsite. She had on enough layers, and the coastal fog cleared as soon as the sun broke through and turned the surroundings into a crowded but striking oasis. Unusually tall palm trees towered over her, as she put together the percolating coffeemaker and drew in the chocolaty, rich fragrance of the Italian roast coffee. She figured out how to start the propane stove, one of Todd's long-treasured possessions, and got the coffee going.

Christy tucked her cold hands into the front pouch of her sweatshirt and sat on the picnic table bench, giving way to a string of yawns. She thought about the serious accident Todd had in college and how only two things had survived the crash that totaled the original Gus the Bus. The first was the back bench seat, which had been used to create the Narangus sofa, and the other item was the camp stove Todd had bought right before the accident but not yet used.

No, make that three things that survived. Todd survived. Thank You, God. Thank You, thank You. I can't begin to imagine my life without him.

Moments like this continued to douse the slow-burning embers of frustration Christy felt whenever she thought about Todd's easygoing attitude toward a steady job or building up their savings account. He lived in the moment while she had something in her that propelled her thoughts forward so she was always thinking about what was next and what needed to be done.

Maybe our differences help to balance each other out. That's a good thing, right?

Christy stomped her feet to get the blood flowing. The coffeepot began to percolate. The enticing scent of fresh coffee wafted to her nostrils. Fellow campers stirred. In the space of twenty minutes, the sounds around her went from a few solitary seagulls squawking from atop the nearby lifeguard station to a concert of children's voices, dogs barking, motor-home generators revving up, the clatter of frying pans, and car doors closing.

Christy pulled the small carton of half-and-half from the ice chest and used it to generously lighten her dark, steaming mug of coffee. She savored the first sip while listening to the rising flurry of activity in the campground. Two young boys rode past her on beach cruiser bikes. A woman in a large, floppy straw hat headed toward the beach with a folding beach chair and a Thermos.

What am I doing sitting here? I could be drinking my coffee on the beach and watching Todd surf.

The only thing that stopped her was that she couldn't find the keys to lock up the van. Christy wanted to believe that she could leave everything out on the picnic table and not have to worry. It would be nice if everyone who shared the campground had the same moral code, but she had seen enough in this world to know that everything needed to be locked up.

While she was looking for Todd's keys in the van, she checked her phone and saw that she had missed a video call from Katie ten minutes ago.

Christy clambered into the front seat and plugged in the charger since her battery was almost used up. She dialed Katie and broke into a wide grin when her favorite red-haired friend of all time picked up the call and her face appeared on the screen of Christy's phone.

"You called!" Katie beamed. "Perfect. Seriously. This is perfect timing. Guess where I am?"

"Africa?"

"Very funny." Katie leaned in closer to the camera on her phone as if she was trying to figure out the surroundings behind Christy. "Where are you?"

"We're camping. At the beach. I'm in the front seat of Gussie."

"But you live at the beach. Why are you camping at the beach?"

"It's a different beach. The waves are different here. Somehow. Don't ask me how. We came here after Sierra's wedding last night in Santa Barbara."

"Oh, Sierra! I miss her. How was the wedding?"

"Beautiful. Wonderful. It was outside, and everything felt eclectic and original, just like Sierra. She even had cinnamon rolls instead of wedding cake."

"I wish I could have been there."

"Me, too. Sierra said to tell you that she misses you and the next time you come to California you have to see them." Christy looked more closely at screen of her phone and noticed what appeared to be a stall door behind Katie. "Where are you, by the way?"

"I told you to guess. Where do you think I am? And don't you dare say Africa again. Or Kenya or Brockhurst or any of the other obvious answers."

"It looks like you're in a public bathroom. Please tell me you're not calling me from a public bathroom."

"Ha! You guessed it!"

"Katie, why are you calling me from a bathroom?"

"You're the one who called me."

"But you called me first."

"Yes, because I wanted you to be here in this bathroom with me. But since you're not here, here, having you on the phone like this is the next best thing. I'm so glad you called."

Over the many years of their friendship, Christy had learned that life was slightly wacky with Katie. Her wedding involved a safari and a starlight wedding dinner beside a hippo pool.

Katie zoomed in on the box she held in her free hand. "Do you recognize this?"

Christy squinted to see what was written on the box, and then her heart remembered. It was a pregnancy test. She recognized the same instructions in French that were on the box of the pregnancy test she had taken when she was at Brockhurst. Katie was in the same bathroom where the two of them had gone so Christy could "discreetly" take her test.

"Katie, are you? Really?"

"I don't know yet. I was just about to take the test. Eli is out in a village for another week, but I couldn't wait. I want to know now. I figured the best place to find out was here, where you took your test. And the only other person in the world, besides Eli, that I'd want to have here with me is you."

"Oh, Katie. I love you."

"I know," Katie said briskly. "I love you, too. Are you ready? I'm going to leave the phone on the edge of the sink, and I'll be back in a blink. And this time I won't drop the wand in the toilet the way I did when I dropped yours."

What followed were several awkward minutes of a fixed, close-up view of the underside of the faucet and faint noises accompanied by Katie's play-by-play description.

I can't believe I'm sitting here looking at my phone like this. I should have told her to call me back in five minutes.

"Katie?"

"Almost done."

"You can call me back if you want."

"And not have you share this moment with me? Come on. We Peculiar Treasures have to stick together at times like this. I'm coming out of the stall right now."

The image on the screen changed from the enlarged view of the faucet to a blur of Katie's palm and then a shot of the ceiling. It was a moment before the image on the phone screen came into focus.

Katie held the wand so Christy could see the results clearly. "What does it say? Can you see it?"

"Yes, but you have a much clearer view than I do. What does it say?" Christy held her breath and waited for Katie to report the results.

"Negative." Katie turned the camera to her face. "That means negative, doesn't it?"

Christy could see the disappointment on her friend's freckled face.

"I'm not pregnant."

"Not yet at least."

"I was so sure," Katie said. "Well, reasonably sure. I guess I'm just off kilter, as Eli's mom says. Bummer."

"It could be too soon to tell." Christy tried to sound hopeful since Katie had seemed so excited about the possibility.

"No, it's not too early. It's negative. That's the true result."

"I'm sorry, Katie."

"Well, I'm glad you were here. I mean, sort of here." Katie exited the bathroom and walked outside to her favorite thinking bench on the lush conference grounds. Christy caught bits of the beautiful scenery as Katie walked. "This is going to sound terrible," Katie said as the camera bobbed in rhythm with her gait. "But I'm kind of glad that you guys aren't prego yet either."

"Why do you say that?"

"Because I want to have babies at the same time you have babies."

Christy remembered how Tracy had said something similar about them being pregnant at the same time, and she almost told Katie that Tracy was expecting again. But then she remembered that Tracy didn't want to announce it yet. Plus, if Katie was more bummed about the negative result than she was giving evidence of, hearing that Tracy was pregnant would not be encouraging.

"Our kids have to be close in age," Katie said. "It's because of the way I always said I wanted us to live on the same cul-de-sac so our kids could grow up riding bikes and taking swim lessons together."

"We are both at home in quite different corners of the world. I don't think either of us could have ever predicted that."

"I know. That's why my new dream is that we can both be pregnant at the same time. One of us will have a boy, and one of us will have a girl. Then we'll set up an arranged marriage for them, and in our old age we'll all go live with our children, and all their babies will have the best of you two and the best of us. They'll have Todd's blue eyes and my red hair."

Christy laughed. "That's an awesome dream, Katie. Keep dreaming it."

"Did you just say 'awesome'?"

"No. Wait. Did I?"

"You did. I'll take that as evidence that Doug is rubbing off on you. So tell me more about Sierra's wedding. I don't want to talk about babies anymore right now."

"She was a beautiful bride, and Jordan seems perfect for her."

"I guess that's the end of our PO Box club."

"Your what?"

"We had this thing back in England when we were at Carnforth Hall that we were going to be 'pals only' with guys. That's where the *P* and *O* came from. But I guess the PO days are over for both of us."

The two friends reminisced some more before the video call suddenly cut out. Christy was used to that happening with their connection so she didn't try to call Katie back.

She checked her phone to make sure she hadn't run out of battery or cell service. Todd tapped on the window and she jumped. Christy opened the door and stepped out. "You have seaweed in your hair." She pulled the clump of bulbous pale-green stuff from his matted hair and tossed it toward the bushes.

"Kelp," Todd said.

"What do you need help with?"

"No, I said *kelp*. The water is filled with kelp. It's like surfing through monster spiderwebs."

"Were the waves any good?"

"They were all right." Todd balanced his board against the hood of the van. "Are you still cold? Is that why you were closed up in there?"

"No. I made some coffee, and then I was looking for the keys so I could lock things up and go down to the beach. But Katie called."

"How are they doing?" Todd pulled the zipper down the back of his wetsuit and looked at Christy, waiting for her to continue.

"They're good." Christy didn't want to share the details with him. Instead of Katie's and Sierra's Pals Only club, Christy sometimes felt as if she and Katie were in a GO club—a Girls Only club. She didn't feel the need to tell Todd about the girly stuff she and Katie had just shared.

"You were saying something about coffee?" Todd hung his wetsuit over the end of the picnic table and looked around for evidence.

"Coming right up." She eagerly went about making a fresh pot. She knew Todd would love the strong scent and taste as much as she had.

They might not have a posh, bohemian weekend set up with pillows and pinwheels and antique soda pop bottles lining the picnic table and bursting with freshly cut wildflowers. But they had darling Gussie with her flower-power vintage cuteness. And they had deep, dark, velvety roasted coffee percolating away on Todd's camp stove.

They were living the good life, and Christy loved it.

One More Wish

six

*T*he next few hours were happy ones.

Christy and Todd worked together to made a tasty breakfast as the sun rose overhead. The welcomed warmth on their shoulders flooded their campsite with brazen light. Christy peeled down to the T-shirt and shorts she had on under her sweats. Todd locked up the van, and together they strolled down to the water with their low beach chairs.

Christy brought her *Peter Pan* book with her and a bottle of sparkling lemon water. Todd brought his skimboard instead of his surfboard. He tossed the flat, wooden board onto the firm sand at the shoreline. As the water curled in and slid beneath the board, Todd would run, jump on the moving board, and skim across the sand. His balance was so good Christy only looked up to see him tumble into the water once or twice.

By the time he finally took a break and came to sit next to her in his beach chair, he looked wiped out. Christy handed him her bottle of water, and within a few minutes he had reclined his chair and stretched out his legs. His arms, still glistening with tiny drops of ocean water, balanced on the armrests.

"Do you want some sunscreen?" Christy asked.

Too late. He was already asleep.

Christy read a line from the book to him in a whisper. "'You know that place between sleep and awake, the place where you can still remember dreaming? That's where I'll always love you, Peter Pan. That's where I'll be waiting.'"

The rest of their camping trip was just as dreamy and relaxed. They lounged all afternoon and took note of how most of the other campers were leaving. Todd reminded Christy that since it was Sunday evening, most of the campers had come for a weekend getaway and needed to return home.

For Todd and Christy, it felt as if they were nearly alone on a tropical island when they walked the long curve of the shoreline hand in hand at sunset. They saw only four other people on the beach after sharing the same sand with hundreds of vacationers that afternoon.

Returning to their campsite, they found some oranges and an unopened bag of marshmallows waiting on their picnic table.

"One of our neighbors probably left them when they packed up," Todd said. "I brought a couple of wire coat hangers in case we needed them for the hot dogs."

"Perfect." Christy pulled small russet potatoes out of the food bin in Gussie and asked Todd to start the fire. She had wrapped the potatoes in foil after rubbing them with butter and lots of garlic salt. As soon as the coals turned gray in the standing barbecue by the picnic table, Christy buried the wrapped potatoes. "These should take about half an hour. Do you want to roast the hot dogs now or have some coleslaw?"

"You brought cold slaw? I love your cold slaw."

"It's coleslaw. You know that, right? We've had this discussion before."

"Cold slaw," Todd repeated.

"No, *cole*. With an *e*. Not a *d*. It's coleslaw."

"So, who is Cole anyhow? Did he invent it?"

"No."

"You sure?" Todd's expression in the twilight made it clear that he loved teasing Christy. He put the camping lantern on top of the picnic table and primed it so his lit match started a flame in the chamber. "What about this lantern?"

"What about it?" Christy smoothed the tablecloth under the lantern and put two plates and the bowl of coleslaw in front of him.

"Did this guy Cole invent this lantern as well as the slaw?"

"What?"

"Look. It says right here: *Coleman*. I'm thinking Cole invented the Coleman lantern. Clever guy."

Christy shook her head at her husband. He was happy. That made her happy. The joy of the sacred "now" was definitely covering both of them that evening.

"So, did Cole come up with the idea of putting pineapple and macadamia nuts in the salad?"

"No. We had it this way in Hawaii on our honeymoon. Remember?"

"I don't remember, but I love this stuff." Todd transferred a big scoop onto his plate.

"I'm glad you do." Christy had often thought that this was one of the few vegetable dishes she had successfully integrated into their meals. Most of the time the only vegetables Todd consumed were ones that were swimming in a pool of ranch dressing.

Todd prayed before digging in. He thanked God for the restful day they had shared and offered thanks for the food they were about to enjoy. He thanked God for the gift of the marshmallows, but especially for the *cole*slaw.

He looked up after his "amen" and caught Christy smiling at him. Three bites into the coleslaw he pointed his fork at her and said, "Cole," as if it were a grand declaration.

She thought they already had exhausted the topic and went back to eating.

"Cole Spencer. Admit it. That's a great name. Sounds rad, doesn't it? We should name our first son Cole."

Christy stopped chewing. Over the years they had come up with lots of names for their children. Some were serious and some were silly. Cole had never appeared on any of their lists.

"What do you think?" Todd looked hopeful. "It's a great surfer name. Cole Spencer. Yeah, that's it."

"What if we have a girl?"

"Then we'll name her Cole-ita." He waited for her to respond.

Christy didn't give him the satisfaction. She kept eating without looking up.

"Coleita Gussie Juliet Spencer."

Christy tipped her plastic spoon back and playfully flung a dollop of coleslaw at him. Todd ducked, and the flying cabbage salad missed him. He laughed his best little boy laugh.

"You think I'm kidding," he said." I'm not kidding. Not about the boy's name. I think Cole is the best one we've come up with yet."

Christy didn't dislike the name. It wasn't one of her top five, but she could see why Todd liked the way it sounded. She put another spoonful of coleslaw in her mouth and chewed thoughtfully while keeping her gaze fixed on her husband. For her, it was way too early to settle on a name for their first baby. They needed to figure out their finances and make sure Todd's job situation was established. They needed to talk about when would be the best time to get pregnant and then wait for the miracle to happen. She would be more interested in agreeing to a baby's name after first priorities had been settled. But once again, she knew this wasn't the time to bring up the subject of Todd needing a permanent job rather than agreeing to sand a bunch of surfboards for little or no pay.

Wait until after this trip. Everything has been so perfect. It's always tense, emotional, and painful when we talk about money. Be smart, Christy. Don't bring it up now.

"I'll add the name to the list," she said diplomatically.

Todd thought a moment. "How about Bryan for a middle name? Cole Bryan Spencer. Yeah, that's it. Cole Bryan Spencer."

When Christy didn't respond, Todd asked, "What are you thinking?"

"I think . . ." She cautiously sidestepped leaking any of her tension-inducing comments and said, "I think we could never tell our son that the inspiration for his name came from a cabbage salad we ate on a camping trip."

Todd stopped eating and put down his fork. He looked at the remaining coleslaw on his paper plate and then looked up at Christy. "There's cabbage in this?"

"Yes, of course."

"You never told me you put cabbage in this."

"What did you think it was made from?"

"I don't know. Good stuff. Not cabbage." Todd poked at the remains, isolating the crushed macadamia nuts and bits of pineapple.

Christy shook her head and chuckled at her funny husband.

The deep joy continued through the night as they roasted hot dogs, toasted and burnt a few marshmallows, and gave themselves to each other with their uncluttered hearts overflowing with nothing but love.

Monday morning became a repeat of Sunday, with Todd slipping away to go on dawn patrol, and Christy once again longing to take a hot shower. They ate leftover hot-dog buns slathered with peanut butter and drank mugs of camp-stove coffee.

After a long walk on the beach, collecting bits of sea glass and a few pebbles, they repeated their late-morning routine of Christy reading and Todd skimboarding and napping. By one o'clock they were ready to pack up and head home. Christy had finished her book at the same time that a stacked-up layer of offshore clouds was creeping inland, hiding the sun.

Both of them craved pepperoni pizza from their favorite place four blocks from their house. They thought that if they left now, they could enjoy an early dinner, long, hot showers, and a great night's sleep in their own bed.

The drive home took much longer than they expected due to the Los Angeles traffic. The music mix they had listened to on the drive to Santa Barbara played through twice before Christy asked if they could listen to something else.

Todd turned off the music. "What do you think about adopting?"

Christy felt her heart lunge, as if Todd had put on the brakes. "Adopting? As in, adopting a baby?"

"A baby or a kid. What do you think?"

"I don't know. Where did this come from?"

"One of the guys I painted with last week said he and his wife weren't able to have kids of their own, and they adopted three."

"Three? At the same time?"

Todd nodded. "I think the six- and seven-year-olds were brothers in foster care so they adopted them at the same time. Their daughter is a baby. She was a foster kid, too."

Christy stared out the window at the endless stretch of Los Angeles buildings and billboards that lined this congested portion of the freeway. The topic had caught her off guard. Having children suddenly enter her life who were already walking and talking was something she had never pictured before. She had only thought about having a child of their own one day. Her mental images were linked to tiny feet, midnight feedings, and soft kisses on pudgy little cheeks. Not foster care of young boys.

Todd glanced at Christy and then back at the road. "You look like you just clocked out of the conversation. Are you okay?"

"I never thought about adopting."

"Really? After the year that you worked at the orphanage in Switzerland? I always thought that experience with those kids would have made you want to adopt a dozen before we even tried to have a baby."

"No. I didn't feel that way." As soon as she said those words, she felt as if there was something wrong with her. Christy liked working at the orphanage. She didn't love it, but she liked it. She loved some of the children, not all of them. One little girl had captured her heart, and if Christy could have adopted her and brought her home then, she would have.

"What if we had a chance to adopt a brand-new baby?" Todd asked.

Christy still didn't have an answer. When they were in high school, their friend Alissa gave up her baby for adoption. The birth father, Shawn, was one of Todd's closest friends, but he had died in a freak surfing accident. Christy had fallen out of contact with Alissa, but she often had wondered how both Alissa and her now eleven-year-old daughter, Shawna, were doing. She especially wondered if adoption had been the right choice in that situation.

But she never had wondered if she and Todd should adopt an infant.

"What are you thinking?" Todd asked after Christy had been silent for some time.

"I don't know. I think you and I need to sit down and talk about a lot of things when it comes to babies and plans for the future. Adoption is one of things we should add to the list. But I don't think I'm up for that conversation right now."

"Okay."

They continued at their twenty-miles-per-hour pace down the freeway, both of them silent.

"When do you want to sit down?" Todd asked.

"I don't know. Tomorrow night? Or next weekend? It doesn't matter. Just not now while we're stuck in traffic."

Todd glanced at her. "Are you okay? Do you need stop to find something to eat or drink?"

"That's probably a good idea. I could use a bathroom

break, too."

The discussion of their future ended up on hold for several weeks. Once they were back home in their regular routine, it seemed all they did was work and sleep. Todd stayed busy at Zane's on the surfboard-reshaping project. He was promised a "fair portion of the profit" once the job was completed. Todd was comfortable with that arrangement, and Christy decided that, for now, she would be, too.

She felt that way because Todd finally received a big check from a kitchen remodel he had helped with in May. The amount was twice what he had expected. It had taken so long for the money to come in that Christy had convinced herself they were never going to get paid. They deposited the entire amount into their savings account, and that felt really good. It didn't solve any of the bigger problems, but for now it was a panic reliever.

Christy's schedule left little time for anything else. She didn't like being so busy. She missed having a free day on Saturday and thought she would be relieved when September came and her summer job at the spa would end.

However, on the last Saturday in August when Eva asked if Christy would stay on at the White Orchid through the fall, Christy immediately said, "Yes." She also said, "I'd love to work here full-time, if a position opens up."

Eva looked surprised, but then she said, "If we had an opening, I'd love to have you here full-time. Your personality and your spirit exude serenity. You are a pleasure to be around."

Christy wasn't sure what Eva meant by "serenity," but knowing that Eva thought she was a pleasure to be around was encouraging and gave her reason to hope that maybe she could make the switch and leave the Balboa Treasure Chest sometime in the near future.

She called Tracy before heading home from the spa. Tracy had stayed home the past few Friday nights, and Christy hadn't seen her since their very brief teatime at Julie Ann's, which was more than a month ago. Doug said on Friday night that Tracy's parents had put their house up for sale and were continuing their plans to move to Oregon. When Christy asked how Tracy was doing, all Doug said was, "You should give her a call."

Tracy answered right away, and the first thing Christy said was, "I'm so sorry."

"Sorry for what?"

"For being a terrible friend. I've missed you, and I feel awful that I haven't been able to get over there to see you."

"You don't have to apologize, Christy. Don't feel bad. It's been a busy month for you."

"I know. But I've been eager to get caught up with you. Would it be okay if I came over now? I'm leaving work in a few minutes."

"No, sorry. We're going over to my parents' tonight. Maybe we could get together tomorrow afternoon."

Christy groaned. "We're going down to Escondido tomorrow after church to see my parents. We haven't seen them since the middle of June, and here it is almost September already. I can't believe the summer is gone. I hate being so busy."

"I know. It's been crazy for both of us. My good news is that I finally got a doctor's appointment scheduled for Monday. They had to cancel my last appointment, so I'm hoping this one works out."

"That's good to hear. Should I try to come by Monday when I get off work?"

"No. We have a birthday party we're going to for one of the guys from Doug's work."

"Tuesday, then?"

"That might work. How about if I text you?"

"Sure. Sounds good. I look forward to seeing you."

"I look forward to seeing you, too. Thanks so much for calling, Christy."

Christy hung up and felt a little less guilty for letting the whole month of August slip by without spending any time with Tracy.

The best thing about Tracy is that she's truly a Forever Friend, like Sierra. We're always able to pick up where we left off. I only hope it will feel that way for her, too, once we finally connect next week.

seven

$\mathcal{C}$hristy and Tracy didn't manage to connect until the Friday Night Gathering the next week. The best part was that Tracy felt well enough to come after missing so many weeks. To Christy's surprise, when Doug and Tracy walked in the front door, Lindee was the first to welcome Tracy back with a big hug.

"Doug told us last week," Lindee said. "Do you know if it's a boy or a girl yet?"

"No, not yet."

"I hope it's a girl. Girls rock."

Tracy smiled. It seemed that she wanted to say, "Me, too," but she didn't say anything.

Some of the other girls in the group welcomed her back with equally sweet hugs. Tracy managed to make her way into the kitchen where Christy was refilling a big bowl with tortilla chips. She put down the bag and added her hug to the others Tracy had received.

The first thing Christy noticed was that Tracy already was showing. Christy wanted to pat Tracy's tummy but sensed her shy friend would feel more comfortable without being patted or having any attention drawn to her already looking preggers.

The group stood around the island counter in the kitchen talking and snacking as Tracy fell into her usual role of helping to serve. When the guys started to play the first worship song, Christy motioned for Tracy to follow her into the downstairs guest bedroom where they could close the door and talk in private. They stretched out on the guest bed, and Tracy rested her folded hands on her pooched-out belly.

"So start with the baby news," Christy said. "How did it go at the doctor's?"

"I found out I'm further along than I thought."

"You are? When's your due date?"

"January 10."

"Wow, that's going to come quickly."

"I know." Tracy reached over and gave Christy's arm a squeeze. "There's something more."

"More?"

Tracy nodded and paused as if waiting for Christy to guess.

Christy was certain the "more" was the news that Tracy and Doug were moving to Oregon. She didn't want to be the one to say the sad words so she waited for Tracy to speak.

That's when Tracy uttered a single word with a double meaning. "Twins."

Christy thought Tracy was telling a Doug-type of joke and immediately replied, "Very funny."

Tracy waited, biting her lower lip.

Christy's mouth opened, but no words came out. Her response was to stare at Tracy's belly. When she found her voice she squeaked out the words, "Really? Honest?"

Tracy nodded. "Yes. Really. Honest."

Christy quickly crafted an enthusiastic response. "Wow, Tracy. That's amazing! Congratulations. You're having twins!"

Tracy's sweet face seemed to crinkle up as if it were made

of tissue paper. "What am I going to do, Christy?" Big tears like liquid crystals raced down her cheeks.

"Oh, Tracy, don't cry." Christy gave her a hug. "You're going to do great. You are. I'm so happy for you."

"I'm still in shock. We've only told about five people other than our parents. I just can't believe it. How is this little body of mine ever going to carry twins?"

"You'll do fine, Tracy. You will. No wonder you had such a difficult time with morning sickness the last few months."

"I know. It makes sense now. I'm only in my second trimester, and I feel so big already. But at least I can keep food down now."

"Wow." Christy wished she could come up with other words that might be more comforting. "What did Doug say?"

"I'm sure you can guess."

Christy grinned and took on a low, Doug-like voice. "This is awesome!"

"Exactly. But he's not the one who is trying to corral a rambunctious toddler all day long, and he's not the one who has to tote these two kickboxers around inside for the next four months."

"Are they kicking already?"

"I've felt a few flutters. I'm sure it won't be long, though, before my belly is going to resemble two cats fighting in a gunnysack."

Christy laughed.

Tracy's tears had stopped. She seemed relieved, as if she had been waiting for days to tell Christy, which she had. "I couldn't just text this news to you or even tell you over the phone."

"I'm glad you waited to tell me tonight. I'm especially glad that you feel well enough to be out and about again."

"Me, too."

"So, what's the latest with your parents? Did they decide to stay here now that they know you're having twins and will need lots of help?"

Tracy's countenance clouded over again, and Christy wished she hadn't asked. It was obviously a difficult subject.

"They're still planning to move. They haven't had any offers yet on their house, but they received an offer on the bungalow we've been renting from them. If it goes through, we'll have to move."

"To Oregon?" Christy asked cautiously.

Tracy looked surprised that Christy would suggest such a thing. "No. To another house or an apartment. We want to stay here, in this area, if we can."

"Good. I don't want you to leave."

"We don't want to leave either. As much as we dislike the thought of moving, we know it's probably a God-thing that the bungalow sold when it did because it's forcing us to find a bigger place before the babies come."

They talked a few more minutes about all the changes that were ahead for Doug and Tracy. Christy noticed that Tracy's countenance was turning more solemn and chalky.

"Are you okay?"

"I will be," Tracy said bravely. "It's just a lot to think about. I really wish my parents weren't going ahead with their plans to move. Doug seems to understand their side of things better than I do. He says we need to make our own way as our own family and for me not to be so dependent on my mom. I think he's expecting our lives to go back to being more like they were when we lived in Carlsbad, before we had Daniel."

"In what way?"

"We made our own schedule back then and figured out how to do things on our own. Ever since we moved here he says that my mom's wishes and her schedule dictate what we do and when. And he's right, you know. That is how it's been."

"Do you think it's a good thing, then, in a way, for them to move?" Christy inwardly had to side with Doug on this point. She had seen many times the way that Tracy's mom had quietly inserted herself into Doug and Tracy's lives and directed them based on what she thought was best. She always did so with sweetness, and Christy was sure she had the best of intentions. But Christy could see how it undermined Doug's role in their marriage.

Tracy sighed. "I suppose if my parents lived farther away from us, Doug might feel more like he's the head of our home."

Christy couldn't imagine taking regular direction from her mom the way Tracy did. It was enough for her to have her aunt's input, but even Marti had cut way back on her involvement in Christy's life over the past year.

The two friends sat quietly for a few minutes, letting the complex thoughts settle on them. Christy had struggled with this topic of the husband being the fully vested leader in the family. She knew the model was biblically based, and she also knew that following God's way of doing things always brought the greatest blessing. But she wondered how she could support the leadership of someone who hadn't yet taken on the responsibility for providing the majority of the family's income. And how could they start a family until that happened?

It didn't take much to fan the embers Christy had covered over several weeks ago. Suddenly they turned into a searing, red-hot frustration. Christy wanted to tell Tracy all the things that bothered her about her husband and her marriage. She wanted to unburden herself by sharing with her trusted friend.

But something stopped her.

Was it the feeling that Tracy and Doug and everyone else under Christy's roof that night had such a deep sense of love and respect for Todd? Was it her sense that she would betray him if she opened up the way she wanted to? Or was it a sensor alarm going off in her spirit telling her that Tracy was dealing with enough anxiety and discouragement right now? She didn't need to take on Christy's anger and frustration as well.

"Would you mind if we didn't talk about this anymore right now?" Tracy asked.

"Sure. Of course." Christy drew in a long breath through her nostrils and tried to quell her agitated spirit.

"To be honest," Tracy said. "One of the reasons I was looking forward to coming tonight was so I could hear Todd's message. I haven't been to church or anything for more than a month, and I'm so hungry for some encouragement. It sounds like the singing has ended. Would it be okay with you if we joined the rest of the group?"

Christy nodded but didn't trust her heart enough at the moment to say anything. Just like Tracy, she appreciated hearing what Todd had to say. She always had. He was gifted and had the best analogies. But her feelings about his overly easygoing attitude concerning their future and their finances made it hard to think about sitting down to listen to his talk.

But Christy put aside her frustrations and slipped into the kitchen with Tracy. They sat on the counter stools and faced the large, open living room. More than forty high school and college students were packed in the warm living room, sitting on cushions and close together on the sofa and love seat. They were all listening carefully, intently.

Todd had been going through the Gospel of John, with the study stretching out for years. Some weeks he would camp on a single verse and squeeze out all the meaning and application the way their old-fashioned juicer extracted all the juice from an orange. Other weeks, Todd would turn the passage over to Doug and he would move through the verses more quickly with a focus on the historic context. Christy always learned a lot no matter which of them was leading. She knew the group was learning a lot, as well.

Be still. Listen.

Christy stretched her neck from side to side in an effort to release the tension she had felt building up while she and Tracy were talking. She listened as Todd read the passage from John 13 in which Jesus washes the disciples' feet at the Last Supper.

"Last week I talked about how Peter protested Jesus

washing his feet. Let's move on and see how Jesus responded to Peter." Todd flipped through the pages of his well-worn Bible. "It's in verse 7. 'Jesus replied, "You do not realize now what I am doing, but later you will understand."'"

One of the guys on the floor called out, "later," and some of the group laughed at the inside joke. Todd laughed, too, and said, "Yeah. Later. See? I'm not the only one who uses that term. Jesus said it to Peter. 'Later, Dude.'"

Some chuckles and a few more comments circled the group before Todd pulled their attention back to the passage. "Do you see what's happening here? Peter is confused. He doesn't understand what Jesus is doing. Remember how just a few days earlier, on Palm Sunday, Jesus rode into Jerusalem, and the crowd welcomed Him like a king? They thought He was going to take over and set up His earthly rule right then. They thought their troubles were over."

Todd lowered his chin and looked at the group. "Instead, Jesus took on a servant's role. He knelt down and washed his disciples' feet. Peter basically says, 'Hey! What are you doing?' And Jesus tells him, 'You don't understand now, but you will later.'

"So here's my question for you," Todd continued. "Was there a time this week when you said to Jesus, 'Hey! What are you doing? What's going on? Nothing is going the way I thought it was supposed to. Aren't You the King of everything? Why aren't You solving all these problems right now?'"

The room became still. Christy glanced at Tracy and saw tears tumbling down her cheeks.

"You feel like Peter because you're confused. God is doing stuff in your life, but it's not at all what you thought He would be doing. This verse is for you, for me, for all of us, just as it was for Peter. It's an eternal truth. God's ways aren't our ways. What He's doing now, we don't understand. We don't realize what it means, why it's important, or why it has to happen now."

Christy felt the words her husband was speaking soak

into her weary heart.

Todd looked back at his Bible with a slight grin. "Here's the promise. This is my favorite part; this is why I love God so much. Even though we don't understand, He doesn't say, 'Go away, leave me alone, it's none of your business what I'm doing right now.' No. Instead, God gives a promise. He says we will understand later."

Todd gazed over the group. "Think about whatever it is you're going through. When is it going to make sense?"

"Later," one of the guys called out.

"Yeah. Later. Exactly."

Todd lowered himself back onto the counter stool in front of the fireplace. "I have held on to that promise so many times in my life. Every time I have to wait for God to accomplish His eternal purpose in my life, I think of this verse. I think, right now, I don't get it. I don't understand. What You're doing, God, is not the way I'd do it at all. Why won't You explain to me what's going on? And in my head, this is what I hear . . ."

"Later." One of the guys gave the answer Todd was about to say.

Todd grinned. "You got it. Later. I'll understand later. It might not be until heaven. That's okay. For now, all I need to do is trust God and go with the flow of what He's doing in His way and be at peace with His timing."

Christy was so fixated on Todd she almost didn't realize that an unexplainable calm had covered her anxious heart. It felt as if a sliver of the eternal had been captured in this moment in their living room. What was happening here mattered greatly.

My husband has a gift for teaching like this. It's what he was created to do.

She had thought that many times over the years, but tonight she saw it clearly once again.

I mean, what high school student gives up a Friday night to listen to a guy talk about the Bible?

Those thoughts stayed with Christy as she drove to the spa the next morning. She wanted her life to change. She longed for the privilege of staying home so she could use her gift of hospitality. She wanted to facilitate more opportunities for Todd to use his gift of teaching. She wanted them to do that together, in their home. But how could she when she was never home?

The yearly Santa Ana winds that came roaring in from the eastern deserts of Southern California had arrived for their September visit. The tall palm trees that lined the drive up to the resort rustled their fronds like Tahitian dancers. The skies were clear with an unnerving absence of the inversion layer that usually graced the coast this time of day and that left a fine mist on her windshield.

When Christy parked and opened her car door, the hot winds tugged on her ponytail. She decided that she had waited patiently, but the time had come for her to initiate the long overdue discussion. Todd had to walk away from refinishing surfboards and take on a real job.

She sent him a text.

HEY. LET'S SET ASIDE SOME TIME TO TALK TO-NIGHT, OK?

Todd replied right away with a simple: OK.

Christy thought all day about how to tell Todd everything she had been thinking, feeling, and struggling with for some time now. He knew some of her frustrations, but she wanted him to understand that just because they had a little money in the bank didn't mean that she could or should continue to work so many hours.

At the end of her workday, just as Christy was getting in her car, Todd sent her another text saying that he was staying on at Zane's for an hour and he had already eaten so she didn't need to make dinner for him. Christy drove through a fast-food place that had pretty good chicken sandwiches. It was close to Cheri's, the bakery where Marti had bought Christy's birthday cupcakes.

Christy parked behind Cheri's and ate her chicken sandwich. Then she went inside and bought a half-dozen tiny cupcakes that were decorated with hearts on top. They were way more expensive than she would have guessed they would be, but she liked the idea of having something sweet waiting for when Todd finished at Zane's.

The more she thought about it as she drove home, the more Christy liked the idea of setting up a tea party on the living room coffee table. She would use the "wish upon a starfish" napkins Tracy had given her for her birthday and the two teaspoons with the shells. Christy had some nice china teacups with saucers and a raised cake-stand plate she would arrange the cupcakes on.

Going through her usual routine, Christy went inside and opened up the windows, airing out the house. She put on some music and lit a candle on the kitchen counter before pulling together her coffee table tea party just as she had imagined it.

When everything was ready, Christy scooted upstairs to change out of her all-black spa attire and slipped into the same cute dress she had worn for her birthday dinner at Bob and Marti's. She let down her hair and gave it a good brushing. She would at least look nice even if what they had to talk about wasn't going to be that pleasant.

Christy was coming down the stairs when she heard a knock on the front door.

Did Todd forget his key?

She peered through the side window to see who was there before opening the door.

It was Lindee.

eight

*C*hristy slowly opened the door, with her heart pounding faster than it should in the presence of a teenage girl who had been in her home many times.

With her typical I'll-call-the-shots-here attitude, Lindee slipped off her shoes and left them by the front door, as was the Friday night routine. She held up a book and took a step inside.

"You said I could borrow another one."

As much as Christy felt the hair on her arms bristle whenever she was around Lindee, something about her being a fellow reader smoothed over the rough edges of how brusque she was.

Christy led the way into the living room where the wall next to the stairs was lined with books. Many of them were novels she had collected when she worked at the Dove's Nest bookstore right after she and Todd were first married.

The tea party setup on the coffee table caught Lindee's attention. She stopped and eyed the colorful napkins, teacups, teapot, and cupcakes.

"Are you having a party?"

"Sort of."

"A tea party?"

Christy nodded.

"Is someone coming?"

She felt a little embarrassed to say that she had prepared a tea party for Todd. Without meaning to, she said, "They aren't here yet. Would you like some tea?"

"Me?"

Christy gathered her senses. "You probably need to get going. Do you know which book you would like to borrow?"

"I don't have to be anywhere." Lindee eyed the cupcakes. "I've never had tea before. Hot tea, I mean. Not in fancy cups like those."

Christy scrambled to collect her thoughts. Todd had said he was staying at Zane's for another hour. In the past his "one extra hour" had turned into two or three hours more than once. She might as well sit and have some tea with Lindee. It couldn't hurt. It might even help their relationship.

"Have a seat," Christy offered. "I'll put on the kettle."

Christy turned the gas flame on the stove to high, and the water came to a whistling boil in a few minutes. She chose some loose-leaf English Breakfast tea from a canister on the counter and poured the water over the dark leaves. With steady paces, Christy carried the teapot over to the couch.

Lindee sat perfectly still, taking in Christy's movements as she placed the teacup and saucer in front of Lindee. "We'll let it steep for a few minutes, and then I'll pour for us. The milk and sugar are there, and you can use one of these little stir spoons if you like."

Lindee rounded her shoulders back and sat up straight. "This is like one of those TV shows about England where they wear those fancy outfits and the men always wear tuxes to dinner. Do you do this all the time?"

"No, just on special occasions."

"What's the special occasion? Who were you expecting?"

Christy wasn't sure how she wanted to answer but then decided to say what was true. "I wanted to have a nice dessert ready for Todd when he came home."

Lindee made a squirrely face, as if she thought Christy was speaking in code. "You mean like in the movies, don't you? *You're* really what he's going to have for his special dessert tonight, aren't you?"

Christy hadn't seen that comment coming. Her expression must have reflected her uncomfortable surprise that a young teen would make such a statement about Todd and Christy's private lives. "Lindee, that's—"

"Inappropriate. Yeah, I just figured that out. I forget that you guys don't talk like my friends and my family. Sorry."

Christy knew she shouldn't be surprised that Lindee had little sense of boundaries or manners.

"That's why I like the books you've been letting me read," Lindee said. "They're different than the books my mom has." She listed the titles of some of the more popular erotica novels that Christy knew only because of the focus that had been put on them lately in the media.

Christy's heart ached. "Lindee, I don't want you reading those books. The evocative images you're putting into your mind don't represent true love. Those books show the opposite of what we talk about here at the Friday Night Gatherings."

"Tell me about it. That's why I come here every week. It makes me feel good. I don't feel good anyplace else. Not at home or school."

Christy felt even more off guard now that Lindee was being vulnerable and opening up to her. She wished Tracy were with them. She had a tender way of listening and saying just the right thing. Several of the girls who came on Friday night over the years had sought Tracy's big sisterly advice. Christy never knew what to say.

"I think the tea is ready." Christy reached for the teapot and poured the amber liquid into Lindee's cup and then into hers, hoping they could talk about something else.

Lindee followed Christy's lead as she added milk and a bit of sugar to her china cup and stirred it. Lindee lifted the cup and saucer, holding the saucer awkwardly by the rim with both hands.

Christy reached over and adjusted Lindee's fingers so they released their grip, and the saucer could rest on her flattened, opened palm. "There. It's easier that way." Christy lifted her cup and saucer and demonstrated by balancing the saucer and lifting the china cup to her lips.

In halted unison they took a sip. Christy waited for Lindee's response.

"This is weird." Lindee looked over her shoulder, as if to make sure no one was watching.

"Do you need more milk or sugar? I usually make the tea kind of strong."

"No, I mean, it's weird because I always wanted to go to a tea party and drink real tea from one of these kind of cups. I didn't know anybody ever did this at home."

Christy found something lively and cheery rising inside her, and she thought of a random verse she had read in Proverbs 31 a few days ago.

"She is clothed in strength and dignity; she can laugh at the days to come."

Christy wondered how many other young women like Lindee didn't have anyone to show them what strength and dignity looked like in a woman. If all their role models were from books and movies that depicted women making violent and perverse sexual choices, how would they even know that they could develop a deeper beauty in their spirits?

"Lindee, I want to tell you something."

Lindee put down her teacup and saucer in a wobbly way. They clanged against the edge of the coffee table. "Sorry."

"That's okay." Christy tried to make sure she was wearing her most compassionate, kind, and sweet expression. Basically, she hoped she looked like Tracy. "Lindee, you are a one-of-a-kind, memorable, and lovely young woman."

Lindee blushed. "I'm not lovely."

Christy closed her eyes for emphasis and nodded. "Yes you are. You are lovely."

Lindee scowled, as if this were some sort of joke.

"Do you see how we're drinking out of lovely, uniquely decorated china cups? Mine is different from yours, but they're both fine china. We're not drinking our tea out of Styrofoam or throwaway paper cups. It's like that with you. You're not a Styrofoam or throwaway paper girl. God made you to be a lovely, uniquely designed, fine china cup. That's how He sees you, and that's how I see you."

Lindee had no words. She stared at Christy, as if waiting for the punch line of a cruel joke.

Christy smiled calmly. She lifted the plate of cupcakes and offered it to Lindee. "Would you like one?"

With slowed movements, Lindee reached for one of the dainty sweets with the heart on top. She peeled back the colorful paper and ate it in one bite. She awkwardly folded the paper and put it on the edge of her saucer. Then she reached for one of the "wish upon a starfish" napkins and turned her face away from Christy as she wiped her eyes.

To give Lindee a chance to focus on something else, Christy asked, "Did you have a chance to decide on which book you want to borrow?"

"No. I'll get one now." She slowly stood and went over to the bookcase. It seemed that she didn't even look at the titles but pulled out a thick book.

"*Redeeming Love*," Christy said with a smile. "That's one of my absolute favorites. I think you'll love it."

"At least it has love in the title, so maybe my mom will read it, too."

"I hope she does." Christy stood and shepherded Lindee toward the front door.

Lindee paused. "Do you need help cleaning or anything? I could stay and do the dishes or something."

"No, that's okay. Thanks for the offer."

"What are you going to have for snacks on Friday night? Everyone likes your peanut butter cookies."

"Then I'll make peanut butter cookies this week."

"I could come over early to help you make them."

"That's okay. I'll probably make them Thursday night."

"I'll come Thursday night then. What time should I be here?" The tone in Lindee's voice had turned back into her pushy, edgy way of getting her point across.

Christy was trying to think of the best way to say that Lindee didn't need to come at all when she heard the sound of the garage door opening. Todd was home. Lindee's dark eyes looked hopeful. She went over to one of the kitchen stools and plopped down just as Todd entered. Christy stood alone at the open front door, not quite sure what to do.

"Hey." Todd looked at Lindee and then at Christy as if trying to figure out what was going on.

"Christy is letting me borrow another book." Lindee held up the proof, as if she needed an excuse for being there.

"Cool. I hear that's a good one." Todd went over to Christy and gave her a kiss. He looped his arm around her shoulder and stood by her, looking at Lindee.

"I really came over because I wanted to talk to you guys. I mean, I wanted to borrow a book, but I also wanted to ask you something."

Todd led Christy back to the kitchen counter, and together they waited to hear what Lindee had to say.

"The thing is . . ." Lindee looked up and made eye contact with them. "I want to live here. With you guys."

Christy felt her jaw go slack. Once again, she hadn't seen that one coming.

Without missing a beat, Todd asked, "Why would you want to live with us?"

"Because you guys love each other." Lindee said it as if it should have been obvious. "You have an extra room downstairs, and I could help with chores. Christy could teach me how to cook and stuff."

Christy felt ripples of sympathy for Lindee because of the pleading sound in her voice. Todd, however, cut the discussion off in midair, which Christy was grateful for later.

"We're not in a position to take you in, Lindee. My parents divorced, so I know how rough it can be to live with only one of your parents. It's lonely. It's awful. I know. But coming to live here won't solve any of your problems with your parents in the long run."

Lindee's expression went from surprise to anger. "I thought you guys were on my side. I thought you would help me."

"Helping you doesn't mean we do what you want, when you want it."

Lindee rose to her feet and folded her arms. "I said I would help with chores and stuff. Why did you shut me down without even thinking about it?" Her face clouded over, and her dark eyebrows positioned themselves like lightning bolts. "If you don't let me live here, I'll run away."

Todd didn't even blink. "We don't negotiate with terrorists, Lindee."

"What did you say?" She lengthened her neck, as if trying to stand taller.

"You can't bully us into making us do what you want us to. It doesn't work like that in our home." He motioned for her to sit back down, but she remained standing.

Christy couldn't believe how firm Todd was being with Lindee. She never would have said the things to Lindee that Todd was. If he hadn't come home when he did and Lindee had made her plea to Christy alone, she might have had Lindee halfway moved into the guestroom by now.

"Look," Todd said calmly. "We're having a conversation here. Not an argument. Please sit down."

Lindee reluctantly retreated and sat down. She stared at Todd, as if she wanted to appear tough but in truth she seemed mesmerized by the kindness that permeated his direct words.

"When you make threats like that or act like a spoiled kid, it makes me want to stop talking with you," Todd said. "You're a guest in our home. If you want to keep coming over and be our guest, and we hope you do, then you need to honor the way we do things."

Lindee looked over at Christy and then back at Todd, as if verifying that the two of them were a united front. She seemed stunned and unable to think of anything to say. Without a word, she stood, took the book, and headed for the door.

"See you on Friday," Todd called out from the kitchen.

"If you're lucky," Lindee called back. She let herself out.

"That was interesting." Todd went to the refrigerator and started moving items on the shelves. "Do we have any more of that lemonade?"

Christy couldn't believe how calmly Todd had responded to Lindee's drama. She was still trying to figure out what had happened.

"Chris, do we have any more lemonade?"

"No, we drank it. I made tea for us. And I bought cupcakes from the place Aunt Marti likes. Do you want to go sit in the living room?"

"Sure. Let me find something to eat first."

"I thought you said you ate at Zane's."

"I did. I'm still hungry. Do we have any more . . .?" Todd opened a storage container and gave a hoot as if he had struck gold. "Leftover tuna melts."

He placed one on a paper plate in the microwave. "What do you think about having Bob and Marti over for dinner tomorrow?"

Christy had gone to the cupboard and pulled out a bottle of ibuprofen.

"Do you have a headache?"

"Yes." She made a blah face. "Cramps, too."

"Sorry to hear that. How long was Lindee here?"

"Only about forty-five minutes. Maybe less. She saw the tea party I'd set up for us, and I ended up inviting her to have tea. It was nice."

Todd looked slightly amused. "You and Lindee had a tea party?"

"Yes."

The microwave beeped, and Todd removed his steaming food. He always set the time for longer than he needed to, and some part of the food exploded in spits and splats that Christy had to clean up. "I wish you would put a paper towel over the top so it wouldn't leave tuna shrapnel all over the microwave."

"Tuna shrapnel, huh?" He pulled way more paper towels from the roll than he needed, wet the big wad in his hand, and gave the inside of the microwave a quick wipe down.

"Better?" He kissed her on the side of the head and walked into the living room where the remains of the tea party were still strewn across the coffee table. Todd reached for the remote and turned on the TV.

"Todd, we were going to talk tonight. Remember?"

"Let me eat something first, okay?" He switched the channel until he landed on a sports channel.

Christy cleared away the teapot and cups. She realized now what a bad idea it was to think that Todd wanted to sit on the couch and leisurely sip a fine cup of English Breakfast tea while discussing their future.

What was I thinking? Boys are not like girls. Never have been. Never will be.

Christy rinsed out the teapot and realized she had two choices. One, she could forget about the discussion, the way she had over the last few months. They could watch a movie, eat all the cupcakes, and go to bed with full bellies. Or two, she could push the point and ask Todd to turn off the TV and give her his full attention.

She chose the second option, and the night turned into an event like she had never experienced.

nine

Christy waited until Todd had finished his tuna melt and the program he was watching had rolled into a commercial. Those were two small kindnesses she had learned from her mother whenever her dad was engrossed in either his food or a TV show. It was always wise to wait for a break.

"May I talk to you?" Christy asked.

Todd put the TV on mute.

"I asked earlier today if we could talk tonight because we have some pretty significant things to discuss."

Todd turned off the TV. "Okay. Sure. What's going on?"

Christy didn't know how to dive into the sensitive topic of the need for him to find another job without sounding like Lindee. Stalling until she could come up with the best opening, Christy said, "First, can you go back to what you said earlier about Bob and Marti coming over tomorrow?"

"I wanted to know how you felt about having them over. We haven't done anything with them since your birthday, and I wanted to thank your aunt for the referral for Zane."

"What referral?"

"I was over there last week borrowing a sander from Bob, and I showed Marti a picture on my phone of the boards I've been working on. She told somebody she knows in Laguna Beach about them. He contacted Zane and placed an order. It's pretty cool. I thought if we had them over it would be a nice way to thank her. Is that okay with you?"

Christy nodded. "Okay. I guess that will work out. What time?"

"Five. Five thirty." He grinned at Christy and reached for one of the petite cupcakes on the coffee table. "I realize it's not a fancy tea-party way of saying thank you, but I'm better at barbecuing ribs than making cupcakes."

Christy took the small opening about the surfboards as her chance to ease into the topic they needed to discuss. "So, has Zane given you any idea when you might start getting paid for the surfboard project?"

"I'll get paid after he gets paid. With this new order from Marti's friend, it's going to take a while."

"Are you saying it's going to take a while before you're paid or it's going to take a while for you to finish working on another surfboard?"

"Both. And it's multiple surfboards. I'll be at it for at least a month. Maybe longer."

Christy felt her jaw clench. She breathed in through her nose and could feel her nostrils flare. "Todd, I think we need to talk about whether that's a good idea."

"Okay. Talk about what, exactly?"

Christy's head was pounding. The painkillers weren't yet doing their work, and she wanted to get this conversation over with as quickly as possible. "We need to talk about your job. For more than two years you've had an assortment of jobs that don't pay consistently or well, and none of them has provided benefits. When you do get a project that pays well, we have to wait months before a check shows up."

He looked unconcerned.

"I need you to step up your leadership role in our family

and find a real job."

Now he looked confused. "What do you mean by a real job?"

"One that's consistent and has benefits."

"Where did this come from?"

"It's been obvious for a long time, Todd. I can't keep working six days a week. I just can't. If we ever decide to start a family, I don't want to have to work full time. We talked about this before we got married. I want to be home with our kids at least the first few years of their lives. For that to happen, you need to find a real job."

"Are you saying you think it's time for us to try to have a baby?"

"No, that's not at all what I'm saying. I'm trying to tell you that you need to find a job."

"But I have a job."

"Not a consistent job with benefits. You need to find a real job, like Doug."

"You want me to sit in an office and sell insurance?"

"If that's what you need to do, yes."

He looked uncomfortable at the thought and adjusted his position on the couch. "What if we're able to put away a lot of money in savings from the various jobs I'm doing? Would that calm your fears? Do you think you would be ready to start a family then?"

Christy felt her thin emotions stretching out like a high note on a violin. "Todd, you don't get it, do you?"

"I get it. You want to feel secure financially before we have kids, and you see the way for that to happen is for me to get a job with medical benefits. And you're tired. I get it."

"Yes, I'm tired because I'm working six days a week."

Which I wouldn't have to do if you carried your weight in this marriage by bringing in a consistent income.

She noticed that he still had the remote control in his hand, as if he expected this conversation to be over soon so he could click back on the sports event. "Christy, you chose to keep working six days a week. All along the plan was for you to quit working at the spa at the end of the summer."

"Don't you see? I'm still working at the spa because you still don't have a permanent job. If you did, I wouldn't feel the weight of the main financial responsibility around here."

Todd's face turned red. "We share that responsibility, Christy. We always have."

"No, we don't. We haven't for a long time. The majority of the weight is on me." Christy could hear her voice rising. "Don't you see that we can't keep on going like this? You have to grow up sometime, Peter Pan."

"What are you talking about?"

Christy felt the tears burning in the corner of her eyes and couldn't form another sentence right then.

Todd said, "Look. You're taking on a lot of worry about nothing. When you get pregnant, we'll figure out what to do next. God will take care of us the way He always has. You're super emotional right now because your hormones are whacked out."

That's when she snapped.

The way they ended up speaking to each other was everything Todd had told Lindee they didn't do in their home. A string of terrible accusations and hurtful words volleyed between the two of them. It was the worst argument they had ever had.

At one point Christy felt as if she were outside the fight, watching someone else in her skin, spewing things she would never say. When she seemed to take possession of her body once again, she stood up and shouted, "Leave me alone! Just leave me alone!"

She closed herself in the guestroom and gave way to a waterfall of tears. When the initial round of sobs receded, she could hear that Todd had turned the TV back on. That made her even angrier.

Why doesn't he come in here and try to resolve things with me? Why is he staying away?

Christy flopped on the bed and gave way to the exhaustion that had overtaken her. She curled up and cried until she had no more tears. Sleep soon came and pulled her down into a soul-aching silence. For the first time in their marriage, Christy spent the night away from Todd, alone in the guestroom. It was the worst night of her life.

The next morning Christy woke with a monstrous headache. The guestroom felt stuffy, and a heavy sadness covered her when she tried to get up. Vivid memories of their argument circled her. Her shoulders ached and her jaw hurt. She used the bathroom adjacent to the guestroom and listened, trying to determine if Todd was up yet.

Her eyes filled with tears again as snippets from their argument came to mind. She wished she had never said the things that flew out of her mouth. She also wished she had resolved things with Todd last night. It was even more painful now to try to figure out if she should go to him or if he would finally come to her. Someone had to make the first move toward reconciliation, and last night Christy had refused to be that person.

She drew in a cool breath through her pursed lips and repeated a verse in the Psalms that had been her go-to prayer whenever she didn't know what to say to God.

"Create in me a pure heart, O God, and renew a steadfast spirit within me."

After quietly unlocking the bathroom door that led to the kitchen, Christy inched it open. She saw Todd seated at the kitchen counter, watching the door. Her heart gave a thump as their eyes met.

She couldn't tell if he was still upset and was about to tell her, as he'd told Lindee, that he didn't negotiate with terrorists. She hoped he had thought about the meaning behind her words last night and now understood her frustration.

Christy took the first step forward. Todd stood. His screaming silver-blue eyes were clouded and red. He looked as exhausted and miserable as she was.

With a steady step toward Christy, Todd's arms seemed to spontaneously reach for her. She went to him and buried her face in his chest. Todd wrapped his arms around her and whispered, "I'm sorry."

"So am I."

They held each other a long time and swayed slightly as if the rocking motion was a comfort to them both after their long, inconsolable night spent apart. Christy knew she had been over the top in her reactions last night. Todd was, too. His usual calm and logic had been absent, and once they both started rocking the boat, neither seemed to try to make it right. All the frustrating thoughts they both had buried inside came out last night in their rawest form without a speck of grace.

In the cool morning light, grace covered them like a blanket. It felt like the blanket they had wrapped around them the night they had arrived at the campground and dashed down to the beach still wearing their clothes from the wedding. Now they were, once again, trying to navigate as two independent individuals inside a horse costume. This time the "horse costume" was their marriage.

Christy kept holding on to Todd. She didn't know what to say. It seemed that neither of them wanted to bring up any of the points they had argued over last night. She knew they would need to talk about it all again. But not now.

Christy squeezed her arms around Todd's midriff, and he squeezed her back. They drew apart slowly and looked at each other with bleary eyes.

"Let's never do that again," Todd said.

"Never."

He ran his thumb across her cheek, sweeping away her last tear. "You okay?"

She nodded. "You?"

He nodded.

They kissed hesitantly. It wasn't an expression of passion but rather a contrite offering of reconciliation. Christy leaned her head on his chest once again.

Todd offered to make Christy some tea. She said she only wanted water and went upstairs to take a long, hot shower. After she dried her hair and pulled on her most comfortable sweats, she went back downstairs ready for some tea and toast.

Todd was gone. A note waited for her on the counter.

Went to Zane's to get in some extra hours. Call me if you need anything at all. I love you.

Christy felt a mix of guilt and relief that Todd was gone. They were missing church that morning. She couldn't remember a time when either of them had worked on a Sunday. Todd was a lot like Christy's dad in that he was adamant that the Sabbath be honored by not making it a day of work but rather a day of rest.

For Christy, the possibility of spending the whole day resting felt luxurious. She wanted to stretch out on the sofa with her tea and toast and watch Jane Austen movies all day. To her, that was the most luxurious thing she could think of doing when she was so exhausted emotionally and physically.

Balancing a tray with toast with honey and a mug of chamomile tea, also sweetened with honey, Christy retreated to the living room. She noticed the crumpled-up blanket on the sofa. Todd apparently had slept on the couch last night. Christy slid under the blanket and got cozy.

Todd's Bible was open on the coffee table. The old Bible, with smudges and torn pages, was falling apart and had been written in and marked up over the years that Todd had read from it and taught from it.

Christy reached for the battered Bible and felt as if she were lifting Todd's soul as she rested it on her lap. He had turned to God's Word in their worst moment as a married couple. She had always admired the way he turned to God first in everything.

Todd, how can you be such a sensitive spiritual giant in some areas and so stubborn and frustrating in others?

Christy started reading the page the Bible was open to, Psalm 130. She stopped at verse 5 and felt a butterfly fluttering in her heart. Todd had underlined this verse:

"I wait for the LORD, my whole being waits, and in his word I put my hope."

I don't want to wait, her heart whispered with unguarded honesty. *I want these issues to be settled in our lives right now.*

It struck Christy that her thoughts were sounding a lot like Lindee yesterday. Christy wanted what she wanted when she wanted it. But she knew she shouldn't make such demands of God. She didn't want to act like one of His spoiled daughters when things weren't going the way she wanted them to.

I don't know what to do, God. Am I pushing Todd too much to find a full-time job? I just feel like everything is out of balance. Should I quit the spa? Or the gift shop? The thing is, I don't feel as if I can trust Todd to provide for me.

Christy froze. She realized what the real problem was.

I don't trust Todd.

She could see it clearly. In her fearful little heart, for months now, she didn't believe she could rely on Todd to take care of her and provide for her.

That's why I get so skittish whenever I think about being pregnant. If Todd isn't providing for me, how can I believe that he'll provide for a baby and me?

Christy realized that was why she felt the burden of their finances rested on her shoulders since she made the most money.

Looking down at Todd's Bible in her lap, Christy had a clear, precise thought that ran straight through to her core. She never had been one who could say that she "heard" God speaking to her, but at that moment, that's what it seemed like. The thought was like a whisper that was weighted with authority.

I want you to trust Me more than you trust Todd.

The words simply came and sat upon her for an instant, and then they were gone. A resonating sense of truth lingered. She wanted to cry, but no tears came to her eyes. She wanted to hear the thought rush through her one more time, but she knew it was the Holy Spirit, and He didn't need to repeat Himself.

"Okay," Christy whispered in the empty room. "I will trust You, God. I'll trust You more than I trust Todd."

She looked down and read the verse once more. "I wait for the LORD, my whole being waits, and in his word I put my hope."

Christy sat quietly for several humbling minutes. It struck her that she should pray for Todd. She prayed that God would empower her husband with a sense of leadership and show him how God wanted Todd to provide for their family.

She prayed again for wisdom to know what to do about her job situation. As soon as she did, she felt as if a quilt of much needed restoration was tucked around her, and she was beckoned to sleep some more.

Christy returned the Bible to the coffee table and stretched out under the blanket. Tea, toast, and movies all forgotten, Christy closed her eyes and gave in to the deep weariness that had not been satisfied during the night.

Much later she heard the sound of the back door closing. Raising her head, she squinted at the sight of Todd placing a bag of groceries on the kitchen counter. He came over to her on the couch as she tried to focus her eyes. He smelled of resin and paint. Familiar scents from the surfboard shop.

"Hey." He reached down and stroked her hair. "How are you feeling?"

"Better. I slept all day."

He smiled. "Good. Can I get you anything?"

"No. I think I'll get up." Christy yawned.

"I bought some groceries. I'm going to take a quick shower, and then I'll put them away."

"I can unload them, Todd."

"Okay. Thanks."

Christy slid her feet out from under the covers and yawned again.

"Are you sure you're ready to get up?"

"Yes. Otherwise I won't sleep tonight."

Todd headed upstairs. Christy was grateful that everything felt like it was getting back to normal. She was glad they weren't rehashing the torrid argument from last night. She felt as if, in her heart, she was trusting God now more than she was trusting Todd, and that seemed like the way it should have been all along.

Christy stretched her stiff neck and padded into the kitchen. The first thing that caught her eye was a big bouquet of white carnations bursting from the bag of groceries. She smiled as she lifted the puffy flowers and buried her nose in them, drawing in their sweet and slightly peppery fragrance. It took only a few minutes to find a vase and cut the stems. She enjoyed arranging them evenly and placing the beautiful bouquet on the end of the counter so it could be seen from the living room as well as the kitchen.

She had just finished putting away the assortment of canned beans, two boxes of cereal, some ground beef, and a gallon of milk when Todd came bounding down the stairs.

"Oh, hey, you found them. I was going to surprise you."

"You did. I was surprised. Thank you. I love them."

Todd grinned. He looked relieved, as if he had done something right. As if it was written somewhere that when young married couples have the blowout argument of their lives, the husband is supposed to come home with flowers the next day.

"I bought hamburger for dinner," Todd said. "Unless you had something else you thought would be good."

"No, hamburgers would be fine." Christy realized she never had finished her toast and tea. They were still on the coffee table. It felt strange to be planning for dinner already.

"I thought I would barbecue," Todd said.

"Even better." Christy remembered Todd's suggestion last night about Bob and Marti coming for dinner. "Are my aunt and uncle coming?"

"No. I called and asked if they could come tomorrow night instead. I thought it would be best if you and I had a night to ourselves."

Christy pulled out some of the items she had just put in the refrigerator. They worked side by side as Todd made the hamburger patties and Christy sliced a tomato and put two hamburger buns on a cookie sheet so she could toast them in the oven. Todd had tried toasting them one time on their grill, but the buns caught fire.

When Todd went out to the front deck with the burgers, Christy put on some music and lined up the condiments for their dinner. They ate out on the deck, and since it was still early enough to catch the sunset, they put on sweatshirts and walked down to the beach, hand in hand.

The night was calm. The sunset clouds were tinted in bronze with ambitious streaks of amber illuminating their undersides. Christy and Todd stood barefoot in the cool sand, with their arms around each other, gazing at the beauty.

"This happens every night," Christy said.

"For free," Todd added.

"I'm so glad we came down. It's been a long time since we've seen the sunset."

"I made some calls today," Todd said. "Most places won't be open until tomorrow, though."

"What places?"

"The places with job openings. I'm going to see what I can get that will be more permanent." He seemed to be approaching the subject of his work carefully so nothing would tip either of them into the abyss they had fallen into last night.

"Thank you, Todd."

"I told Zane I'd keep helping him until I can find permanent work. I'm almost finished with the first big order. We'll have everything ready to ship by Thursday. Friday at the latest. I'll have more time to job hunt then. You'll see. It'll all work out."

"I know," Christy said.

Todd pulled back and looked at her.

She gave him a clear-eyed nod of confidence in the diminishing light of the sunset. "I believe God will provide for us the way He always has. We have to do our part, of course. And I deeply appreciate your checking out better work options. But I know that ultimately He's the one who takes care of us."

Todd looked at her with an expression that seemed to say he had never loved her more than he did at that moment.

ten

Christy returned to work on Monday morning feeling revived after her day of rest. The day floated by gently. On her walk back to the ferry to retrieve her car, a text came through from Uncle Bob.

HEY, BRIGHT EYES. WHAT CAN MY BEST GIRL AND I BRING OVER FOR DINNER THIS EVENING?

Christy responded: NOTHING. I HAVE IT COVERED. JUST BRING YOUR BEST GIRL.

Christy added a smiley face because she thought it was cute that he referred to Aunt Marti that way. She added, SEE YOU AT SIX THIRTY.

Christy picked up her pace and boarded the ferry just before it began its short crossing. She stood by the railing and watched as the vintage Ferris wheel in the Balboa fun zone made its slow turn beside the water's edge. The ferry bumped into its lock, and the ramp was lowered for the three cars that had ridden across. Christy was about to disembark when she realized the attendant hadn't come by to ask for her fare. She kept a change purse with her all the time so she could pull out the exact amount.

With the coins in hand, Christy waited until the cars had motored off the ferry and then went to the young guy who was on duty. "Here. I didn't pay yet."

"You ride all the time, and you always pay. This one's on me."

"Oh. Thanks." Christy smiled her appreciation. She hadn't paid attention to the attendants before and certainly never would have guessed any of them would have noticed her repeated rides.

"You have really beautiful eyes, by the way," he said.

Christy mumbled, "thanks" and made a swift exit, briskly walking to her car.

Was he flirting with me? That was awkward. I should have insisted that I pay.

Todd was home when Christy arrived. The first thing she did was tell him. He playfully rolled back his shoulders and said he was going to go tell the "dude" to back off and not get any ideas about his beautiful wife.

"You're cute when you're jealous." Christy gave him a kiss on the side of his scruffy jaw and pulled a box of frozen lasagna from the freezer. She set the oven temperature to the directions on the box. "I think he was just being neighborly."

Todd lowered his chin and gave Christy a fatherly sort of look. "Guys never do stuff like that or say stuff like that just to be neighborly. Don't let your innocence blind you. Plenty of wolves are out there. Be careful."

"I will. I always am." Christy put the lasagna in the oven and made a salad.

Todd emptied the dishwasher and told Christy about the three calls he had made that day for various jobs that were listed online. One of them was at the hotel where the White Orchid was located. "All three told me the positions were filled already. I'll keep looking, though."

Christy reached for his hand and held it tightly. "I'm sorry."

"For what?"

"For doubting you and doubting God. I regret all the things I said when we argued about work and money."

"You said a lot of stuff that was true. I do need to find something steady with enough income so you won't have to work so much."

"Yes, that's what I'd love to see happen. But the way I expressed my feelings wasn't kind. And that's what I'm sorry about."

Todd wrapped his arms around her and gave her a tight hug. "Forgiven," he whispered in her ear.

As they pulled apart, Todd gazed at her intently. "You really do have beautiful eyes, you know."

Christy glanced to the side, suddenly feeling self-conscious.

"No, I mean it. They're more striking than usual today. They match the blue in your necklace." Todd leaned over and kissed her.

"Does this mean I'm you're best girl?"

"My what?"

Christy playfully put her hand on her hip. "Your best girl."

"What do mean are you my best girl? You're my only girl. Why? Are you thinking of throwing me overboard for the skipper?"

"The skipper?"

"Yeah, the guy on the ferry."

Christy laughed. "No. Never. You're stuck with me, Todd. Forever."

"What does that even mean, your 'best girl'? Does it mean I should have a 'worst girl'? Or a 'so-so kind of average girl'?"

"No, it's just something Uncle Bob called Aunt Marti, and I thought it was cute."

"Cute, huh?" He raised an eyebrow. "It makes no sense."

"Love and sweet affection don't always have to make sense." Christy kissed him on the end of his nose and grinned. She felt so happy to be back in their familiar routine, just the two of them, at home and at peace with each other in spite of the future being no more resolved than it was two days ago.

What had been resolved was Christy's choice to trust God and wait on Him. Her circumstances hadn't changed, but she had changed.

"When your aunt and uncle arrive, remind me to thank Marti for hooking Zane up with the designer guy in Laguna Niguel."

"What designer guy?"

"The designer guy who ordered all the benches. Marti referred Zane to him."

Now Christy was even more confused. "What benches are you talking about?"

"The ones I've been making at Zane's."

"You're making benches? I thought you were reshaping surfboards."

"I am. I'm reshaping old boards into benches. A while ago I showed Zane a picture of Narangus. He'd been trying to figure out how to do a bench with just the surfboard and no backrest, but he couldn't get the old boards to sit right. That's why he asked me to come help on the project."

Christy stopped cutting up the cucumber for the salad and stared at Todd.

"What? I thought I told you the night you were reading that book upstairs about the kid who runs around wearing green tights."

Christy lowered her chin. "His name is Peter Pan. And don't say green tights like it's a sissy thing. Finish what you were saying about the benches."

"Zane had a bunch of old surfboards, so I showed him how I reshaped Naranja for our bench, and he and I figured out how to weld on a substantial base. It's a better base and frame than the one I put on our bench. Zane has all the tools to do it right."

"How many benches have you guys made?"

Todd thought a moment. "About sixty. Zane is cranking out the bases, and I've been shaping the boards."

"Todd, all this time I thought you were fixing boards for the high school guys and your surfing buddies. I didn't know you were making dozens of benches."

"I'm sorry. I honestly thought I told you." He pulled out his phone and showed Christy several photos of the finished surfboard benches. "We started with four that Zane put up for sale online. Those sold in a few days, and we had an order for twenty from the parks department in Seal Beach. Then we made fifteen for Marti's interior design guy, and a developer ordered another fifteen for a shopping center in San Diego. We keep getting orders online. I think they turned out great."

"They're really nice." Christy enlarged one of the pictures. "The details are beautiful. I can see why Marti's designer guy likes them. Todd, this is a big deal. Why didn't you say anything when we were arguing and I said all those things about you not bringing in any income?"

"Because you were right. I haven't had any income for two months. The money from the benches won't come through for another few weeks because Zane had to take the initial profit to buy more boards."

"He is going to pay you, though, right?"

"Yes. I have no doubt he'll pay me. I don't know how much it's going to be, but it should be a pretty good amount."

Christy gingerly asked, "What exactly do you think would be a pretty good amount?"

Todd took his phone back and tapped on the calculator app. He told Christy the amount the benches were selling for and what their profit was. He said that Zane had promised to split the profit with him fifty-fifty.

Todd raised his eyebrows and said, "Wow. I hadn't added it up yet." He turned the phone screen so Christy could see the projected total he would make.

It was a lot.

"Are you serious?"

Todd nodded. "It'll be less than that, of course, because of the expenses for materials. But Zane raised the prices so on the next order we'll have a better profit margin."

Christy didn't know if she wanted to throw something at him or throw her arms around him and give him a big squeeze. "I'm stunned. This is incredible."

"It's all happened really fast. I'm sorry, Christy. I thought I'd said more about what we were doing. No wonder you've been so freaked out, thinking no money was coming in."

Christy looked at the phone screen again and looked at Todd. "Even if you received half that amount it would be amazing."

Uncle Bob arrived just then. He entered with a pastry box from Cheri's and placed it on the counter. "Sweets for the sweet, from the sweet."

Todd opened the box. "Pink. They're little pink cookies."

"Raspberry macaroons, actually," Bob replied. "A small gift of apology from your aunt. She'll be late due to a mix-up with the time on her hair appointment. She tried to re-schedule, but we're heading out to Palm Springs on Thursday for our annual golf weekend, and this was the only time she could get in. Something smells good in here."

As if on cue, the timer sounded on the oven. Christy pulled out the lasagna and placed it on the stovetop to cool.

"We can go ahead and start with the salad," Christy suggested. "Please help yourselves. We can eat at the table or out on the deck, if you like."

Bob looked at Todd and then back at Christy. "Would you guys mind if we caught the end of the ball game? Dodgers are doing great this year. Tonight's game is a big one for them."

"Sure." Todd went over and turned on the TV.

Christy put out bowls for the salad and plates for the lasagna, but both guys used the bowls to dish up the lasagna and skipped the salad altogether. They positioned themselves on the couch, and Todd took a bite with his eyes riveted on the TV. He took another bite and turned to Christy. "What is this?"

"It's vegetable lasagna. It's made with spinach, zucchini, and eggplant, I think. Do you like it?" She joined the guys in the living room with her bowl of lasagna.

Todd had a forlorn, little-kid look as he stared at the rest of his dinner. "When did we turn vegan and nobody told me?"

"I thought it would be healthier for us than the usual kind with the heavy pasta and sausage." Christy didn't want to sound like a fan of this particular vegetable lasagna because she had tried a bite and wasn't crazy about it either. She had thought her aunt would appreciate it.

Todd carried his bowl into the kitchen. When he returned, Christy could see that he had poured ranch dressing over the rest of his lasagna. She forced herself to eat the small portion she had dished up for herself and refrained from saying anything about Todd's favorite great, white, creamy solution for eating anything green.

Thankfully, Uncle Bob was so focused on his beloved Dodger Blue baseball team that he ate the lasagna without commenting about it.

With a slight sense of defeat, Christy went back into the kitchen with the emptied bowls and put the covered salad in the refrigerator to keep it fresh. If Marti hadn't had dinner yet when she arrived, she might at least be interested in the salad.

Her phone buzzed on the counter. She read the message just as Todd's phone buzzed. Christy checked Todd's phone and read the same message she had just received.

"Doug just asked if we could go over to their place, Todd. He said they heard some bad news today, and Tracy isn't doing well."

"Do you think she's okay?"

"I don't know. I can go over there, if you don't mind hanging out here and waiting for Aunt Marti. There's lots of salad, if she's hungry. I put it back in the fridge."

"Why don't you both go?" Bob suggested. "A friend in need is a top priority. I'll head on home and tell Marti to meet me there instead of coming over here."

"Sorry this didn't work out very well tonight."

"Nobody's fault. Life is full these days. How about if I catch up with you when we get back from Palm Springs?"

"That sounds good."

"What do you say we have dinner at our place a week from Wednesday?"

"Are you sure?" Christy asked.

"Absolutely. Any special requests?"

Christy was going to say that she loved her uncle's grilled salmon with lemon and capers, but Todd beat her to making a request. "Lasagna. Without vegetables."

For the second time that night Christy wanted to throw something at her husband. She gave her uncle a hug before he headed out the door. Todd turned off the TV and closed up the house while Christy did a quick cleanup in the kitchen. She checked her phone again as Todd drove them the short distance to Doug and Tracy's bungalow.

"I hope she's okay."

"Why don't you text Doug and tell him we're on our way." Todd had to park four blocks away due to the lack of parking in their area. He locked the car. Christy fell into step with his quick pace.

When they entered, they found the small space was stacked with boxes. A pile of clothes overflowed one side of the couch and none of the lamps had shades on them. Daniel was seated on the floor in front of the TV with a cracker in both fists. When he saw them he jumped up.

Todd lifted the crumbly toddler and looked around. "Hey, Danny boy. Where's your mom and dad?"

"Tracy? Doug?"

No one answered.

eleven

*C*hristy and Todd exchanged confused glances.

"Maybe they're out on the back patio," Todd suggested.

Just then the bathroom door opened, and Tracy came out. She looked awful.

"Hey," Christy greeted her. "We let ourselves in. Are you okay?"

"Just stressed."

"What's going on?" Christy led Tracy over to their tiny kitchen table and moved the basket of laundry off the chair so she could sit down. Todd came and stood beside the table while Christy instinctively went to the refrigerator to pull out the pitcher Tracy used to purify the tap water. The pitcher wasn't there.

"Doug went to get some ginger ale for my stomach. Did he tell you what's going on?"

"No, but it looks like you guys are moving."

"We were supposed to be going on vacation. Doug found out yesterday that he has vacation time, and if he didn't use it, he would lose it. We decided last night that we would drive up to Oregon with my parents to see where they want to live. Then this morning the new owner of this place went back on his original offer to let us rent month to month. He told us we need to either sign a lease for a year or be out by Saturday."

"Can he do that?" Christy asked.

"We have to move eventually before the twins come. All five of us can't fit in this tiny place. We just didn't plan to move this weekend. Neither of us has the time or energy to argue with his decision."

"Where are you going to move to?" Todd asked.

"We don't know yet."

Christy noticed that Daniel had wiggled out of Todd's arms and was opening and closing the refrigerator door. It seemed he wanted attention.

"Do you want me to clean up this little guy and put on his jammies?"

"That would be wonderful. Thank you, Christy."

"Come on," Christy said, taking Daniel's hand and leading him out of the crowded kitchen. "It's bath time for you."

She was surprised he didn't protest as they inched their way past the stacked-up moving boxes and suitcases. Christy let the warm water flow into the tub as Daniel played with some of his bath toys. She found some baby shampoo that smelled like green apples and quickly lathered up his hair before he had a chance to protest.

Christy had a sudden flashback to when she was in high school and staying with Aunt Marti and Uncle Bob. Marti had taken Christy to a salon to have her hair done in what Marti described as a "current style." When Christy returned to their house, Doug was there. She remembered how he had leaned over and smelled her hair.

"Smells like green apples," Doug had said.

The memory made Christy smile. Never in a million years did she ever think that one day she would be giving Doug's son a bath and that he, too, would smell like green apples. She loved little Daniel like a nephew, but something made her whisper a secret request to the Lord that when the time came for her and Todd to have a child, he wouldn't be as much of a handful as Daniel.

Daniel splashed wildly, drawing Christy back to the present and causing her to turn into the firm auntie. "Okay. Bath time is over." She poured one more pitcherful of warm water over his head to rinse him thoroughly and drained the tub.

Christy quickly wrapped Daniel up in a towel the best she could. She roughed up his short hair and slid on a pair of his Superman big boy pants before she went looking for clothes for him. As soon as she opened the bathroom door he was on the run, laughing and enjoying the freedom.

With quick steps Christy tracked him to the kitchen where he had gone to Tracy and was giving his mommy kisses.

Tracy looked up at Christy. "Thank you so much."

"Of course. What else can I do? Does he need a T-shirt or a pair of jammies?"

"His clothes are in the suitcase. I packed all the clean stuff because I thought we were going on vacation."

Christy looked through one of the two large, open suitcases on the floor. "Are you guys thinking you'll still drive up to Oregon with your parents?"

"I was just telling Todd that I don't know how we can leave. Doug thinks we should go, but I think he should take the time off and find a place for us to live."

Christy victoriously extracted a set of pajamas from the suitcase and wrestled Daniel into them. When he was set free, he ran to Todd and pulled him by the hand, begging him to go out on the patio to play cars.

"Hang on, Danny boy. Let me finish talking to your mom." Todd picked him up and held him close to his chest, then patted his back as if he knew the little guy needed comfort and security now more than anything. Daniel put his head on Todd's shoulder and rested calmly for a few brief moments.

"Doug thinks we should put everything in a storage shed

and just go. He says we need to get out of here. We'll probably move into a hotel anyway until we find a place to live so he thinks we might as well go on vacation first. It's probably a good idea, but I can't even think right now." Tracy stood and headed for the bathroom. "I'll be right back."

Todd looked at Christy and motioned with a slight tilt of his head for her to follow him out on the patio. "Okay, Danny boy, let's go play cars."

Christy followed Todd and felt her heart pounding. She knew what he was thinking. She had been thinking the same thing.

Todd put Daniel down on the small patio and scooped up two toy trucks.

"I want dat one." Daniel grabbed the fire truck.

"What if we invited them to stay with us so they don't have to live in a hotel?"

"I was thinking the same thing." Christy's mind was spinning. She knew what it would be like to welcome them into their home. They had a taste of Hurricane Daniel whenever Doug and Tracy came over with him. He already had written on their bathroom wall with permanent marker and broken a lamp.

"You're okay with offering this? Just until they find a place." Todd seemed to be trying to convince himself as well as Christy as he said it. "They would do this for us, if we were in the same situation. Actually, when we were in this situation a few years ago, they did offer to let us stay with them, didn't they?"

"Yes, they did."

"So, you're okay with this, really?"

"Yes. We have an empty guestroom. And to be honest, I've been thinking lately about how I could be doing more hospitality-type things. This is something I was hoping we would be able to do."

Todd said, "I was thinking we could give them our room."

"Our room?" Suddenly Christy wasn't so sure she liked

the idea of providing a safe haven for their friends, now that Todd had made that suggestion.

"It would work better for them because they could put Danny in the little room upstairs, and he would have his own place to sleep."

Images of the current state of her upstairs sewing-and-crafts room loomed before her. When she went to work at the gift shop, she had stopped sewing, and the room had turned into a storage room.

"We would have to do a lot of cleaning out and organizing," she said slowly. "I don't think I could have everything ready in two days."

"It doesn't need to be ready by this weekend. If Doug and Tracy put their stuff in our garage, they can move out of here and still go to Oregon. While they're gone, we'll get our place ready for them."

"That could work. It's a lot to do, but it could work." Christy was already dreaming up some decorating ideas and figuring out how to move the furniture around in the guestroom.

From inside the bungalow they could hear Doug's voice calling out a booming, "Hey, I'm home."

Daniel looked up, and his expression turned to pure sunshine. "Daddy!" He popped up and ran inside.

"Let's go tell them," Todd said. Christy linked her arm through his. He kissed her and whispered, "You're the best."

Christy pulled back and gave him a teasing grin. "So I am your best girl after all."

"That's not what I said."

"It may not be what you said, but I'll take it as being what you meant." She winked at him.

Todd's wide grin faded. He stopped before going back inside. "You're sure that you're okay with this? Everything is going to change for us, you know."

"Yes, I know. But it's the right thing to do."

"Okay. Let's tell them."

As Christy and Todd imagined, Doug and Tracy were immensely grateful. After a round of hugs and a few tears, the plans kicked into high speed. Doug was pretty excited that they could go to Oregon. His logic was that since the doctor had told Tracy she might need to plan on bed rest during the last month of her pregnancy, they wouldn't be able to go be with her parents for Christmas. Even though she was still struggling with nausea on days like today, Tracy was feeling well enough to travel, and this was the best chance for them to go.

The two weeks that Doug and Tracy were in Oregon provided Christy and Todd ample time to clear out the upstairs craft room and turn it into a bedroom for Daniel. They moved all their things into the guestroom and cleaned out the upstairs bathroom. Christy couldn't believe how dirty things were. She thought she was a fairly tidy housekeeper. But some dust, hair, and dirt weren't found unless everything was moved to the side.

The only unfortunate occurrence during their nightly renovation and cleaning sprint was that both of them forgot about going to Bob and Marti's for dinner. They were in the middle of a sweaty, messy cleanout of stuff in the garage when Bob called to see when they might be heading over.

"We blew it," Todd said after he ended the call with Bob. "He said we could set it up for another night, but I told him we would have to wait until we made it through our to-do list. He said he understood. I hope your aunt does."

Christy wasn't overly worried about Marti being upset. She was the one who had to cancel last minute because of her hair appointment. Surely she understood what it was like when things came up and schedules had to be changed.

"We can set another time with them after Doug and Tracy are settled in," Christy suggested. "I feel like we barely have enough time each day to accomplish everything here that we need to do."

Todd agreed.

The two weeks sped by and everything they needed to do was completed. Good things seemed to be happening all around.

Todd came home on the first Friday in October and had a huge grin on his face. Christy was in the kitchen listening to some of her favorite music and making oatmeal cookies for the Friday Night Gathering.

Todd sidled up to her, pulled a folded envelope from his back pocket, and handed it over. "The first payment. It's only for the first thirty benches, but look at that, Christy."

She unfolded the envelope and pulled out the check. When she saw the amount, she spontaneously threw her arms around Todd's neck and gave him a big kiss. The song playing in the background was one that always made her think of Katie's wedding in Africa because of the complex drumbeat.

In an uncharacteristic burst of craziness, Christy broke into a little happy dance, and Todd joined her. They tried to reenact some of the moves they had learned at Katie and Eli's wedding reception when a group of Kenyan singers had the whole party on their feet and dancing. Todd tried to pull off a head-bobbing motion while simultaneously keeping his crooked elbows and bent knees grooving to the beat.

It was one of the funniest things Christy had ever seen. "You look like a chicken on drugs."

They laughed so hard they had to stop dancing to catch their breath.

"You've got moves there, girl." Todd wiped a laughter tear from his face with the back of his hand.

"And you don't. But you have some serious moola there, dude. So I think I'll keep you around." Christy picked up the check and looked at it again, still grinning wildly. "This is incredible, Todd."

"I know. God's timing on this is flawless. And we received another order today, this one for twenty benches. Zane just hired a high school guy to come in part time so we can keep up."

Christy handed the check back to Todd and set the timer on the oven. Inside she was still dancing to the joyful beat.

Todd helped himself to a scoop of cookie dough. He looked so excited. "I heard back from a construction job I'd applied for a few weeks ago. The general contractor was apologetic about not having any work for me, but I told him about the benches, and he's going to buy four of them."

"That's so fantastic, Todd." Christy grinned broadly and looked coyly at him. "I have some news, too."

Todd lowered his chin and looked at her tenderly. "You're pregnant."

"No, I'm not pregnant." She swatted his arm. "And if I were, that's not the way I'd tell you."

He looked disappointed. "Everything else is going so great. I thought that might be the next great thing that should happen to us."

Christy wasn't ready to think about that or form a response. She moved on to the news she wanted to tell him. "I found out that one of the women at the spa is moving next month. That means her hours will be available. I'm going to talk to Eva tomorrow and see if I can take those hours, and if they would be enough."

"Enough what?"

"Enough hours to allow me to leave the gift shop."

"Do it." Todd put the check back in his pocket. "Even if it doesn't add up to forty hours, do it."

Christy appreciated his confidence and enthusiasm, but she still had to meet with Eva in the morning and get the whole story.

"Hey, we're not doing anything Sunday afternoon, are we?"

"Doug and Tracy arrive that day but not until the evening. Why?"

"Zane knows a guy in San Clemente who has a bunch of old surfboards he might be willing to sell to us. Zane asked if I could go down on Sunday and have a look. You want to go with me?"

"Of course."

The doorbell rang, and Todd looked at the clock. "We have an hour before the Gathering starts up."

"It's Lindee. I told her it would be fine if she started coming early." Christy headed for the door.

"You're doing what you always wanted, aren't you?" Todd said.

Christy looked at him over her shoulder, not sure what he meant. She and Lindee had come a long way in forging a working relationship, but she wouldn't say she always wanted her around. Lindee was like a big puppy who was always curious and always bumping into things with her big feet.

"You're using your gift of hospitality," Todd said. "Isn't this what you've been saying you always wanted to do?"

Christy thought of the dream that sprouted in her heart at the youth hostel in Amsterdam. It wasn't that she disagreed with Todd's comment. She just never thought a life of hospitality would look like this.

One More Wish

twelve

*T*he Sunday afternoon traffic on the 5 freeway was light as Todd and Christy motored their way to San Clemente in Gussie. They already had discussed all the great changes coming up in two weeks when Christy started working more hours at the spa. Eva offered the hours to Christy as soon as she arrived at work the day before, and Christy immediately accepted. She stopped by the gift shop on her way home to give her two-week notice. She would only work thirty hours per week at the spa, but right now that was perfect. Everything in their lives felt pretty perfect.

With a grin that showed his dimple, Todd glanced over at Christy. "Is it okay if I bring up a topic that might be a little sensitive for you?"

"Okay."

"The other night when you said you had good news and I guessed that you were pregnant, you looked frightened."

"Frightened? I'm not afraid. Why do you say that?"

"It wasn't the way you looked. I've seen the look a couple of times. I wasn't sure how to talk to you about it."

Christy reached over and gave his brawny arm a squeeze. "You can talk to me about anything."

He glanced at her again. "Okay, I'll just say it. Do you want to have a baby?"

"Yes, of course. Not right now, but eventually, yes."

"Why not right now?"

Christy knew she couldn't say it was finances or her working too much. She sat quietly thinking about what her deeply imbedded apprehension was.

"Is it okay if I make some observations?" Todd asked.

"Sure."

"During your birthday in July, when you were blowing out the candles on the carrot cake Tracy made, that was the first time I saw the timidity in your expression. You made some sort of comment about wishing for a baby, but then you shut down."

"That was because of all the tension I felt then about our finances. And to be honest, I still feel some of it. I mean, things are incredible now with what's happening at Zane's, but what if this is a phase, and the orders suddenly stop?"

"We've talked about that. Zane has a couple of other outdoor items he's designed but never tried to sell. We're thinking we could branch out when the time comes." Todd shook his head. "Let's not talk about that right now. We were talking about you and what your feelings are about having a baby."

Christy sighed. "I guess I don't want to be done being 'us' yet. I know that probably sounds selfish, but I saw how much Doug and Tracy changed, and the way their relationship changed after Daniel was born. I'm not sure I'm ready to take on those kinds of changes."

"Fair enough." Todd kept looking straight ahead.

"When I hear myself say that, it sounds pretty shallow. I don't want to sound like I don't have room in my heart for a baby."

"I think I'm tracking with what you're saying. If we had a baby, our camping trip in August would have been completely different. Not worse. Just different. I like having time with you like this, too."

They drove in silence for a few minutes before Christy asked, "Do you feel like you're ready for us to have a baby?"

Todd was slow to respond. When he did, there was no doubt that his answer had been deeply considered. "Yes, I am. I'm ready."

Christy hadn't expected that response. She was more familiar with his answers to such questions being along the lines of, "Hey, let's wait on God for His timing... Let's be patient... Let's trust and not worry about it..." This time his answer was definitive and strong. He was taking the lead.

Todd glanced over at her. "It's more important, I think, that you be ready."

Todd had always been generous and patient in his love for Christy. Whenever she heard the popular verse from 1 Corinthians 13, "Love is patient," she felt that she could insert Todd's face in the margin next to those words.

I wonder if there's a deeper reason I'm hesitant about this. Am I afraid? Afraid of what? Or am I just not ready? There's nothing wrong with not being ready to take on the responsibility of bearing and nurturing a new life. Is there?

Christy considered the possibility that making this big decision, like most other big decisions in her life, as well as lots of little ones, was paralyzed midway through because of her inability to feel confident she was making the right choice.

"Maybe I am afraid." She said the words aloud before she intended to reveal them.

"Afraid that something could go wrong?"

"I guess. Or afraid that I won't be a good mother."

"You can throw that one out right now," Todd said firmly. "You're going to be an incredible mother. Sometimes I watch how you are with Daniel, and I think you're more in tune to what he needs than any of us." He quickly added, "That's not to say that Doug and Tracy aren't doing a great job as parents.

But you have a way with kids that's evident. I think your term at the orphanage in Switzerland gave you a deeper understanding of kids than most women your age."

"Thanks for saying all that, Todd. I probably need to hear stuff like that more than I realize."

"Then I'll keep telling you. You're going to be an awesome mom, Christy. You really are."

"You did *not* just say 'awesome,' did you?"

"I did, didn't I? Guess I'm getting ready for when Doug moves in tonight." Todd put on his turn signal and pulled off the freeway. Christy read the directions that Zane had scratched on the back of an envelope.

Gussie wound her way up a steep road, and Todd turned into a driveway that led to an old ranch-style house. To the side of the weathered house was an expanded garage. The door was up, and as Todd turned off the engine, he gave a low whistle.

"What is it?" Christy asked.

"Look at all those vintage boards! I think we hit the mother lode."

The next four and a half hours turned into the most fascinating time Christy had ever had with one of Todd's surfing pals. This guy's name was "Bones," and he was eighty-two years old. Tall and skinny, he had a head of white hair that rivaled the best Santa Claus wig around. His skin was spotted and leathered like an old guitar case. He was missing a front tooth on the bottom and said his filly of a board kicked it out when he was surfing last month down the hill at Trestles.

Christy was enamored with him. Todd kept looking at Bones as if he were a legend. He offered them bottles of water or root beer, and they both went for the water.

Along with stacks of hundreds and hundreds of old-school surfboards that were no longer seaworthy, Bones had dozens of framed photos of himself surfing in places like Borneo and South Africa. Every board had a story and every photo had a story.

Within the first five minutes of their conversation, Todd asked if Bones would mind if he recorded their conversation. "I want to capture your stories," Todd explained.

"Take all you want," Bones said. "I've run outta people around here to tell. They've heard 'em all."

When they finally were ready to leave, and the deal had been sealed with a handshake, Christy initiated a hug with Bones. He smelled a bit like the way Todd did on summer mornings when he returned from surfing. A little salty, a little sweaty, a little twangy from the seaweed that had run its fingers through his hair every time he dove under deep enough to startle the mermaids.

"You two married?" Bones looked at Christy with his funny, tooth-missing grin.

"Very married," Todd answered for them both.

Bones shook his head, loosening his long, snowy-white hair that was tied back with a narrow strip of leather. "The good ones are always taken."

"I wasn't interested in the good ones." Todd reached for Christy's hand. "Only the best one. For some reason she agreed to have me."

Bones seemed to like Todd's comeback. "Babies yet?"

Todd looked at Christy. "Not yet."

"You're burning daylight, sweetheart. You need to give this old-soul surfer guy of yours a grommet or two while he can still paddle out and show 'em how to take on the big ones."

Christy smiled a close-lipped smile at Bones and then looked at Todd to see his reaction. Todd was ready. She could see it all over his face. She had dreamed of growing up, marrying Todd, and duplicating the hospitality lifestyle they had experienced in Amsterdam.

Perhaps Todd's dream had been all this and a son of his own as well.

Cole. Cole Bryan Spencer.

For the first time in their married life, Christy's heart fluttered at the possibility. It was like she had a crush on some-one she hadn't met. Someone who wasn't even in her life yet.

"That was incredible," Todd said as soon as they were in Gussie and heading back toward the freeway. "I can't believe he was willing to part with all those boards for such a low price. Zane is going to be stoked. His stories were the best. Don't you think?"

"They were. He is like no one I've ever met before."

"Were you okay when he said the thing at the end about having a baby soon?"

"Yes." Christy turned and faced Todd so he could see her honest expression and clear eyes as she repeated her answer. "Yes."

Todd glanced at her with a discerning eye. "What exactly are you saying yes to?"

"I think I'm saying yes to trying."

Todd glanced at her again. "You're saying you're ready to start trying to get pregnant?"

"Yes."

"Just like that?"

"Yes."

He laughed. "What changed your mind?"

"I don't know. You. Bones. And well, ultimately God, of course. I guess our conversation on the way here helped me realize that I've been afraid of something I can't even define. It's the old insecurity I have about making decisions."

"Fear can be stupid that way."

"When we got married, I had this feeling that if I became pregnant, I'd be happy about it. The decision would have been made for me—for us. I know that must sound cowardly or something. I think I've been afraid to try to get pregnant and then find out when it happens that it wasn't a good time, or we didn't have enough money saved up."

"I don't see it that way."

"I know you don't," Christy said. "You've always found it easier to trust God and His timing. For me, I have to keep learning to trust over and over. I feel like a faith wimp."

Todd laughed. "I have never thought that about you. I think you're cautious because you really care about people, and you want to honor God."

"I do."

Todd reached over and squeezed her knee. "May I tell something else?"

"Of course."

"Ever since our camping trip in August, I've had this sense that something, or rather, someone, was missing from our lives."

"Do you feel that way now?"

"It's different now. I don't feel that someone is missing. It's more like someone is coming. I'm looking forward to it more than ever."

Christy smiled at her tenderhearted husband. She didn't expect to tear up as they talked about having a baby. They had had this sort of conversation many times over the years. But their talks had never felt like this. This time the tears were right there, on the rim of her eyelids, ready to spill over the side like a spring waterfall.

Todd pulled off the freeway. He turned into the first parking lot they came to, which happened to be a rather run-down, sketchy-looking motel.

Christy blotted her tears and laughed. "Todd, when I said I was ready to start trying to get pregnant, I didn't mean right now, right here."

He looked confused at her comment until he noticed where they were parked. He winked at her and put her at ease by saying, "I stopped so we could pray. I wanted to hold your hand. Come here."

Christy slipped her soft hand into Todd's rough paw. She closed her eyes and bowed her head. Todd's strong words rolled over her, smoothing out the final wrinkles in her emotions. He asked for God's continued blessing on their marriage and for God to gift them with the miracle of a new life, according to His plan for them and on His time schedule.

"I'm looking forward to meeting our first 'someone,' and together Christy and I wanted to say that we're ready, Lord. We're willing and available if You should choose to bless us with a child."

"Amen," Christy echoed when he concluded. She looked up to see Todd grinning at her with teary eyes.

"Our son just got pre-prayed," Todd said.

"Our son? What if our first someone is a daughter?"

"Our son or our daughter," Todd agreed. "Either one. Or both."

"Please, Lord, not both at the same time."

Christy's phone buzzed. She read the text message as Todd directed Gussie back onto the freeway.

"Doug said they just arrived at our house and used the hide-a-key to get inside. Tracy loved the Welcome Home sign I made for them."

"This is a big day. Lots of changes are coming."

Christy felt a sense of satisfaction that their house was clean, organized, and all ready for Doug, Tracy, and Daniel. She had dreams of lots of laughter around the dinner table and many shared moments of sitting on the deck around the fire, singing the way they did on Friday nights.

Her high hopes for a fun, new, youth hostel-lifestyle were dampened when she and Todd returned and saw Doug's car parked in their driveway. Tracy's car was in the street behind Christy's car. That left no place to park Gussie, and the garage was filled to the brim with Doug and Tracy's belongings. Neither of them had thought about the parking problem.

The only option was for Todd to prowl the narrow streets in hopes of finding a place.

"I have a feeling our lives are about to radically change even more than we thought they would," Todd said solemnly as he locked Gussie. He took Christy's hand in his and held it tightly as they started the five-block walk back to their home in the dark.

Todd's prophetic statement was true. Truer than either of them could have imagined. After only a few days of sharing their abode with their friends, Christy felt drained. She never guessed it would be so difficult to relinquish her time and especially her space to other people who had different ways of doing everyday life.

The trip to Oregon had been exhausting for Tracy emotionally and physically. While they were there, Tracy's parents put money down on a house. They also lowered the price on their home in Newport Beach so that it would sell quickly.

Their final decision to move had caused a rift between Tracy and her mom and had sent Tracy to Christy's couch where she camped out all day. Her energy was low and what she did have was all used up on little Captain Rambunctious, as Doug had started to call Daniel.

On the first Friday night of the new guesthouse living arrangement, the Gathering was more chaotic than usual because Daniel didn't want to stay upstairs in his room. He wanted everyone to know that was *his* couch, and he wanted to watch *his* TV. Lindee took him out to play on the deck while Todd did the teaching part of the night. Tracy coaxed Daniel upstairs around nine thirty, and both of them went to bed, leaving Christy to clean up.

Lindee pitched in and helped Christy to put everything away. "I like kids," Lindee said. "If you think Tracy would ever want me to babysit after school, I'd do it. She wouldn't have to pay me either. I like coming here."

"That's really nice of you to offer. I'll tell Tracy."

Christy asked Lindee about school and her parents and was glad to see the way she looked when she answered. Lindee gave the same sort of "Oh, it's okay" answers, but she didn't have the same angry shadow over her face like in the past.

Christy commented on the apparent change in Lindee's attitude when Todd got up early on Saturday morning to go surfing with Doug.

"Sometimes all a kid like that needs is some attention and

love. You and Tracy have been giving her that." Todd tried to slide past Christy as she pulled her hair back in a ponytail. The space in the downstairs bathroom was much smaller than in the bathroom upstairs. Without meaning to, she fwapped him in the face with her long hair.

"Sorry!"

Todd gave her a forgiving kiss on the cheek and murmured, "I love you" in her ear. Christy wondered if he was secretly thinking what she was thinking. Being in the downstairs bedroom had made it difficult to feel the freedom to be as romantically expressive as they were used to. The guestroom was just off the kitchen and not nearly as private as the master bedroom. The guest bathroom had two doors so it could be accessed from the kitchen as well as from the guestroom. With an early rising toddler, a late-night snacker, and a little mama with a squished bladder camped out on the downstairs sofa most of the day, Todd and Christy's new corner of the house was a hub of activity.

Just not the kind of activity that could lead to a baby for them.

Christy reminded herself that this was only a temporary setup. Doug was on the hunt for a permanent place for them to live, and Tracy was daily checking the online listings for their area.

The next week scooted by at the same pace. Christy finished out her final workdays at the gift shop and left with a heartfelt good-bye from the ladies she had worked with. Todd received his second payment from Zane's and put it directly into their savings account. Lindee had become an additional, frequent guest. She turned into a welcome nanny for Daniel and came over every afternoon after school. She usually stayed for dinner and hung out until Daniel went to bed. He adored her, and in her boisterous way, she helped to keep up with the laundry and quickly learned where all the dishes went when she unloaded the dishwasher.

Two and a half weeks into the new-normal lifestyle at

Christy and Todd's home, Christy came home after a five-hour shift at the spa and brought with her a half-dozen helium balloons that were leftover from an event at the resort. She tied the bundle to the handle of Daniel's little bike on the back porch, thinking he would like the festive touch.

For some reason the balloons sent him into a tantrum.

"I think it's the movie I just watched with him," Lindee said. "The old guy had balloons on his house, and he floated away. It's okay, Danny. Your bike isn't going anywhere."

Christy was untying the ribbons from the bike's handle when Aunt Marti suddenly appeared on the deck. Daniel was still wailing, so Christy couldn't hear what her aunt was saying.

"I said, have I come at a bad time?"

"No, you're always welcome, Aunt Marti. How are you?" Christy handed over the balloons to Lindee. Daniel tempered his wailing to a moderate fuss.

"I haven't seen you in such a long time." Christy motioned for her aunt to join her back inside. She closed the sliding glass door behind them, hoping it would cut down on the noise from Daniel as well as give Lindee the hint to keep him out there a little longer.

"That's precisely why I came over. You haven't answered any of my calls today. I left two messages."

"I just got home from work. I was planning to call you back." Christy shuffled the pillows on the sofa and kicked the toy trucks under the coffee table. Tracy had vacated her usual spot, so for the moment Christy and her aunt had the living room to themselves. "How was Palm Springs?"

"That was more than a month ago, Christina. It was fine. We had a nice time. We always do." Marti eyed the paper plate on the coffee table with the half-eaten sandwich and the half-emptied yogurt carton.

"Your hair looks nice," Christy said. "Did you get it cut?"

"Styled," Marti corrected her. "And yes, I just came from the salon. My new stylist feels the warmer highlights are more complimentary to my skin tone."

"It looks great."

"Thank you. As for Palm Springs, it was relaxing." Marti seemed slightly more relaxed and chatty. "I always enjoy the spa at the resort we stay at now. I sometimes find it hard believe we used to stay at the other hotel. What was the name of that one? You remember, Christy. The one we stayed at when you were in high school, and your disreputable friends came along for the weekend."

Christy didn't want this to turn into a discussion about her "disreputable friends" from high school. Nor did she want Lindee to overhear anything about how Christy had been picked up by the Palm Springs police and falsely accused of shoplifting. Her new friends from school had set her up and then ditched her.

Tracy, Doug, and Todd had been there for her after the whole fiasco.

For a brief moment, Christy wondered how different her life might have been if she had continued to hang out with the girls from school who were determined to push the boundaries and break the rules. It made her realize how important it was that Lindee was watching Daniel instead of hanging out with some of the girls at school she had told Christy and Tracy about.

"I guess it doesn't matter what the name of that hotel was." Marti pulled Christy back into the conversation. "I came by to see if you were available on Saturday. I believe I owe you a lunch. I thought I'd treat you to a pedicure as well."

"That sounds so good right now, Aunt Marti. But I have to work this Saturday. It's my last Saturday at the spa."

Marti looked befuddled. "I understood that you were leaving the gift shop, not the spa."

"I did leave the gift shop. But my new schedule at the spa doesn't switch over all the way until next week."

"I see. Is there a day that would work better for you?"

"My days off will be Saturday, Sunday, and Thursday. I could go next Thursday, if that works for you."

"No, not Thursday. That doesn't work for me."

"Next Saturday, then?" Christy suggested.

"No," Marti said quickly. "That's too soon. I mean, I'm already obligated for that day." Marti stood and glanced around at the cluttered area. "We'll have to try to arrange something for another time." She headed for the door, as if she were late for an appointment.

Christy scurried to keep up and followed her aunt out the front door to where her Mercedes was parked in the driveway. She knew something was up with her aunt. She just didn't know what it could be.

"Is everything okay, Aunt Marti?"

Her aunt turned to her with a piercing look of disapproval. "You've turned this house into a commune. It's a disaster. What were you and Todd thinking? And where did you find that disagreeable nanny? She's far too young, and in the name of all that is civilized, why doesn't someone tell her to get those atrocious eyebrows waxed?"

Christy's jaw went slack. She had no words for her outspoken aunt.

"I never intended for this house to be turned into a circus when I bought it for you and Todd. I hate to think of the expense I'm going to incur for all the inevitable repairs. It was bad enough when you started hosting your Friday-night block parties. Now this." Marti maneuvered into her car, still shaking her head. "I don't understand, Christina. I don't understand you at all."

Marti started the engine and backed out of the narrow space. Christy watched her go and stood in the driveway, reeling from what had just happened.

One More Wish

thirteen

The next day, instead of leaving the spa as soon as she finished work, Christy tucked herself away in one of the well-insulated massage rooms and closed the door. The sense of privacy felt good. She had contacted Katie earlier and had arranged for them to have a video call. Seeing Katie's face appear on her iPad made her tear up, as it always did.

The two friends started off the call with their usual litany of how much they missed each other, and then the video feed went out.

"Let's keep going," Katie said. "The audio is working fine. Tell me what's up with you."

Christy dove in and told Katie everything she hadn't been able to talk about at home: her encounter yesterday with Aunt Marti; how Todd was hardly home now that the bench business was on such a steep upward trajectory; and how Doug and Tracy hadn't found another place to live yet, nor did either of them seem anxious to do so.

"I thought it was going to be so great," Christy concluded. "Everything was coming together. We finally had money in the bank, and I thought that hosting Doug and Tracy was what I'd always dreamed of doing. Hospitality is my thing. What's happening at our home right now is not my thing."

"Living in community has its downsides, that's for sure."

Christy realized that Katie lived with inconveniences like this all the time at the conference center.

"How do you do it, Katie? How do you keep your own life and marriage protected?"

"You just have to adjust all the time. It sounds like that's what you're doing. Don't worry if it's messy. What you're doing is worth it. I'm sure this has been a difficult time for Doug and Tracy, especially with her mom and dad moving."

"Her parents left two days ago. Their house hasn't sold yet, but they packed up and left. Tracy was over there helping whenever she could last week. Then she would come home and collapse."

"I'm glad she could come back to your place and know that she had a listening ear and lots of love."

Christy felt comforted by Katie's confident words, but she didn't think she had been especially loving or understanding of Tracy. Christy tried to explain her sense of failure to Katie.

"Don't be so hard on yourself. You're doing well, Chris. And don't worry about Aunt Marti. She has issues. We've all observed that at one time or another."

"But it is her house, technically. She owns it. She has a right to be concerned about its condition. It did feel like a cluttered three-ring circus when she came over yesterday. Daniel was in the middle of a meltdown."

"The poor kid has been displaced," Katie said. "We see it a lot here with missionary kids that are in transition. It's the same in the refugee camps. Being without a permanent home is hard on anybody. It was hard on me when I first moved here."

"That's a good point."

"Here's what I know, Christy. Being in a close community with people is hard. Even if they're people you really love, it's still bumpy because everybody is different and everybody has her own way of doing things. You have to talk through stuff all the time. This can be the biggest blessing time for both of your families, or it can ruin your friendship forever."

"You're right." Christy felt bad for venting. She should be talking to Tracy about the things around the house that were getting under her skin, not to Katie. "Thanks for saying that. We love Doug and Tracy. We want this to work."

"I know. And you love Eli and me. But if we moved in with a toddler, our two families would be having the same issues your two families are having. It's different from two roommates living together or a husband and wife figuring out their mojo. It's two families. It's a different dance."

"You're right."

"May I ask you a question?" Katie asked.

"Sure."

"Did you guys pray about having them come live with you?"

Christy thought a moment. "We talked about it briefly. I don't remember if we prayed about it. I know we both thought that if we were in the same situation, we would be grateful if our friends opened their home to us."

"Eli's mom is always saying, 'Inquire of the Lord.' I'm starting to see the wisdom in praying before any major decision. But the fact is, you guys are all under one roof now, and you and Todd have an opportunity to serve in a big way. Serving Tracy can be something beautiful."

Christy didn't feel as if anything she was doing at home was particularly beautiful.

"I mean, really, when you think about," Katie said, "you're serving a woman who is in need. That's a beautiful, womanly thing to do. You're the one who taught me that. It's just as honorable for you to serve Tracy there in Newport Beach as it would be if you were a missionary here in Africa and helping to care for a sick woman in a hut."

Christy let Katie's words sink in.

"And don't worry about your house being a circus. Just let it be what it is for now."

"That's pretty much how it is all the time. A noisy circus. I miss my space. I miss quiet. Complete quiet."

"That's because you need to be alone to recharge. I remember when we shared a dorm room back at Rancho. You would contentedly stare out the window or write in your journal. I'd try to convince you to go with me to the softball field or to get chimichangas to eat, but you were happy just dreaming."

"I forgot about those killer chimichangas. They sound so good right now."

Katie laughed. "At least you can go back to Casa de Pedro and buy one. It's going to be a long time before an authentic chimichanga finds its way into my belly. I wonder if you could wrap one in dry ice or something and mail it to me."

"I could try," Christy said.

"It probably wouldn't make it through customs. Thanks for the thought, though."

"Do you miss living here?"

"Sometimes. Not often, though. I have a new thing here that's been so fun. I play the African drums."

"You do?"

"One of the guys from Ghana taught me. Christy, I love it. It's crazy. I never tried playing any instrument before. Especially not drums. But the experience is soothing. It really is. You stand and use your hands, not sticks, and all the tension goes out my fingers and makes something powerful."

"I can see you playing one of those tall drums. That's cool, Katie."

"You should try it."

"Oh, right. That's all we need at our house. A set of drums." Katie laughed.

"What's the latest for you guys on the topic of babies?" Christy asked.

"We're still thinking that if it happens, it happens. If it

doesn't, that's good, too. At least for now. What about you guys?"

"We decided that we're ready to start trying."

"Really?"

"Todd told me he was ready a couple of weeks ago, and it did something in my heart. I can't explain what exactly, but I knew I was ready, too."

"And?"

"And what?"

"And what results do you have to share with me?"

"Nothing yet." Christy left out the part about how challenging it had been to find a time to actively pursue their shared dream. "It could take a while. We don't know."

The connection on the call suddenly broke. Christy tried to phone Katie back, but the call didn't go through. She sent Katie a message, thanking her for her listening ear and practical encouragement. YOU WERE A DEEP WELL OF WISDOM FOR ME TODAY, KATIE. THANK YOU.

Katie replied, YOU'RE USUALLY THE DEEP-WELL WOMAN FOR ME, AND I'M THE OH-WELL-WHATEVER WOMAN. MAYBE THE UNIVERSE IS SHIFTING.

Christy smiled and messaged back, AND MAYBE WE'RE BOTH BECOMING MORE THE WOMEN WE WERE CREATED TO BE BECAUSE OF THE WAY WE'VE RUBBED OFF EACH OTHER OVER THE YEARS.

Katie sent a little frowny face with tears. I MISS YOU.

Christy's immediate reply was, I MISS YOU, TOO. MORE THAN YOU'LL EVER KNOW.

Katie lightened up her final message by saying that she was going to find an online recipe for chimichangas and take on the challenge of making one using local ingredients.

Christy left the spa craving Mexican food. Her new habit when she left work was to connect with everyone at home to see what was happening. Tracy said that Doug had picked up pizza on his way home, and they already had eaten. Christy relayed the update to Todd. He said he was heading home.

Just as Christy was starting the car she received a text from Tracy asking if Christy could stop at the grocery store.
SURE. WHAT DO YOU NEED?
Tracy replied, I'LL TEXT A LIST IN A MINUTE.
Christy drove to the grocery store, selected a cart, went inside, and stood in the produce section, waiting for Tracy's text. I'M AT THE STORE. READY FOR YOUR LIST.
Christy picked up items she knew they needed. She was halfway down the cereal aisle when Tracy's text came through. The list was long.
Returning to the produce section, Christy wove up and down the aisles all over again. Something ugly settled on her weary spirit. It didn't matter if Katie thought that Christy's life was something "beautiful" and "womanly" because Christy was serving another woman in need. Christy felt tired of it. She wanted her old life back, the life in which when she came home, she ate what she wanted to eat and watched what she wanted to watch on TV.
In her old life, she and Todd didn't have to worry about being awakened at five thirty in the morning by Captain Rambunctious. She didn't have to lock every cabinet with childproof devices that made it nearly impossible for her to open them. When it was just Todd and her, she didn't come home to an emotional friend who was processing her parents' move or an uncoordinated teenager who had already broken two glasses and one plate while helping with the dishes.
The frustration inside her grew.
By the time Christy had finished shopping, filled the car with gas, and managed to double-park in front of their house so she could unload the groceries, she was done. Done for the day. Done for the week. Done. The only saving grace was that she had tomorrow off, thanks to her new work schedule at the spa.
Todd offered to park the car, and Christy gladly let him take on the irritating task of driving around the neighborhood until he found a place. Doug and Tracy had offered not

to park in the narrow driveway, but the four of them had agreed it made the most sense to keep the car with the child's seat closest to the house.

Christy unloaded the groceries. Daniel was running wild through the kitchen wearing a plastic bowl on his head. Lindee wasn't there, and Tracy and Doug were apparently upstairs. Two open boxes of pizza took up one side of the counter. Only three slices remained. Christy wasn't interested in pizza.

She decided all she wanted for dinner was French vanilla ice cream with a sprinkling of cinnamon on top. Last week Todd had brought home a carton, but it had been eaten before she had any of it. She knew it was ridiculous to obsess over ice cream, but she wanted to make sure she had a serving from the carton she had just brought home before it disappeared.

Christy put the last few items away and pinned the receipt to the message board on the wall. Four other receipts were underneath it. They were from shared meals and other trips to the grocery store. Doug had suggested that Christy keep all the receipts together so they could figure out later who should pay what amount. So far, they hadn't settled up, and Christy's grocery budget for the month was nearly spent.

Todd came in through the front door, and Daniel ran to him as if he hadn't seen Todd in weeks. Todd picked him up. "Should we show Auntie Christy what your daddy got you today?"

"I got a beach," Daniel said.

His "beach" was a plastic sandbox that commanded the entire left corner of the deck.

"Wow," Christy said unenthusiastically. "Just what we needed."

Todd put Daniel down and frowned at Christy. "What's wrong? Are you okay?"

"Everything is bugging me." She wanted to rail against the addition of a messy sandbox and point out that the sand was going to end up in the house and that she would be the one who would have to clean it up.

"Did you call Katie like you said you were hoping to do today after work?"

"Yes, we had a great conversation. I don't know what happened when I was at the grocery store. I just started feeling super tired."

"Hopefully you can sleep well tonight." Todd looked over at Daniel, who was playing with a truck in the sand. "You have tomorrow off, right?"

"Yes."

"I was thinking about taking Daniel to the zoo tomorrow afternoon to give Doug and Tracy a break."

Christy stared at Todd. She wondered if he had listened to her say she was tired. She needed a break tomorrow, too. "You didn't promise them that we would take him, did you?"

"No." He looked hurt. "Not without talking it over with you."

Christy felt her shoulders relax slightly. "Thanks."

"Of course. We agreed that you and I need to talk things through and not volunteer each other for anything while we're doing this community thing. That's why I'm talking to you now. I'm trying to improve my communication skills. I really am."

"I know." Christy rubbed her forehead and watched Daniel scoop up sand and pour the sand on the deck. "You're doing a much better job than I am right now. How about if we decide tomorrow?"

"Sure." Todd rubbed her shoulders. "You are tense. Why don't you schedule a massage for yourself? You've been talking about doing that ever since you started at the White Orchid."

"I should," Christy said.

"Yes, you should."

"How was work for you today?" Christy asked.

"We received all the boards, the ones that we bought

from Bones. He came in and saw what we're doing. He said he wants to help us to promote the benches to his extended surfer community."

"That's awesome," Christy said.

"Odd-sum!" Daniel piped up from the sandbox.

Todd laughed. "That's right, Danny boy. It is *odd-sum*! Our God is *odd-sum*!"

"I'm glad everything is going so well for you, Todd. I really am."

"And I'm glad you were able to switch to just working at the spa. You'll feel the relief of working fewer hours next week."

"I hope so. I'm going to get something to eat and go to bed." Christy went back inside and was content with having a nice, big, happy bowl of French vanilla ice cream for dinner, which she ate alone in her bed with the door closed. It was a small way of taking a break, but it recharged her batteries.

By the next morning everyone else, including Daniel, was sick to their stomachs. Tracy was already pounding a trail to the bathroom, but this bad-pizza food poisoning was doubly hard on her. Daniel was sick in the middle of the night, and so was Doug. Todd, who always said he had an iron stomach, finally succumbed just before dawn.

Since Christy was the only one who wasn't green and dehydrated, she did what she could to help the battered crew. It was pretty awful.

Lindee agreed to come after school to take care of Daniel. The guys were still queasy and sleepless, but neither of them wanted to miss work.

Outwardly, Christy was operating with polite kindness. But in her heart, all the charming was gone. She wished she and Todd never had agreed to open their home to their friends. She hated cleaning up everyone else's messes.

At two that afternoon, Christy put Daniel down for a nap in his cleaned and sanitized room. She felt pretty good about that accomplishment and headed downstairs to stuff another load of towels into the dryer.

On her way down the stairs, she saw Tracy trying to get up from the sofa and shuffle her way to the bathroom. She was weak, and her motions were wobbly.

"Are you okay?"

Tracy's knees seemed to give way, and she flopped onto the love seat.

"Here, let me help you." Christy hurried to offer a bolstering arm. Together they made the trek to the bathroom where Christy left Tracy alone. When she didn't emerge for what seemed like a long time, Christy knocked on the door.

"You okay? You need anything?" Christy cautiously opened the door.

Tracy was lying on the bathroom floor with her arms clenched around her middle.

"Tracy! Trace, are you okay?"

She didn't answer.

With her heart pounding in her throat, Christy dashed for her phone and dialed 911.

*f*ourteen

$\mathcal{C}$hristy patted Tracy's face. "Trace, can you hear me? I called the paramedics. They'll be here in a few minutes." She slipped her hand into Tracy's. "Your hand is cold. Are you in any pain?"

A faint whisper of "no" passed through Tracy's dry lips.

"Okay, you're conscious. That's good. Do you want a drink of water?" Christy wasn't sure why she asked that except she knew she always wanted a drink of cool water after she was sick to her stomach. She thought it might help Tracy's parched lips.

Tracy weakly nodded, and Christy gathered a bottle of water, a blanket, and a pillow.

"Here's some water. Can you lift your head a little?" Christy slid her arm under Tracy's matted blonde hair and found her neck was damp with perspiration. "Try taking a sip. There. That's good. Let me put this pillow under your head. Okay, now go ahead and lean back. I'm going to cover you."

The doorbell rang. Christy wanted to call out, "Come in" to the paramedics, but she didn't know if the door was locked.

She scurried to open it and found Lindee on the doorstep, slipping off her shoes, ready for her afternoon of hanging out with Daniel.

Christy quickly explained the emergency situation and spontaneously gave Lindee a hug. "Daniel's sleeping right now. I'll go with Tracy, and I'll call you as soon as I know anything."

Lindee looked terrified. "Do you think she's going to lose the babies?"

Christy hushed Lindee's loud voice and tried to sound calm. "Just pray, okay? Pray."

Christy hurried back to the bathroom where she had left her cell phone. Tracy looked as if she were sleeping. "Trace, are you warming up?"

"Hhhha."

"It's okay. That was Lindee. She'll stay with Daniel. I'm going with you to the hospital. I'm texting Doug right now to let him know."

"Aaaah."

"Shhh. It's okay. Just rest."

The first-response crew arrived in a fire truck that blocked the adjoining street. Two paramedics entered and checked Tracy's vitals. Christy stood back and replied to Doug's text and sent a text to Todd. The next ten minutes were a chaotic shuffle as an ambulance arrived and the expanded medical team lifted Tracy and strapped her onto a stretcher.

They expertly whisked her out the front door while Christy followed with her purse and phone. On her way out the door, she grabbed a sweatshirt that was flung over the back of a chair and gave Lindee a wave good-bye.

"I'm praying," Lindee called out after them.

The ambulance attendant suggested that Christy drive her own car and meet them at Hoag Hospital. She sprinted the two blocks to where her car was parked. As she drove the short distance to the hospital, she seemed to hit every red light. Her pulse was racing even though she found it impossible to speed through the afternoon traffic. She could hear her phone buzzing with incoming messages, but she resisted the urge to look at them while she was driving.

By the time she had parked and was hurrying into the emergency room, Christy noticed that her lower lip was sore and swollen. She had been biting it the whole time.

To Christy's surprise, Doug was already in the emergency room. His office was closer to the hospital, and he had left the minute Christy first texted him. He enveloped Christy in a tight hug.

"They said I needed to wait. What did the paramedics tell you?"

"Nothing. They took her pulse and checked her eyes and put her on the stretcher. She's very weak."

"She didn't hit her head in the bathroom, did she?"

"I don't think so. I don't know. I didn't see any blood. I asked if she was in pain, and she said no. It looked like she just collapsed."

Doug's eyes clouded with tears. He gave Christy another tight side hug, and together they shuffled over to two empty seats. A dozen people were waiting. One woman rocked a crying baby in her arms. An older man in a wheelchair had his left leg raised and was moaning. They waited an agonizing twenty minutes before they heard Doug's name called.

He bounced up and Christy followed. The nurse stopped her from entering the back area and asked if she was family.

"No," Christy answered.

Doug reached for her hand to pull her in with him and said to the nurse, "She's closer than family. We're part of the same household."

The nurse frowned and remained firm. "Relatives only."

Doug let go of Christy's hand, and she stood alone as he went in with the nurse. The entry doors creaked slightly as they wobbled back and forth. Returning to the waiting area, Christy pulled out her phone and responded to Todd's text messages. She didn't have much to say because everything was still a mystery.

Leaning back in the uncomfortable waiting room chair, she took a deep breath. Tinges of the scent of disinfectant came in through her nostrils along with the smell of dusty air-conditioning vents. A distinct memory of another visit at this hospital came back to her. The summer she was fourteen, Todd's closest friend, Shawn, was brought here after a late-night surfing accident when he was stoned. Christy hadn't found out about the incident until the next day, but when she did, Uncle Bob had driven her to the hospital. But it was too late. Shawn had passed away.

Christy hugged her arms and remembered how deeply Shawn's death had affected Todd, especially a few months later when Alissa revealed that she was pregnant and Shawn was the father.

Please, God, protect Tracy and the babies. Please don't take any of them. Please, Father.

She cried silent tears. The tears were for Tracy and the twins growing inside her. But the tears were also for Shawn, Alissa, and their baby girl, who had been given up for adoption.

A single moment can change a life forever.

Christy scrounged through her purse to find a tissue. She didn't try to stop the tears because deep inside she felt as if she had carried a small reserve of tears for Shawn all these years. She hadn't spent those tears yet because she somehow felt back in her adolescence that she was being strong. Todd had closed up the night Shawn was wheeled into this emergency room. Part of Christy had done the same.

She understood now a little more of what Todd had dealt with since she was the one sitting here, waiting for the report from the doctor. When you have someone you care for deeply and who is part of your everyday world, you can't imagine what life would be like if they were taken from this earth. That's what had happened with Shawn. It didn't mean that was what was going to happen with Tracy. Christy had to remind herself of that.

Sitting back, she thought of something she had read in a book she and Tracy had gone through together last year when they were meeting regularly at Julie Ann's. They had both underlined the same passage and shared it as their main takeaway from the chapter: *The Teacher is always silent during the test.*

This definitely felt like a test to Christy. A test of nerves. A test of faith. A test of her love for her friend.

She regretted that she had harbored a sour attitude when everyone was sick and had treated her chance to serve as a toilsome affair. Opening their home had been her dream. Having her chance to offer hospitality was something she had wished for. She never would have guessed it would be as difficult and complex as it was.

Christy closed her eyes and silently prayed her go-to verse from Psalm 51, asking God to renew a steadfast spirit within her. Right before she opened her eyes, she heard the voice that had stirred her soul a thousand times.

"Hey." Todd gently touched her shoulder before sitting beside her and reaching for her hand. "Any news?"

"Not yet. I'm so glad you came." Christy leaned her head against his shoulder. He rested his head on hers. His grown-out, wavy blond hair fell across her closed eye, and she felt comforted.

It took another half hour before Doug came through the swinging doors. She could tell immediately by his expression that Tracy had improved. Their faces expectant, Christy and Todd both rose and went to him.

"She was severely dehydrated. They have her hooked up to an IV to get her fluids and electrolytes back to where they need to be. It looks like she's going to be okay. They want to keep her overnight."

"And the babies?"

"They're okay." Doug gave them a relieved grin. "It seems the twins took everything she had, and she was the one who got depleted. It's going to be okay."

"Can we see her?" Christy asked.

"They want her to rest. They kicked me out and told me to come back in a few hours after she's more stable."

"Is there anything we can do?" Todd asked.

Doug looked at the time on his phone. "It's almost five. You guys want to get something to eat with me?"

"As long as they serve chimichangas," Christy said.

The three of them took Gussie to a Mexican restaurant in Costa Mesa. Christy called Lindee and made sure everything was okay with Daniel. For the next hour it felt like a blast from the past as the three of them shared a meal without interruptions. Although it seemed odd not to have Tracy there.

Doug and Todd apparently were still recovering from the effects of the pizza plague because they didn't devour the basket of tortilla chips and salsa the way they usually would have.

"I have one more thing to tell you guys," Doug said. "I don't think Tracy will mind my saying anything." He leaned back. "They did a sonogram to make sure the babies were okay, and it looks like we're having two boys." Doug's expression brightened with a look of timid enthusiasm.

"Hey, congrats!" Todd reached across the table and gave Doug a firm handshake. "You weren't able to tell from the last sonogram, right? That's great news."

Christy added her congratulations while trying to picture Tracy with three little boys

"The thing is, they're kind of small for how far along she is. The doctor recommended that she take it easy. Really try to rest more. I told him how she's been going through a lot lately with her parents moving and how she helped them pack up. He thinks she needs to get more rest for the next couple of weeks with only moderate exercise. She needs to eat more nutritious food, too."

"So, no more toxic pizza, huh?" Todd's joke didn't go over well.

Doug moved onto the point that he seemed eager to

make. "So, here's the thing. I found an apartment today that's available next week, on November 1. It has two bedrooms and is in Santa Ana so it's about a twenty-minute drive to work when it's not rush hour. The place isn't exactly in the best area of town, but the price is right."

"That doesn't sound like the answer you were looking for." Christy looked at Todd. He dipped his chin as if inviting her to say what was on her mind.

"Doug, we meant it when we said you guys are welcome to stay with us as long as you need to."

"I know. But we both feel like we've overstayed our welcome. It's been too much to ask of you guys. Especially you, Christy, after the way you had to take care of all of us."

"But who is going to take care of Tracy in an apartment in Santa Ana while she is on bed rest and you're at work? Lindee won't be able to walk over every day like she does when she helps out at our house."

"Christy's right," Todd added. "Save your money. Don't add a stressful move to your lives. Didn't the doctor say she's supposed to take it easy?"

Doug raked his fingers through his short, sandy-blond hair. "It's hard, because this whole thing about her parents moving to Oregon has messed up a lot of stuff. In some ways it's been great for our relationship because Tracy is coming to me first now, instead of always going to her mom. She and I are talking things through and making our own decisions instead of her mom backseat driving all the time."

"That is a good thing." Todd nodded.

"But the other factor in all this is that her mom made it clear that she would come back and help out as soon as the twins were born. If we take the apartment, I was thinking I could call her and see if she could come now to help out."

Christy frowned at Doug's suggestion. She had spent enough time around Tracy's mom to know that she wasn't the sort of woman who would leave her husband for three months, especially after their big move, to live in an apartment with her weakened daughter and overactive grandson. She was a sweet woman, but not one who was made of the tougher stuff that Doug and Tracy's situation called for.

"Why don't we all pray about this?" Todd suggested. He immediately bowed his head and asked God for wisdom and direction for all of them. He asked for God's protection on the twins and a solution that would work best for everyone involved.

As Todd was praying, Christy knew in her heart that she should say something. As soon as he concluded with, "May it be as You wish, Lord," Christy reached across the table and rested her hand on Doug's forearm.

"Doug, just stay. Stay with us. Don't get an apartment. Don't call your mother-in-law. Be at home with us during this season."

Doug looked as if he might tear up the way he did when they had first arrived at the emergency room. "Are you sure, Christy? It's asking a lot of both of you. You guys have already been so gracious to us."

Christy glanced at Todd. His returned gaze was filled with affirming admiration for her.

"Yes, I'm sure."

"We're both sure," Todd added.

"We want the three of you, or I guess I should say the five of you, to stay with us. I agree that it's been difficult and uncomfortable at times these past few weeks. But we can work through all the rough spots." Christy felt an uncommon peace as the words were coming out in a smooth, even tone. This was her gift. She was wired to show hospitality. For the first time since Doug and Tracy had moved in, she felt as if her heart and her attitude were in sync.

"We'll all have to do some adjusting," Todd said. "But that's okay. Why don't we move you guys to the downstairs bedroom since the stairs have been difficult for Tracy? We could put a TV in that room, if you want."

"That would be awesome." Doug's Beachcomber Burrito

arrived, and he cut into it with his fork. "We can put Daniel in with us. You guys shouldn't have to feel like he's in your space upstairs."

"We can think about that before deciding," Christy said. "What matters the most right now is giving Tracy what she needs." The waiter placed a ginormous chimichanga in front of Christy.

Both guys laughed.

"What did you order?" Doug asked.

"A chimi-chimichanga." Christy pulled out her phone and took a photo. She rarely took pictures of food, but this time she tapped out a text. THIS ONE'S FOR YOU, KATIE GIRL. Christy sent the photo with a big grin of satisfaction on her face.

"I'm not going to ask what that was all about, but I am going to let you order for me next time," Todd said.

"No need. You know I'm only going to make it through a quarter of this. You're looking at your lunch tomorrow."

Doug added one more serious thought to their conversation before the subject changed completely. "About the invitation for us to stay on with you, thanks, you guys. Really. Thank you."

"It'll all work out." Christy felt good about the decision. If it was true that the Teacher was silent during the test, it was also true that when she was brave enough to fill in the blank with what she believed to be the right answer, she could feel confident enough to keep going and finish the exam.

She suspected the real test going on in all this was an examination of her heart. She said she loved her friends to their faces, but did she love them behind their backs while she was serving them?

The answer had been no. Not when the going got tough. She had caved in to discouragement and a critical spirit way too easily.

Now that she was retaking the test, she knew the answer was to draw all her strength, love, and patience from the

Lord, not from her own meager reserves.

Christy took a big first bite of her chimichanga. A long string of cheese looped from her fork to her chin and decided to stick there. She looked up just as Doug snapped a photo of her with her cheeks pooched out and the cheese hanging from her chin.

"That was awesome." Doug laughed and checked the photo on his screen. He turned it around to show Todd and Christy.

The shot was about as unflattering as it could be. At that moment, Christy didn't care. She swallowed the bite. "Send it to Katie."

"Katie? I was going to send it to Tracy."

"No! Don't do that. Let the poor woman get over her food poisoning in peace. Doug, you don't send gross pictures of people with food hanging out of their mouths to someone who is hooked up to an IV and trying not to throw up."

Doug blinked. "But it's okay to send it to Katie?"

"This time, yes."

Doug looked at Todd with a perplexed look on his face. "I will never understand women."

"Neither will I," Todd said. "But with this one, it's definitely fun trying."

fifteen

*T*hat night, with Lindee's help, the switch was made so Doug and Tracy could settle into the guestroom downstairs and Christy and Todd were back in their own haven. That felt good to Christy. She realized that if she was going to have what it took emotionally to live a life of hospitality as a rather introverted personality, she needed to protect her hideaway. She hadn't realized, until they had given it away, that their spacious bedroom with the snuggle chair by the window was her sanctuary.

Tracy was released from the hospital the next morning, and Doug took the day off so he could be there for her while Christy was at work. He installed a TV on the wall above the dresser, did the dishes and laundry, and even made three batches of brownies with Daniel from boxes of mix Christy had in the cupboard.

By the time Christy walked in the door from work, her home felt like a different place. She was still sharing it with other people, but the hospitality felt like it was back in balance. Daniel was content to hang out in the guestroom with

Tracy and watch a movie while the Friday Night Gathering was going on in the living room. Lindee got to be part of the group again, and Todd's talk was funny and poignant.

They had almost fifty kids that night—more than they could comfortably fit in their living room. The sliding doors to the deck were opened, and students outside were sitting on blankets and lawn chairs. Todd found a place to stand and teach so that everyone inside and out could hear him. Christy snapped a few pictures of the group as well as the faces of some of the teens while they were listening to Todd teach.

This is thrilling, God. It's so cool to see this happening in our little home. Please draw these young hearts to you. Deliver them from evil.

As the group was dispersing, one of the new guys came up to Christy and introduced himself as Trevor. He looked familiar, but she wasn't sure why, since he said this was his first time at the Gathering.

"How did you like it tonight?" she asked him.

"It's rad. I've been looking for a group like this ever since I became a Christian and got serious about living for the Lord."

"That's so good to hear," Christy said.

"You're a Christian, too, aren't you?"

"Yes, I am."

"I thought so." He grinned awkwardly. She tried to figure out if he was a little slow in the social-skills department or if he was just nervous about being in a new situation. Christy remembered those moments during her teen years.

In an effort to make him feel at home, Christy said, "I'm glad you came."

"So am I."

"Do you live in this area?"

"Yeah, not far."

"Did you come with anybody?"

"Yeah, Ryan and Brett."

Christy recognized Ryan and Brett as two of the guys Todd had taken surfing on Saturdays. "Do you surf?"

"Yeah. I'm not saying I'm any good."

"Have you ever gone with Todd on Saturdays?"

"Yeah, last week. That's how I found out about this."

"Well, I'm glad you came." She realized she'd already said that, but she was having a hard time finding a way into a conversation with Trevor that didn't feel like she was back in high school. The poor guy seemed so self-conscious and nervous.

That's when she remembered where she had seen him before. He was the "skipper," as Todd had jokingly referred to him. Trevor was the guy who had told Christy she had beautiful eyes and that she didn't have to pay for her ride on the ferry.

"So, I was wondering," Trevor said in a low voice. "A bunch of us are going to the movies tomorrow night. Would you like to go?"

Christy took a moment to let his invitation sink in.

Wait. Is he asking me out on a date?

When she didn't reply, he said, "We're going to the Irvine Spectrum. You could meet us there, or if you want, I could pick you up."

He is! He's asking me out.

Christy tried to hide her stunned surprise and quietly said, "Wow, Trevor, thanks for the invitation." She tried to reframe the moment, hoping it would relieve the inevitable embarrassment Trevor would feel when she spoke the next sentence. "I can ask Todd, my husband." She pointed across the room just to make the connection clear. "We might be able to join you guys, but I think we were already planning on doing something tomorrow night."

"Oh. Okay. Yeah. Well, you know, everybody really likes you guys, so if you do want to come, that would be great." His face had turned crimson.

"Thanks, Trevor." Christy thought he would bolt.

Instead he looked down and rubbed the back of his Bible. "Who am I kidding? I'm an idiot. I had no idea. I honestly didn't know you were Todd's wife. Or that you were married at all I thought . . ." He looked up. "I don't suppose there's a way you could somehow forget everything I said and pretend none of this happened?"

"Pretend none of what happened?" Christy tried to look as if she already had forgotten the embarrassing moment.

Trevor caught on and nodded, looking grateful. He gave her one more scrutinizing look. "I probably shouldn't ask this either but, how old are you?"

"Twenty-six."

He looked stunned and still a bit mesmerized by her.

"And now I'm embarrassed to admit my age, so I think I should ask you to forget you ever heard that."

"Heard what?"

They shared a mutual, good-natured grin.

"I'll see you around." Christy reached for the empty pitcher of iced water on the counter and went over to the sink to refill it. She hoped by turning away it would give Trevor an easy exit. She didn't think anyone had heard their awkward conversation. She hoped for his sake no one had.

Her question was answered the next morning when she came downstairs, dressed and ready to work her last Saturday at the spa before she moved to a regular schedule. She found Tracy was already in the kitchen, sitting at the counter, eating a sliced-up cucumber and some raisins.

"Hey, good morning. It's good to see you up and about. How are you feeling?"

"Pretty good."

"That's a welcome improvement." Christy nodded at the cucumber slices and raisins. "Interesting breakfast choice."

"I woke up craving cucumbers. It's the only thing that tastes good to me right now."

"That's new. You haven't had many cravings, have you?"

"The first few months I wanted barbecue potato chips dipped in Greek yogurt. But that was before I realized I was pregnant, and I couldn't figure out why I liked the combo so much. Since then, as you know all too well, I haven't wanted to eat much of anything."

Christy looked around. "It's so quiet around here. The guys went surfing, right?"

"Yes. They took Daniel with them, which is a first. Doug said a bunch of kids were going, and they could take turns watching him."

Christy's phone buzzed, and she saw a text from Eva. "Well, this is another welcome bit of good news. I don't have to go into work today. Eva just realized that she made an error on the schedule."

"That's nice."

"Yes, it's really nice. Maybe I'll go back to bed." Christy stood by the kitchen counter, not quite sure what to do with a free Saturday morning.

"By the way, I heard what happened last night." Tracy looked at Christy over the top rim of her glasses.

"What happened?"

"You were asked out by one of the guys in the group."

"Oh, that." Christy waved her hand as if trying to tell the incident to scat. "How did you hear about it?"

"I heard the whole conversation. You know you can hear everything that goes on in the kitchen when you're in the guestroom. I feel bad now about all the times that we were noisy in here at all hours of the day and night while you guys were trying to sleep."

Again Christy swatted at the air in an effort to dismiss the past.

"Good save, by the way," Tracy said. "I was impressed with how you tried to keep the guy from total embarrassment." She bit into one of her circles of cucumber with her eyes locked on Christy's.

"What?"

"Aren't you going to say anything?"

"What is there to say?"

"That you were kind of flattered that he thought you were

part of the group?"

"I am part of the group."

"You know what I mean. Go ahead, admit it. You were flattered."

"Flattered? No. Embarrassed? Yes."

Tracy went to the cupboard and pulled out a box of peppermint teabags. "I know I shouldn't say this, but I felt jealous."

"Jealous?" Christy laughed.

Tracy put out her arms. "Look at me, Christy. No high school guy would ever think I was the same age as the rest of the group. I look like I'm forty-six, and you look like you're sixteen."

"I do not look like I'm sixteen. And Tracy, you definitely don't look like you're forty-six."

"Okay, thirty-six then. But I feel like I'm forty-six."

"Stop it, Tracy. Just stop. You are so beautiful. Your body is doing very important work right now. You're making four itty-bitty kidneys right this very minute."

Tracy laughed. "I think God is the one who is doing all the work on making the kidneys."

"Yes, He is. But it's your wonderful body that's participating in that miraculous work. That's a sacred kind of beauty, and you know it."

"Sacred beauty," Tracy repeated with a laugh. "Who knew that sacred beauty included varicose veins and acid reflux? So attractive."

Christy placed her mug on the counter as if putting down a gavel to halt the direction Tracy was taking this conversation. "Not every woman gets to do what you're doing. Not every woman can get pregnant just because she decides she's ready to be a bearer of new life."

Tracy's expression sobered. She blinked at Christy as if realizing for the first time that Christy might be slightly jealous of her, as well.

"Sorry that came out so grizzly," Christy said.

"No, it's truth, and I needed to hear it. You're right. Some women I know would give anything to get pregnant as easily as I have."

"Let's not forget, you're having twins. A double blessing."

"I know. It is. I guess I just miss feeling young. While some women wish for a baby, I wish I could feel attractive again and not as if my whole being is under siege."

"Under siege," Christy repeated. "Is that what it feels like?"

"Today, yes. Definitely." Tracy shuffled over to the small kitchen table and moved a stack of mail and papers aside. "Oh, did you see this yesterday? I accidently opened it. It was your mail, not ours. Sorry."

She handed Christy what looked like the kind of envelope that might hold a birthday card. The return postmark read *New York*. Christy guessed it was one of those bait-and-switch kinds of mailings in which the address is handwritten, but the envelope contains a flyer offering low-priced life insurance.

This mail was personal. But it wasn't a super-belated birthday card. It was a birthday announcement. The printed, single-sided card had scalloped edges with a pair of tiny pink little girl shoes embossed at the top. The announcement read:

Rick and Nicole Doyle invite you to share their happiness
as they welcome their daughter
Maisey Jacqueline Doyle
7 pounds 10 ounces, 19 inches
Born September 20 at 7:49 p.m.

Christy sat down at the table across from Tracy and read the announcement a second time. "A baby girl. Did you read this? Rick and Nicole had a baby girl."

"I did see it. They sent us an announcement, too. What do you think about going in together on a gift for them?"

"Sure. That's a great idea." Christy hadn't thought about

Rick and Nicole for some time. They had weathered some difficult stops and starts in their relationship before they finally married on a sea bluff in La Jolla last summer. They moved to New York right after the wedding, and Christy hadn't done a very good job of keeping up with them. She didn't even know they were expecting. If they had announced it on their social media, she had missed it. The only photos Christy remembered seeing posted were ones of their growing restaurant renovation business.

Rick and Nicole had a baby girl.

Christy suddenly felt as if she was the hypothetical woman she had just been holding up as an example for Tracy. Tracy wanted to feel young again; Christy wanted to have a baby. For the first time she sensed an ache inside when she thought about having a child. Twenty-six suddenly seemed old. She wanted to be young and energetic when their kids were little. If that was going to be the case, she and Todd needed to get going.

"What do you think?" Tracy asked.

Christy realized she had blipped out and missed what Tracy had been saying. "I'm sorry. Say that again."

"I was saying that maybe if you have time this morning since you don't have to work, we could dash out and find a gift for Rick and Nicole's daughter."

"That's a great idea."

"I'll let Doug know." Tracy stood, and a youthful glow suddenly returned to her cheeks. "Maybe we can even go to lunch somewhere."

"You must be feeling better. Should I try to find a place that serves cucumbers and barbecue chips?" Christy teased.

"I was thinking Julie Ann's might be nice, actually. We could go there before we head out shopping."

"This is sounding better and better. Are you sure you're feeling well enough to do this?"

"Yes. I'm supposed to get some moderate exercise. I'll be fine as long as I don't try to do too much."

"Okay. If you're sure you're up for it. Why don't you let the guys know what we're doing, and I'll go change out of my work clothes."

Christy and Tracy started off their spontaneous free day by sharing a carrot cake muffin at Julie Ann's. Tracy's appetite returned, and she ordered a second pastry as well as a glass of fresh squeezed orange juice. They easily fell into the chatty sort of sharing they used to exchange when they went to Julie Ann's regularly.

The theme of the day turned into babies, babies, babies.

Christy asked Tracy a dozen questions she had wondered about pregnancy and doctor's visits. She told Tracy some of the recent changes that had happened in her heart and about the conversation she and Todd had on the way home from Bones's garage almost a month ago.

"I'm so glad that you feel ready," Tracy said. "I know I've been a horrible example of what a blessing being pregnant is, but at least you've seen it from all angles. It's wonderful and kind of awful at the same time. At least it is for me."

"Do you remember around my birthday when you said you wished we could be pregnant at the same time?"

Tracy nodded.

"To be honest, it kind of freaked me out when you said that. It doesn't anymore. I'm getting more eager for it to happen."

"That makes me happy, Christy. It really does."

They decided to go to the baby shop on Balboa Island where Christy bought the *Peter Pan* book. Tracy had never been there, and Christy knew they would find the sort of gift that would work for a posh little baby girl growing up in New York. They took their time, looking at everything and enjoying the chance to shop for something girly and pink.

"This is the only thing I'm bummed about now that we found out we're having two boys." Tracy held up an adorable, pink-and-white polka-dotted bathing suit that came with a pink tutu attached. "Doug would never let me put one of the twins in this."

Christy laughed. "That is so cute. Let's buy it for Rick and Nicole. What size do you think we should get so she'll be able to wear it next summer?"

"Twelve to eighteen months seems like a good way to go. What about a book for her, as well?"

Christy held up a beachy-looking book entitled *Who Made the Ocean?* It had adorable illustrations. "How about this one?"

"Love it. Let's include some lotion or a little seashell bracelet for Nicole, too."

Christy loved shopping with Tracy. She had great taste and good instincts in how to turn a simple present into a complete gift. Several years ago when Katie had entrusted Christy with the task of finding a wedding dress for her, Christy had taken Tracy along, and the shopping spree was a great success. Today was a repeat performance and a much needed break for both of them.

Their mission was accomplished before eleven o'clock, and the two friends didn't quite know what to do with themselves. Tracy called Doug, and he said they were doing great at home. Daniel had run himself out at the beach that morning and was taking an early nap. Todd was working on something that had to do with a story Bones had told him, and Doug was watching football.

Tracy hung up and looked at Christy. "Doug said we should treat ourselves to lunch or go get our pinkies painted."

"Is that what he calls a pedicure? Getting our pinkies painted?"

Tracy gave a cute shrug. She didn't seem to care what her husband called it. Her eyes were glowing with hope. "Should we?"

"Absolutely," Christy said. "Where should we go?"

"I have no idea. I can't remember the last time I had a manicure or a pedicure. Those little luxuries were the first thing taken out of our budget a long time ago."

Christy snapped her fingers. "What is wrong with me? I work at a spa!"

They both laughed.

"Let me call and make sure we can get in on such late notice. If they can, I want you to let this be my treat for you. And before you protest, let me tell you that if I pay for both of us, I'll receive my employee discount."

Instead of protesting the way Tracy often did when they took turns covering the bill at Julie Ann's, this time she simply said, "Thank you."

"You're welcome. That is, you're welcome if they can fit us in." Christy made the call while the two of them took their time walking to where they had parked the car several blocks away in the residential part of Balboa Island.

"Good timing," Christy's coworker told her on the phone. "We just had a cancelation for two pedicures at eleven thirty. We can slide both of you in, if you can get here right away."

"No problem. We're on our way now. Thanks so much."

Tracy didn't stop smiling the whole way there. "My feet are already so grateful."

For Christy, it felt a little strange showing up as a guest instead of an employee at the White Orchid. All her fellow employees were warm and friendly and asked if this was a special occasion.

"We're celebrating that Tracy is having twins," Christy decided aloud.

The ladies made all the right cooing and congratulating sounds. Christy found it fun to treat her friend like this and it was insightful for her to see how it felt to be on the other side of the tour of the facilities and the warm welcome.

They were ushered into the spa's salon area and directed to two plush reclining chairs. The curtains were drawn on either side of the two chairs to cordon off the other guests who were receiving pedicure and manicure services. The curtain between their two chairs was tied back, making it feel as if Tracy and Christy were in their own luxuriously appointed area, having a private party.

Christy was surprised at how secluded and lush it felt. She had only seen how the setup worked from the service end, when she was the one drawing the curtains.

"This is like a dream, Christy. Thank you so much."

Christy leaned back in the comfortable chair and slipped her feet into the warm water. "You're welcome. It's my pleasure. I'm so glad I didn't have anything else to do today."

Just then the curtain next to Christy was pulled back with a brusque swish. The woman on the other side leaned over in Christy's direction and in an exaggeratedly cheerful voice said, "Yes, it's wonderful that you didn't have any other plans or invitations for today, Christy darling."

sixteen

"Aunt Marti!" Christy chirped in surprise as she sat up and took a closer look at the spa customer leaning toward her.

"Hello, Christy. Hello, Tracy." Aunt Marti was all smiles. A salon employee was massaging one of Marti's feet while the other one soaked in the warm water.

Christy had forgotten all about her aunt's invitation earlier that week. That was before the pizza poisoning, the trip to the hospital, the baby announcement from Rick and Nicole, and definitely before the call from Eva that morning telling Christy of the scheduling error. Christy scrambled to explain why she was here, even though something inside kept telling her that she didn't need to apologize.

"I found out I didn't have to work today."

"How nice for the two of you." Marti was smiling and her tone was hushed, but Christy felt icicles hanging from every word. "I won't interrupt your special time. I'm sure it must be difficult for the two of you to find many opportunities to be together."

Christy's heart was pounding. She hated it when her aunt twisted things so that Christy felt as if she had done something wrong when all she had tried to do was something nice.

"She just found out this morning about the schedule change." Tracy came to Christy's defense with her trademark sweetness. "You can imagine how excited we were to get out for some girl time while we had the chance."

"Oh yes. I can quite imagine."

Christy cringed, but Tracy kept riding on the sweet train, determined to take Aunt Marti with her all the way to the station. "We just went shopping for a gift for Rick and Nicole."

"Shopping, as well. My, you are making quite a day of it."

Undaunted, Tracy said, "Did you hear Rick and Nicole just had a baby girl? We'll have to show you what we bought her."

Marti seemed to flinch a bit. "Rick and Nicole had a baby?"

"We just received the announcement this week. They named her Maisey."

"Maisey," Marti repeated. "What an unusual name."

Christy suddenly recognized the source of the pain in her aunt's voice. She was jealous. Jealous of Christy choosing Tracy over her on Christy's day off. Jealous that the two of them knew about Rick's baby even though Marti had generously doted on both Rick and Nicole when they lived in the area and came regularly to the Friday Night Gatherings.

Christy wasn't sure how to purge the effects of a green-eyed jealousy monster, but she did understand it a little after the conversation she and Tracy had in the kitchen that morning.

"Well, enjoy your spa time, girls." Marti reached for the curtain to pull it back and separate them.

Christy reached out and kept the curtain where it was. "Join us, please. Our decision to come was fun and spontaneous, and it will make it even more fun and spontaneous if you'll be part of it."

Marti looked as if she had been silenced with kindness.

"Yes," Tracy said. "It's been an awful week. We need you to help both of us relax. I ended up in the emergency room on Thursday and had to stay overnight. My parents have moved to Oregon, and I want you to know that your niece has been a lifesaver for us."

Whether it was Marti's maternal sensitivities kicking in or a stunned curiosity, her demeanor softened, and her voice turned gentle. "Tracy, dear, what happened? I wish you had let me know you were having difficulties. Are you all right? What about the twins?"

Christy leaned back and released a sigh of relief as Tracy filled Aunt Marti in on all the latest, including how difficult it had been for Tracy since her parents moved to Oregon. As Christy listened, she could easily imagine the "How Can I Rescue Tracy" project that was formulating in her aunt's brain right then.

My aunt wants the same thing all of us want. She wants to be valued. Needed. Included. Now that my work schedule is back to a more humane pace, I want to think of a way that I can express how much I appreciate her and want to spend time with her.

Christy's chance to make good on her wish came the following Thursday when she had the day off. The serendipitous meeting at the spa had been followed by lunch beside the pool and Marti purchasing expensive bottles of body lotion for Christy and Tracy from the spa boutique.

Marti hugged them both good-bye with a youthful, genuine smile. "You both know where to find me. Do promise that you'll notify me immediately if you have any other trips to the emergency room. Better yet, call me or come by anytime. I mean that."

That was when Christy decided she was going to take all the elements of a girly tea party over to Marti's house on Thursday afternoon to surprise her. Christy had Todd check with Uncle Bob to make sure they would be home that afternoon. Tracy had a doctor's appointment and wasn't able to come along for the tea party, but she helped Christy with the preparations.

The two of them had a lot of fun collecting all the pieces that would tailor-make the party for Marti. Christy bought an assortment of macaroons and tiny cupcakes at Cheri's Bakery and found some special party napkins with a fleur-de-lis emblem that looked like Marti's style of decorating. Tracy prepared special little egg-salad sandwiches cut into small, crustless triangles. Christy used gluten-free bread since that was Marti's new preference and added fresh dill she bought at an upscale grocery store.

Packing everything, including her well-wrapped fine china teapot and cups and saucers, Christy headed over to her aunt's at four o'clock wearing her nicest dress. She rang the doorbell twice. When no one answered, she did what her aunt and uncle had invited her to do long ago and opened the unlocked door. She stepped inside and called out, "Hello!"

Christy traipsed into the living room and laid out the party on the coffee table. When everything was just right, she called out another "hello" and went to the kitchen to start the water boiling so she could complete the final touch and make fresh, steaming tea. Her uncle walked in just then from the garage with a bag of groceries in his hand.

"I thought that was your car out front. How are you?"

"I'm good." Christy gave him a side hug as he put the bag on the counter. "I have the day off so I came over to surprise Aunt Marti with a special little tea party."

Uncle Bob had merry eyes with lots of laugh lines radiating like sunbeams. His eyes suddenly changed from smiling to a curious stare. "Does she know?"

"No. I let myself in because I guessed that you guys couldn't hear the doorbell. Where is she? Upstairs on the bedroom deck?"

"I'm not sure." Uncle Bob hesitated, smoothing the side of his face with his open palm. "Well. Only one way to find out how this is going to go. Let me lead the charge."

Christy wasn't sure why he was responding in such a cryptic way. Was he concerned that Marti wouldn't do well with a surprise?

Maybe I should have called earlier in the week and set up an appointment. She does like being organized. I thought the surprise would make it more fun.

Uncle Bob headed for the stairs, and Christy followed. When he looked into the living room and saw what Christy had set up, complete with a vase and a single pink rose, he paused.

"Looks pretty fancy. Little pink rose and everything."

"I wanted to make it special. Do you think she'll like it, Uncle Bob? I'm getting the feeling that I shouldn't have done this. Or at least, not have done it so spontaneously."

Bob quickly looped his arm around her shoulders and gave her a hug. "You're always welcome here, Bright Eyes. You know that. The way I see it, when you have something to celebrate, you stop everything and celebrate. You wait here. I'll go talk to Marti."

Christy could hear the electric teakettle sounding a pleasant ping, indicating the water was ready. "I'll make the tea and wait for her in the living room."

He gave her a wink and continued upstairs.

Christy prepared the tea and carried the china pot into the living room. The autumn sunlight gathered at the bottom edge of the expensive shades that were almost always kept lowered to protect the furniture. On the rare occasions when the shades were lifted, the two large windows that faced the beach provided a stunning view of the long stretch of sand that rolled out like a carpet to the water's edge. It seemed to Christy that the sunlight was as timid as she was beginning to feel about coming in for a visit.

She looked around at the immaculate and tastefully decorated room. There were no toys or clutter or noise. This tranquil setting was the antithesis of what her home was like.

However, it also struck her that the room felt faint of breath, as if it were sleeping with a placid expression void of dreams.

As familiar as this room was and as peaceful as it felt to sit alone, Christy decided she preferred the mostly happy chaos that was always happening in the living room at her home. She liked the crazy collection of guests who filled the space with life. She and Todd lived in a home, not just in a house. Their living room was awake, not asleep.

Uncle Bob came down the stairs and entered the living room with a look that Christy recognized. He was trying to be cheery and upbeat, but something was wrong.

Before he could say anything, Christy asked, "Is Aunt Marti okay?"

He nodded but seemed still to be on the hunt for what he wanted to say.

"Did I come at a bad time? She's not sick is she? Or does she have one of her migraines?"

Uncle Bob lowered himself into the chair across from Christy and rubbed his hands together.

"What is it? Something's wrong. Just tell me what it is."

"Your aunt had some minor surgery this morning, and she's resting. The pain medication makes her quite loopy."

"Surgery? I didn't know. Is she okay?"

"Don't worry, she's fine. Absolutely fine. There was no reason for her to alert you about the procedure. She was eager to have it done before we leave for Maui in a little more than a month." Bob eyed the plate with the tiny sandwiches. "Those look tasty. Is that dill?"

"Yes. Egg salad. You're welcome to have one, if you like." Christy felt like a little girl, sitting here at a tea party with her uncle. She wasn't satisfied with his limited explanation, so she kept asking questions.

"Do you think it would be good if I took a cup of tea upstairs to Aunt Marti? I can understand that she might not want anything to eat. It might cheer her up, though, to have a hot cup of tea and some company. What do you think?"

Bob had fit the whole wedge of sandwich in his mouth and was chewing slowly. As he was swallowing the well-pulverized egg salad, Christy heard Marti's light footsteps on the stairs. She rose to her feet, prepared to help guide her aunt to the couch after her brave journey down to the living room.

However, when Marti entered the living room wearing one of her long, flowing kaftans, Christy's feet turned to cement and anchored her in stunned silence.

Both of Marti's eyes were circled with dark black-and-blue bruises. The area was so swollen, her eyes were nearly shut. She looked as if she had just lost a prizefight to the current heavyweight champion of the world.

"Aunt Marti," Christy whispered, "what happened?"

Bob rose and went to Marti, helping her to navigate the last few steps to the sofa. She sat down and faced Christy with a silly, pain-killer-influenced sort of crooked grin.

"So." She placed a hand on Christy's leg. "Tell me. What's the good news? Hmmm?"

"The good news?" Christy turned to her uncle for a clue as to why that would be Marti's first sentence when obviously her appearance was the only news any of them should be discussing.

Talk about an elephant in the room!

"I don't know what you mean, Aunt Marti. I came over because I wanted to surprise you with a tea party." Christy motioned to the arrangement on the coffee table.

"Well, surprise!" Marti pointed to her face, as if Christy hadn't noticed Marti's shocking appearance.

Christy saw that a long piece of black thread ran in an arched curve through the middle of both of Marti's eyelids. When Christy looked closer, she could see the stitches.

You had plastic surgery!

All the odd comments from her uncle and avoidance from her aunt made sense. Marti had something done to her eyelids and hadn't wanted anyone to know. Instead of Christy surprising her aunt, Marti delivered the biggest surprise that afternoon.

Marti reached across the coffee table. Instead of taking one of the pink macaroons, Marti lifted the pink rose out of the vase and twirled it in front of her nose. Her silly grin seemed to be fixed in place.

"Well?" Marti said. "Well, well, well?"

Again, Christy looked to her uncle for a clue.

"I may have given it away. Sorry, Christy. It seemed the only way I could convince her to come down. You went to so much trouble, I didn't want to spoil your announcement."

"What announcement?"

"The baby!" Marti held the long-stemmed rose up like a fairy godmother wand. "The baby, of course. The baby!"

"What baby?"

"Why, yours." Marti tapped the end of Christy's nose with the soft, pink rose. "I do hope it's a girl."

Uncle Bob kept his gaze fixed on Christy, his eyebrows raised, his expression expectant.

"I'm not having a baby." Christy could almost feel the disappointment in the room falling like a glass on the kitchen floor. It shattered all the earlier joviality.

"Why else would you go to all this trouble?" Marti fixed her squinty-eyed glare on Uncle Bob. "You said she had a rose. A pink baby rose and an announcement."

"I thought she was going to tell us she was expecting." Bob's expression of disappointment turned to one of chagrin. "My apologies to both of you. I honestly thought . . ."

Marti tossed the rose at him, but it fell short and landed on the carpet. "You just wanted to trick me into coming down here and humiliating myself in front of our daughter."

"Our niece," Bob quickly corrected her. "Christy is our niece. And I wasn't trying to trick you."

Marti reminded Christy of someone in a movie who was intoxicated and had released all her inner sensibilities.

No wonder Uncle Bob tried to keep me from seeing her. If my aunt remembers this bizarre encounter, she is going to be furious at me as well as more humiliated than I've ever seen her. For her sake, I hope she won't remember.

When Christy thought about the whole fiasco later, she wasn't sure why she did what she did in that awkward, suspended moment. But her instinct was to pour her aunt a cup of tea, and that's what she did. The gesture had tamed the sassiness out of Lindee. It might have a neutralizing effect on Marti as well.

"It's Darjeeling," Christy handed Marti the china cup and saucer. "I like mine with a little milk and sugar. Would you like yours the same way?"

"Oh no. No thank you. No sugar for me." Marti seemed to slip into her socialite role without a tick. "I'm off sugar. Completely off. We're going to Maui, you know."

"Yes, I know. I'm sure you'll have a wonderful time."

"Only if I can fit into my bathing suit. I refuse to buy a new one a size up. I simply refuse."

Christy nodded, trying to show strong support of whatever her aunt had to say at that point. She offered Marti the plate of tiny sandwiches. "These are egg salad on gluten-free bread. I know you prefer gluten-free."

"Actually, I'm not eating any bread whatsoever. It's a carb, you know. Gluten-free brands are the worst. They have to add so much sugar to their rice flour. You might as well eat a cookie. Two cookies! Are those cookies?"

Christy lifted the plate of cupcakes and macaroons and brought them closer so Marti could see them through the slits that her swollen eyelids had become. It was the first time Christy realized the sweets were all pink. The desserts along with the pink rose and the unexpected visit—it made sense to her why Uncle Bob had jumped to the conclusion that this was a baby announcement.

"None for me. Thank you." Marti took a sip of tea and reached for one of the small napkins to delicately dab the corner of her mouth. Her slightly downturned lip seemed to make it difficult to get the sip of tea to cooperate and go down her throat. The effect reminded Christy of the last time she went to the dentist and then tried to drink from a cup before the Novocain had worn off.

Uncle Bob rose and quietly slipped out of the room. He gave Christy a wave behind Marti's back and pointed to the kitchen as if to indicate that he would be standing by if things turned wonky and Christy needed him to intervene.

As it turned out, the tea party was one of the most entertaining experiences Christy had ever had with her aunt. Marti dished on scandal-worthy information about a woman in her Pilates class. Then she reached for a macaroon and held it between her thumb and forefinger as she confessed to Christy that she had been receiving Botox injections for six years now.

Marti drew the pink dainty to her lips and then lowered her hand without taking a bite. "What I'm most excited about is a new skin treatment my esthe . . . ecta . . ."

"Esthetician?" Christy ventured.

"Yes. That's her name. Esther . . . whatever you said. She's going to give me the treatments before we go to Maui. I have to wait until I heal from my eye-lift surgery, of course."

"Of course," Christy agreed.

"It's a special pumpkin-enzyme peel from Switzerland. She said it's guaranteed to make me look ten years younger." Marti popped the macaroon into her mouth as if the motion would add an exclamation mark to her comment. She seemed to be sucking on the macaroon but only for a moment before opening her lips, uncurling her tongue, and depositing the deflated goodie into her party napkin. She discreetly placed it on the side of the coffee table and slid a magazine over the top, as if Christy wouldn't notice it that way.

Christy wanted to laugh at her aunt's peculiar behavior. Instead, she decided that since her aunt was being unguardedly honest, Christy might as well take a chance and be equally unfiltered.

"You know, about the plastic surgery and everything, I

think you are beautiful, Aunt Marti. You always look lovely. And youthful, too. I don't think you should try to change the way you look."

"You only say that because you're not my age. You'll see. It's traumatic getting older."

"But aging is natural. Don't you think so? If anything, I think that sometimes women your age who try to do too many improvements end up looking odd. It's like those pictures you see online of plastic surgery gone wrong." Christy made an exaggerated pouty face and opened her eyes wide to demonstrate her meaning. "They look like they can't blink or like their lips were stung by a bee."

Instead of defending the plastic surgery industry or her own procedures, Marti put her cup and saucer down with a shaky hand and reached for a cupcake. She peeled back the pink floral paper and took the tiniest of nibbles. "I should expect such an opinion from someone living in a commune."

"I don't live in a commune, Aunt Marti."

"It certainly looks that way to the common observer. The wear and tear on my house is what concerns me the most. The next time I come over, I wouldn't be surprised to find you've all put flowers in your hair and are raising goats."

Christy finally let the big laughter bubble inside of her burst. She had to put down her teacup because she was laughing so hard.

"I fail to see what is so humorous." Marti lifted her chin as if she were the queen of Newport Beach and she had nothing but disdain for the rowdy subject sitting on her couch. "I shouldn't tell you this, but I was going to raise your rent after my visit last year."

"Don't you mean your visit last week?"

"I mean five thousand dollars, that's what I mean. That was my plan."

Christy wasn't tracking with her aunt. She gave her a perplexed look.

"What are you doing? I can barely see your face. I must be

allergic to these pumpkins."

Christy wanted to laugh again, but she held it in. "We're not eating pumpkins. You were saying that you're going to have a facial with pumpkins. We're eating raspberry maca- roons and strawberry cupcakes."

"None for me, thank you. I'm off sugar. Entirely."

Christy had a feeling the time had come for her to pack up and take her leave. Marti needed to rest. Christy stood and began to clean up the items on the coffee table.

"Wait. I didn't tell you the end. Or did I? About Tracy and why I didn't raise the rent."

Christy sat back down.

"When I saw the two of you at the spa I was very hurt."

"I can understand how you would have felt that way, Aunt Marti."

"I changed my mind about everything, including the five-thousand-dollar rent increase. Because you are like sis- ters. And sisters need each other when they are having ba- bies. You never had a sister. I did. My sister was there when I had you. You need to be there for Tracy. She's a good sister to you."

Most of what Marti said made sense. Except the part about Marti being the one who gave birth to Christy. Marti had given birth to a baby girl, but sadly she died in infancy, right before Christy was born. Bob and Marti never had any other children. Christy had become the focus of the love and generosity they never could pour out on their child.

Christy had felt more than once that Marti had project- ed onto herself the role of being Christy's birth mother. This was the first time Marti admitted that was her view of their relationship.

Christy let the odd comment go and thanked her aunt for not raising the rent in an effort to roust Doug and Tracy out of their home. She stood again and began to clear the table. When she did, Marti polished off the rest of the cupcake she had been holding and stretched out on the couch. "Would you put a blanket over me, dear? My head is pounding, and I feel as if my eyes are on fire. Oh, wait. You will leave a few of those pink cookies for my husband, won't you? He likes sweets. He says that's why he likes me."

A silly smile rested on Marti's discolored face, as she closed her eyes the rest of the way and fell asleep almost instantly. Christy pulled an angora throw blanket from its decorative spot draped over the back of one of the chairs. She smiled as she tucked in her aunt.

What a crazy, Mad Hatter tea party this turned out to be! I hope you don't remember any of this when you wake up, Aunt Marti. No, wait. I take that back. I hope you remember the part about not raising our rent!

One More Wish

seventeen

$\mathcal{F}$or the next few weeks Christy felt as if she were living the life she had always wished for.

According to Uncle Bob, who had been listening in to the whole wacky conversation at the tea party, Marti had little recollection of their conversation. She remembered that Christy had come by, but she thought it was before the procedure. Marti didn't bring it up, and she didn't raise the rent.

Tracy seemed to develop an appetite overnight. She was eating all the time, and her belly kept growing. She took it easy, as the doctor at the emergency room had recommended, and as soon as she entered her third trimester, she seemed to feel better than she had the first two trimesters. Most of the time, though, Tracy lived the half-waking, half-sleeping life of a homebound, precariously pregnant, mother of a pre-schooler. She slept whenever she could and spent most of her waking hours with her feet up.

Doug arranged his schedule so he could work at home two days a week, which was a big help to Tracy. He turned the kitchen table into his remote office and spent more time with

Daniel, which had a calming effect on the displaced little guy.

The biggest surprise to all of them during this season of shifting priorities was Lindee. She faithfully came over every day after school and turned out to be Daniel's best pal. He responded to her brusque approach in unexpected ways She taught him how to put away his toys when told and got him to wait his turn and not interrupt when the adults were having a conversation.

Tracy developed a deep appreciation and a bit of awe for the unlikely Mary Poppins who had come to them in the form of teenage Lindee.

Work clicked along at a steady pace for Todd as he and Zane kept up with the orders for their surfboard benches. He adjusted his hours so he could spend time with Christy on the days she had off. They met for lunch, went to a matinee one Thursday afternoon, and had more time together.

More time together meant more possibilities of a baby.

On the Tuesday before Thanksgiving, Christy left the spa at five and joined the hordes of grocery shoppers with her long list. She had put plans in motion to host a grand Thanksgiving feast. Her parents, Bob and Marti, Lindee and her mom had agreed to come, and Zane said he was a "maybe." The only one who wouldn't be there that she was looking forward to seeing was her brother, David. He had plans to go on a camping trip with a bunch of guys from his dorm at Rancho Corona. Christy knew that when she did see him at Christmas, he would be older and cooler and nothing at all like the pesky little brother who had bugged her so much when she was in high school.

One of the items on Christy's shopping list was "ptst." She had written it in code in case Doug ended up shopping for them. She knew that it meant "pregnancy test." For now, that was all that mattered.

In the squash to move up and down every aisle, Christy forgot to get it. She didn't realize her oversight until she was home, unloading the bags.

Oh, well. I should probably wait until after Thanksgiving to take it anyway. Although if it's positive, it would be fun to tell everyone around the table. When we all take turns saying what we're thankful for, I'll have something really great to share. If I am pregnant and if we decide to keep it a surprise until Christmas, it would be so fun to wrap up a gift of some sort that gives it away and send it off with my parents to Maui.

But the more Christy thought about it, the more she wanted to see her parents' faces when they told them. She went back out to the store, saying she forgot something, and returned home with the pregnancy test tucked into the bottom of her purse.

She didn't take the test that night. She waited until morning, thinking of how fun it would be to get up before Todd and then wake him up with the results. The only problem with that plan was Todd was an early riser, and he was already downstairs by the time she woke up. It seemed best to wait until the next day, Thanksgiving morning. She and Todd didn't have to work so no one would be rushing out the door. The news would be fresh without the possibility that either of them had leaked the details to Doug or Tracy.

The test was still in the bottom of her purse. When she was on a break at work that day, she considered taking it to get it over with. The suspense was starting to bother her.

She called Todd and when his phone rolled to voice mail she left him a message. "Hey. I know this is crazy, but I haven't told you something. I bought a pregnancy test, and I'm thinking of taking it here at work. I know you told me a long time ago that you wanted me to tell you when—" Christy's phone indicated Todd was trying to call her.

"Hey," he said. "What's going on?"

Christy repeated the message she had started to leave for him.

"Take it."

"Really?" Christy asked. "Do you think I should take it here at work?"

"Yeah. Take it now and then come over here on your lunch break and tell me the results. I don't want to find out in a text."

"Okay. I'll see you around noon."

Christy slipped into one of the stalls in the spa restroom. Relaxing violin music was playing as she closed her eyes and made a wish. Opening her eyes, she checked the wand.

Not Pregnant..

Christy had taken a dozen pregnancy tests over the last few years, and every time the negative result gave her an unspoken sense of relief. But she had never taken one when she and Todd were being intentional about getting pregnant. This time when she saw the results, she cried.

At noon Christy hurried over to Zane's new warehouse, which was only a five-minute drive from the spa. She walked into the cavernous, dusty, noisy workshop and waved till she got the attention of one of the guys.

All four of the men working that day were wearing expensive breathing masks to protect them from the resin on some of the old boards they worked with. They also wore large earphones that protected their ears from the noise of the sanders, and they had on protective goggles. The benches were lined up along one side of the warehouse looking bright, shiny, and ready to go be a work of art in some shopping center or public park. They were impressive.

Todd strode over to Christy and walked her out to the parking lot. As he pulled off his face mask, goggles, and earmuffs, he gave her a look of anticipation.

Christy shook her head. "No," she whispered. "It was negative."

Todd's eyes welled with tears. "It's okay." He wrapped his arms around her and held her close. "It's okay."

Christy felt her earlier sadness double when she shared it with Todd. They pulled apart, and she noticed that her black work clothes were now covered with the fine dust that had clung to Todd's clothing. She brushed off the particles and told herself to brush off the disappointment as well. It surprised her again how deeply disappointing the results were. She had wanted so badly for the test to be positive.

They reached for each other's hand and stood close together in the parking lot.

"God's timing," Todd said calmly. "We have to wait on Him. We have to believe His timing is flawless."

Christy gave Todd's hand three squeezes. She wanted to tell him that the best thing she had discovered in this was that she cared about having a baby more than she ever had before. Her disappointment at the gut level and the tears in Todd's eyes showed Christy that they really were ready for the next season of life.

It felt cumbersome, though, to try to put those feelings into words on her lunch break while standing in the parking lot. So Christy waited.

Their home was a hive of happiness the next day. Tracy had done a lot of the Thanksgiving meal preparations on Wednesday. She was the first in the kitchen on Thursday, and by one o'clock the feast was ready. The house was permeated with the scent of pumpkin pies, seasoned stuffing, fresh-baked rolls, the roasted turkey, and cinnamon-spiced apple cider warming on the stove.

The celebration was a grand success, and Christy felt grateful that they had invited everyone over. She was especially grateful that Tracy loved to cook so much and that she had some amazing recipes for all the items that really mattered, like the garlic sour cream mashed potatoes and the Italian sausage-and-cashew stuffing.

The surprise of the day came after all the guests had gone home and Tracy and Daniel had both gone to bed early. Doug was washing the last of the pots and pans, and Todd stood by his side with a dishtowel in hand. The guys had turned it into a competition of some sort and were giving each other a hard time about who did the most to help around the house. It reminded Christy of when the two of them shared an apartment with Rick in college.

She was about to make a comment about who would have won the competition back in their college days, but her phone buzzed. She read the text and said, "It's from Sierra. They spent today at Jordan's parents' home in Irvine. She wanted to know if they could stop by in the morning on their way back to Santa Barbara."

"That would be great," Todd said. "Don't you think so?"

"Yes, absolutely. I'd love to see them."

"Tell them to come. We all have the day off, so it's perfect."

"See if they want to come for breakfast," Doug suggested. "I'll make leftover omelets."

"Oh, yeah. Put some of Tracy's killer Italian sausage stuffing in an omelet and add some cheddar cheese. I'm all for that," Todd said.

"How can you guys even talk about food?" Christy patted her still-full stomach and texted to Sierra. The plans were made, and at eight o'clock the next morning the gang celebrated what Doug called the "Thanksgiving After Party."

"You've got some skills there with the spatula," Sierra teased.

Doug flipped her omelet and looked pretty proud of himself. The kitchen counter was covered with all the Thanksgiving dinner leftovers, and a couple of cartons of eggs sat by the stovetop ready to be cracked open.

"Who's next? Jordan, what do you want in yours? And are you going for two eggs or three?"

"Two eggs, and I'll take turkey, mashed potatoes, cranberry sauce, and jalapeños."

"I don't think we have jalapeños," Christy said.

"We do." Doug held up a jar on the counter. "I found these in the back of the fridge. I don't know how old they are, though."

Christy checked the expiration date and saw they should be okay. Doug was making a mess with dropped food on the floor, as he transferred Jordan's ingredients to his side of the kitchen and added them to the skillet. Christy pulled some cereal bowls from the cupboard and said, "How about if everyone puts what they want in a bowl and hands it over to the master chef here."

"You're next, Trace. Get your bowl ready."

Tracy opted for a simple leftover dinner roll for breakfast. She was too wiped out from all the prep and celebration. A glass of milk and a permanent corner on the sofa where she could put her feet up made her happy.

Breakfast was a loud and messy affair, and Christy loved it. She loved having vivacious Sierra and reserved, gentlemanly Jordan in her kitchen, picking up the conversation where it had paused at their wedding reception. They had fun stories to share, and Sierra's laugh seemed to brighten up the whole downstairs.

Daniel was eager to show Jordan his "beach" sandbox out on the deck and his assortment of trucks. The other guys drifted outside to join them while Christy and Sierra cozied up on the couch with Tracy.

"Are you getting excited?" Sierra asked Tracy.

"Excited?"

"Yes. Excited to meet your new boys?"

Ever the calm and pensive woman, Tracy said, "I'm probably not as excited as I should be. I keep imagining two more miniature Daniels running around, and I'm grateful for every minute they're still inside."

Sierra laughed. "Okay, first, they don't come out running around. And second, every child is different. You could have two little bookworms in there that will like to sit and look at books or make LEGO houses all day."

"And then their big brother will come along and demolish them with his monster trucks."

"That little guy?" Sierra looked out the sliding glass door at Daniel, who was sitting on his daddy's lap with his head resting against Doug's chest. "He's going to be the best big brother around."

Tracy gazed at her husband and son fondly. "I know. He's grown up so much in the last few months. It's been life changing for our family to be here at Todd and Christy's." Tracy told Sierra about Lindee and about how upset Tracy had been when her parents announced they were moving to Oregon.

"I look back now," Tracy said, "and see that this is the best thing that could have happened. Daniel has bonded with Doug like never before. I feel like Doug and I are much closer than we've been in a long time."

Christy agreed.

"Not everyone can live with two families under one roof," Sierra said. "When I was in Brazil, I ended up in a situation like this. I was the Lindee, I guess you could say. It didn't go well. It destroyed the friendship between the two couples."

Christy and Tracy exchanged glances. "We've had our moments," Christy said with a warm smile.

"Todd and Christy have been so gracious to us," Tracy said. "That's why this has worked. Christy has more patience and generosity in her than anyone I know."

Christy felt uncomfortable being praised that way. She knew she had had plenty of impatient moments. Especially during the first three weeks before she viewed this as an opportunity to exercise her gift of hospitality.

"What about you?" Christy asked Sierra, eager to redirect the conversation. "How's everything going in Santa Barbara for you and Jordan?"

"Stupendous." Sierra's long, curly blonde hair seemed to bounce as she enthusiastically talked about their married life. Jordan had just gotten another photo-shoot assignment from a surfing magazine, and he and Sierra were going to Bali in January. She said she loved her job as a waitress at a friend's Italian restaurant because she could chat with interesting people all day long, and the tips were great.

"We live in the tiniest garden cottage you've ever seen."

"I don't know," Tracy said. "You didn't see the Balboa

bungalow Doug and I were in before we came here."

"Our place used to be a pool house on the grounds of an old Santa Barbara mansion in the hills. It's perfect for us because we're hardly ever home, but when we are I feel as if we're playing house. Plus, we can use the pool whenever we want, and both of us love that."

"It's your haven," Christy said.

"Exactly."

"I've come to believe that every woman needs to feel that where she lives is a haven. It doesn't matter how large it is or how it's decorated. What matters is that she feels safe and at peace there and is always happy to be home."

"I couldn't agree more," Sierra said.

"And the other thing every woman needs," Christy added. "Is a snuggle chair."

"What's a snuggle chair?"

"I'll show you. Mine is upstairs in our bedroom." Christy turned to Tracy. "You okay if we leave you here for a few minutes?"

"I was thinking of going to our haven of a bedroom and resting. Sorry to be such a slug, Sierra. I'm just so tired today."

"I understand." Sierra offered Tracy a hand so she could get up from the couch. Her rounded middle seemed to protrude even more as she stood there with both hands on her lower back, saying good-bye to Jordan out on the deck. She gave Sierra a hug and waddled into the guestroom.

Christy and Sierra scooted upstairs. The morning sunlight gave the room a fresh, airy feel, as if a host of fairies had just been in there doing a bit of straightening. The soft shades of beachy-blue and white that Christy had selected when they painted the room several years ago were showing off their ability to make the space look larger. In the corner by the window her snuggle chair looked especially inviting, with one of her playful throw pillows brightening up the scene.

"That is the best snuggle chair I've ever seen!" Sierra went right over and plopped down, then put her feet up on the ottoman, making herself comfortable. "Yes, I definitely need a snuggle chair. I'm not sure where to put it, but a chair like this would be so perfect to come home to after being on my feet all day."

Sierra adjusted the throw pillow and examined the colorful fabric and cute ruffled detailing on the corners. "Where did you get this pillow? I love it."

Christy sat on the edge of her bed and told Sierra about her sewing business that had been put aside almost a year ago. The conversation moved on to more realities of finances and the challenges of being a newly married couple. Both of them were sharing on a deeper and more personal level than they had been downstairs. Christy didn't know if it was because it was just the two of them or if the feeling of sanctuary had come upon both of them when they retreated to Christy's hideaway.

"What about babies for you guys?" Sierra asked. "Jordan and I are thinking we want to wait at least a couple of years before trying."

"We're trying." Christy felt a small sadness welling up, as if she were admitting defeat, even though it had only been a few months of intentional efforts.

"So you're past the wishing stage?" Sierra asked. "And on to hoping?"

"That's one way to say it. Although, right now I think I've lost some of my hope. Maybe we are still in the wishing stage. Not that I should act as if I know the difference between the two."

"I think of it like this," Sierra said. "A wish is like the childhood stage of a dream. It's the most innocent, elementary version of a possibility. It's fragile, like a dandelion in a breeze."

"Or the flame of a birthday candle," Christy suggested.

"Exactly. That's why when you're little, you close your eyes, wish for a unicorn, and blow out the candles. It's like you're opening your heart with childlike joy and giving space for anything to be possible. You know that the wish can be fleeting or fragile, but it makes you happy just to hold it for a moment."

Christy agreed. She wasn't wishing for a unicorn, though. She was wishing for a baby.

"Hope is different," Sierra said. "Hope is a wish that goes to high school."

Christy laughed.

"It's more realistic than a wish. Hope comes to the possibility with a sense of responsibility and understanding of what it's going to take, but at the same time hope leaves room for the unexpected. Hope is always on an emotional roller coaster because, like I said, it's a wish that goes to high school. It's always looking for love, identity, and purpose."

Christy let Sierra's thoughts settle on her. "It sounds like you've considered this a lot."

"I have. That's what five years in Brazil will do to you. I was always wishing and hoping for things when I was doing full-time mission work. I would pray all the time, and God seemed to be awfully quiet."

"The Teacher is always silent during the test." Christy realized that thought was more for herself at the moment than for Sierra.

"I like that. Yes, it's so true. It seems like God is annoyingly silent during the time when you're wishing and hoping. But then I think something happens in answer to all the prayers. I don't know if it's because of God's timing or what. It seems like the wish that went to high school grows up from being hope and turns into faith."

Christy thought of a verse she had always liked in Hebrews and said it aloud, "'Now faith is confidence in what we hope for and assurance about what we do not see.'"

"Exactly! You see? Faith grows out of that adolescent hope, which is such a roller coaster. And that's why I think it's a good thing to pray and keep praying. To wish and keep wishing. Because God answers prayers in His way and in

His timing. The worst thing we can do is to stop praying or dreaming and wishing. We have to start there, with all our childlike, whimsical thoughts. Because I think that every prayer of mine that God ever answered first started out as a wish that grew into a hope and graduated to become faith."

"That's really good, Sierra. You should write it down."

Sierra shrugged. "It's yours now. You write it down. I'm not the kind of girl who keeps a journal, as you know. Life seems to happen in the moment for me. I think about it, and then I go on. Someone else can write the poems for the rest of us. Me? I'm onto the next adventure."

Christy took Sierra up on her offer to be the one to write down her thoughts. She went to bed early that night and snuggled her chilled feet under the covers. With her journal in one hand and her pen in the other, she summarized her conversation with Sierra and put the date at the top of the page. On the next page she added her thoughts about the season of life she and Todd were in. It seemed the best way to express what she felt was in a letter. She had written letters to her future husband long before she and Todd were serious about each other. Now she wanted to write letters to her future child.

Dear Baby of Mine,

You aren't alive yet. You aren't breathing the air of God's beautiful world. You aren't even in my womb yet.

But you are alive in my heart.

You are my wish. My sweetest wish. I can't wait to one day see your little face and feel your tiny fingers wrapped around mine.

Until then, I will wait upon the Lord. With my whole being, I will wait. God does all things well. He gives good gifts to His children in His time and in His way.

For now, you are my wish. Every time I gaze upon a star, I will wish for you. Every birthday candle I blow out between now and when you come to us, I will wish for you. Every time I find a dandelion, I will pluck it, and I will close my eyes before I blow, and I will wish for you.

Every one of those wishes will be wrapped in a prayer. A prayer for the miraculous beginning of you.

Forever,

Your mommy

One More Wish

Two days before Bob and Marti left for Maui, Christy stopped by their house after work to see if they could fit a few small Christmas gifts in their suitcases. She wanted to have something for Bob and Marti and her parents to open since they would be celebrating Christmas across the sea.

Marti looked surprisingly younger, with much smoother skin and fewer lines around her eyes. Christy knew it was the glad results of her aunt's pumpkin-enzyme treatments and eyelid surgery. She wanted to say something but wasn't sure how to compliment Marti without giving away that she knew about the procedures.

"You look gorgeous, Aunt Marti." Christy chuckled inwardly. *Gorgeous* was a word Marti used often. It wasn't a word Christy used, but she knew her aunt would like it. Then because something of a pixie harbored inside Christy when it came to dealings with her aunt, she added, "You look ten years younger. You must be in vacation mode already."

"Why, thank you, Christy darling. You are so kind. I must have gotten up on the right side of the bed this morning."

"Yes, I'm sure that's it. You look rested and ready to go to Maui."

Marti turned her head to the right as if subtly giving Christy a chance to gaze upon her firmed and hydrated skin. "The challenge, of course, will be to stay out of the sun as much as possible."

Christy knew that was a wise route to take, especially since Marti's procedures may have made her skin more sensitive to UV rays. Still, it seemed sad to think about going to Hawaii and avoiding the sun. Christy's happy memories of Maui included lots of days of snorkeling, lounging on the beach, and sailing on a catamaran. She hoped her mom would get to enjoy some of those beautiful opportunities in Maui. It might be difficult if Marti preferred to stay inside every day.

"I hope you guys have a wonderful time," Christy said. "It was a good idea for you to take my parents. My mom is really looking forward to it."

"It will be the trip we should have taken with them years ago," Bob said.

Christy gave her aunt a light-touch sort of hug. "You really do look gorgeous, Aunt Marti."

Marti took a closer look at Christy. "You're not like anyone else, are you?"

Christy laughed at the odd comment. "No, I guess I'm not. And neither are you. We're all unique. We're a bunch of Peculiar Treasures. That's what Katie and I have always called each other."

"That's not what I mean. You seem more mature. More settled than you've been since you moved here. I would have imagined that the schedule you keep and the house full of people that you feed and entertain would have put you under by now. Yet you've found a way to thrive in the midst of all the chaos."

"It is chaotic sometimes. But it's a beautiful chaos. Todd and I feel like we're doing what really matters."

Marti shook her head. "I couldn't live the way you're living."

A thought floated through Christy's mind. *And I wouldn't want to live the way you're living.*

Fortunately Christy didn't let it slip out. She did think, though, that Marti was right. Nearly six months ago she was blowing out her birthday candles and wishing she could fly off to Maui to get away from her life. She had felt worn out from being the main source of their finances. Now that that responsibility felt that it had been lifted from her shoulders, Christy didn't have the same need to push an Eject button on her life. Instead, it was as if she had hit the Reset button and had been reconnected to the source of power that she needed daily. She liked that she and Todd were doing what they could to ensure that two tiny lives would be as healthy as possible when they entered this world in a few weeks.

When your circumstances don't change, you change. And when you change, it's possible that your circumstances will change.

Christy hoped she remembered that thought so she could add it to her journal when she got home.

As Bob walked Christy to the door, he put Marti's comment into his own simple terms. "You know that we're proud of you, don't you? I think that's what Marti was trying to say. We're proud of you, Bright Eyes. Always have been. Always will be. We saw you in your best light on Thanksgiving, and it impressed both of us. Your home is a place anyone would want to be."

"Thanks, Uncle Bob." She gave him a warm hug. "That means a lot to me."

Christy left feeling his affirming words soak into a few parched places in her heart.

She was still thinking of her aunt and uncle's comments later that night, after she and Todd had retreated to their upstairs hideaway bedroom. Christy told Todd what Marti had said about how she seemed more "mature" and more "settled."

"Do you think that's true, Todd?"

"I think we've both had to grow up lately. Responsibility does that."

Christy cozied herself under the covers and kicked her cold feet to warm them up. Todd and Christy liked to sleep with the window open an inch so they could hear the ocean, but tonight the air carried a chill. Todd turned out the light and flopped into bed. "Love you. Good night."

Christy snuggled up to him and kissed the back of his neck. His body felt warm. She gave his earlobe a playful nibble.

Todd reached his arm behind him and patted her on the hip. He seemed too exhausted to add any words to go along with his gesture.

Christy sighed. She gave him one more kiss on his shoulder and whispered, "Later."

Todd's rhythmic breathing was a pretty good indication that he was already in dreamland.

Christy closed her eyes and welcomed the sleep that covered her. All around her were soothing hints of life. Even the house seemed to breathe in the blessing that covered all of them like a warm blanket on this Southern California winter's eve.

Just before she fell asleep Christy wondered what it would be like to be entrusted with a tiny soul that would live and move and have its being inside her. The now-familiar echo of her heart whispered, *wait*. She knew that was all she could do.

The next morning Christy was up early, and so was Tracy. Christy found her on the sofa, reading a book to Daniel.

"Morning." Christy picked up Daniel and gave him a hug. He had a runny nose and seemed eager to demonstrate his cough for her.

"That doesn't sound good." She felt his forehead. He didn't feel too warm. Tracy handed Christy a tissue from the box on the coffee table. Christy tried without much success to wipe Daniel's nose before putting him down.

"And what about these little guys?" Christy patted Tracy's

very plump tummy. "How are they doing this morning?"

Tracy had dark circles under her eyes, and her hair was matted across her forehead. "They've been having a punching contest all night." She reached for Christy's hand and moved her palm to the left. "Feel that."

Christy's eyes opened wide. "Whoa! That was quite a kick."

"I wanna feel, too." Daniel leaned against the couch. Instead of putting his hand on his mommy's belly, he pressed his cheek against hers. A moment later he popped his head up. "I felt it, too. That baby kicked me right here."

Daniel definitely had his moments of cuteness.

"Who would like some oatmeal?" Christy asked.

"Me!" Daniel raised his hand.

"Sure. That sounds good." Tracy slowly swung her legs over the side of the couch.

"You don't have to get up. I can bring it to you."

"I'm headed for the bathroom. I don't know how Doug and I could have ever lived through this pregnancy without all the kindness you guys have shown us," Tracy said as she shuffled along behind Christy and Daniel.

"You don't have to keep thanking us, Tracy. We're all in this together. Those little sluggers are going to make a healthy entrance into this world in less than a month, and for the rest of their lives I will guarantee you that their auntie Christy will remind them of what they did to their poor mama while they were hitching their free ride."

Tracy grinned weakly. "And when we're old and heading for the nursing home, we'll both remind these two that it's their turn to show us a little extra love. And you, too, Daniel. Especially you."

Daniel looked up as if he had no idea what they were talking about.

Christy chuckled. "The nursing home, huh? You took a big leap through life right there."

"Trust me, I feel like I'm ready for a nursing home."

"Well, one thing is certain. You'll be nursing all right."

Tracy gave a small moan and closed the bathroom door. When she came out a few minutes later, she had washed her face and brushed her hair. She looked fresher and more awake.

Christy pulled the milk out of the refrigerator.

"I hope you know that when your turn comes, Christy, you'll be able to count on me being there for you the way you've been here for me every inch of this journey."

"I'm sure I'll take you up on that." Christy took some bowls out of the cupboard.

Doug opened the door of the downstairs bedroom and joined them. "What's cookin'?"

"I'm making oatmeal. Does that sound good to you?"

"I was thinking of making some eggs," Doug said.

"We can have both." Christy readied a frying pan and cracked eggs in a bowl.

Doug wrapped his arms around Tracy and held her close. Daniel tried his best to wedge in between them and become the peanut butter in what Christy had seen the three of them call their "peanut butter and jelly sandwich" hug before.

"Those babies won't let me in!"

Doug reached down and scooped up Daniel, giving him a two-armed morning hug that was equally cuddly to the one he had given Tracy. Todd entered at that moment, and Daniel wiggled out of Doug's clutch. He ran to Todd and grabbed Todd's hand. "Come to da beach with me."

Todd gave Christy a passing wave and let Daniel pull him out to the deck where his sandbox awaited him.

"I have an appointment at the doctor's this morning," Tracy said. "We can stop at the grocery store on the way back. I'll see what we need and make a list before we go. Let me know if there's anything you would like us to pick up."

"Sounds good." Christy checked the time and realized she was going to be late if she didn't leave for work right then. "I'm leaving," she called out. "Love you guys!"

Christy hoofed it to where her car was parked several blocks away. She didn't check her phone all day until she was in the back room, getting ready to leave. She had three missed calls, all from Tracy. At first she thought Tracy was probably calling to see if Christy wanted anything at the grocery store. She remembered the doctor's visit and decided she better call her back.

"Is everything okay?"

"Yes. I have some big news. Are you heading home pretty soon?"

"I'm leaving right now."

"Okay. I'll wait till you get here."

Christy hated surprises and wanted to say, "No, tell me now." But Tracy already had hung up.

When Christy walked through the garage to the house, she noticed a number of large packages of paper towels, toilet paper, and tissues stacked against the garage wall as well as three big boxes of disposable diapers for newborns. She went inside and found the kitchen counter was covered with staple items that didn't need to be refrigerated and an ice chest by the trash can that was packed to the brim with ice and frozen meat.

Christy found Tracy stretched out on the couch.

"Guess what?" Tracy's face glowed.

"I can't imagine. Are we starting a food bank here?"

"No. That's all from your uncle."

"My uncle?"

Tracy bolstered herself up on her elbow and leaned against a stack of pillows on the couch. "He called Todd and said he and Marti wanted their refrigerator cleaned out before they went to Maui. Doug met Todd over there, and they brought all this back at lunchtime."

"Diapers? A year's supply of paper towels?"

"Doug is convinced that your uncle wanted to bless us when your aunt wasn't looking so he picked up all that extra stuff for us when he was buying sunscreen for their trip. Bob told Doug that the boxes of diapers fell into his cart, and he thought we should have them."

"My uncle is the best."

"Yes, he is," Tracy agreed. "Now guess what the doctor said."

Christy sat down. "I have no idea. I hope he didn't say it's actually triplets."

Tracy put her hands on her bulging midriff and smiled. "I'm probably big enough to be carrying triplets. There are two in there. I know that because my obstetrician took another sonogram today. He said that he and the doctor in the emergency room both got it wrong. I'm not having twin boys."

"How could they get that wrong? With all the technology today, can't they tell if there's one baby in there or two?" Christy added, "Wait. I thought you just said you know there are only two in there and not three. I'm so confused."

"There are two babies. I am having twins."

"Then I lost you somewhere."

Tracy was grinning, as if she just swallowed the sweetest bite of pink cotton candy. "Baby A is a boy but Baby B is . . . a girl!" Her eyes teared up.

Christy popped up from the love seat and spouted the happy news. "You're having a girl!"

"A girl and a boy. The boy is larger and has pretty much dominated the earlier images. Today it was clear, though. There is definitely a girl in here."

Christy rushed over to give Tracy a hug around the neck and a pat on the belly. "I'm so happy for you!"

Tracy dabbed her tears. "I know I kept saying it didn't matter as long as the babies were healthy. But now that I know I'm having a girl, I am so excited. So is Doug. We talked about names on the way back from the doctor's. I think we're set on our two names."

Christy waited for the big reveal.

"Annie Lynn for our daughter, and Cole Spencer for our son."

Christy blinked. "Did you say, Cole Spencer?" She knew she hadn't told anyone about the name she and Todd had come up with on their camping trip last summer. She wondered if Todd had told Doug.

"How did you come up with that name?"

"I've always loved the name Annie, and my mom's name is Lynn."

"I mean, the name for the boy." Christy was having a hard time not feeling as if she had just been robbed. She and Todd had shared everything with their friends for weeks without any misunderstandings or feelings of unfairness. But she wasn't prepared to share the only boy's name that she and Todd had agreed on. A few nights ago Christy had a dream of being at the beach with a towheaded little guy in baggy swim shorts who was chasing seagulls. When she called to him in her dream, she called out, "Cole! Cole Spencer, come back here!"

Tracy clearly wasn't aware of the dart that she had unknowingly thrown into the deepest longing of Christy's mothering heart. Tracy looked happy and excited as she said, "Doug has always liked the name Cole. At one point he wanted to name Daniel, Cole, but the name Daniel seemed to fit him from the moment he was born. You remember. You were there right after he was born. He looked like a Daniel, didn't he?"

Christy nodded and forced her still-numb lips to curve up in a smile. She decided then that her friend must never know the enormity of the gift Christy was giving her in that moment when she said, "Cole is a great name."

"And, of course, Spencer is in honor of you guys. I told Doug we should name the girl Anna Christina, but he said it sounded like a nun's name."

Tracy's casual comment wasn't delivered to be a jab, but Christy felt as if another dart had gone into her heart. Her not-yet-conceived son's name had been scooped, and now her name apparently sounded like a nun's.

Christy rose and tried with all the charm she had left to

say, "What great news, Tracy. I'm really happy for you. I better clear the gifts from Uncle Bob off the kitchen counter so I can make some dinner for us."

"Lindee asked if she could stay for dinner, and I said yes. She and Daniel are with Doug picking up the rest of the stuff at Bob and Marti's."

"There's more?"

"Just one final carload," Tracy said. "Oh, and Christy, if it's not too much trouble, could you bring me something to drink? Juice would be great."

"Sure." Christy felt as if she were limping into the kitchen, even though her wounds were invisible. She tried to tell herself it didn't matter. This wasn't something that should cause her so much hurt.

This is ridiculous. If we ever have a boy and we want to name him Cole, we can do that. It's not like only one child in all of history can bear a certain name. Why am I making such a big deal of this?

As she poured Tracy a glass of cranberry juice from their overly filled refrigerator, she realized why the sting was so potent. Tracy was having a baby, and she wasn't. Tracy was having two babies, actually. She and Doug would soon have three children, but Christy and Todd had none.

I'm jealous. That's what this feeling is. I'm hurt because I'm jealous, and it feels like I can't even keep the name that we were saving for our son one day.

nineteen

*L*ater that night, after Todd had fallen asleep, Christy got out of bed and sat in her snuggle chair by the window. She wrapped a throw blanket around her legs and turned the lamp by the chair on low. With her Bible in her lap and her journal beside her, Christy went on a search. She didn't know what she was looking for. Comfort, maybe? Forgiveness for her jealousy? Assurance that God hadn't forgotten her? A promise that He would fulfill the desires of her heart? She couldn't sleep because she needed something, anything, to help her to feel that God was close and that He cared about her and what she was feeling.

Christy opened to the page in her journal where she had been keeping a list of God's promises. Her eyes fell on a verse from Isaiah 49:16 that she had copied several weeks ago. *"See, I have engraved you on the palms of my hands."*

Below that she had written some reflections on one of her favorite chapters in the Bible, in Psalm 139. The note she had included was, *God knows everything about me. He knew me before I was born. He saw me in my mother's womb. He knows me by heart, and He knows me by my name. I am His child, and He has written my name on the palms of his nail-pierced hands. God loves me.*

Tears like a winter mist on the beach clouded her vision. She may have written those words weeks ago, thinking of how they related to God's promises to her, but now she saw how they related to God's promises to the yet-to-be-born Cole Spencer. God already knew him. God saw him in Tracy's womb, and God saw Annie Lynn. He knew that Annie was a girl even when the doctors didn't. God already knew both of those tiny children by heart and *by name.*

Oh, Father God, I believe all this is true, but it still hurts. I'm happy for Tracy and Doug. I really am. Forgive me for being jealous of the way You have chosen to give these two babies to them, entrust Annie and Cole's earthly care to Tracy and Doug. What I yearn to know is, do You have a child for us? Do you already know that child by heart and by name?

No reassuring echo reverberated in her spirit. The Teacher was still being silent.

Christy wished this test would end. It felt worse than the SAT. She wanted the test to be over, whether she passed or failed, she wanted to know if she and Todd were able to have a baby. If not, if something was wrong with her body or with Todd's, then she wanted to know so they could start discussing adoption.

Christy looked up and saw that Todd had rolled over and was squinting at her. "You okay?"

She nodded, even though she was pretty sure the nod wasn't very convincing.

"Is it the name, still?"

Christy swallowed the tears that wanted to rise to the surface. "The name, and the fact that . . ." She couldn't bring herself to say aloud that she was jealous of Doug and Tracy having two babies. "I just feel like we got ripped off."

Todd gave her a sleepy but sympathetic look. He reached over and pulled back the covers on Christy's side of the bed.

"Come to me, Kilikina."

She turned off the light and went to him. Todd smoothed back her long, loose hair with his rough hand. He drew her close and whispered, "I love you."

In the deeply romantic moments that followed, Todd did, indeed love her. He loved her very well. When sleep finally overtook both of them sometime later, Christy's heart was calm. Her strength was being renewed.

She felt that strength giving her peace and grace as the week rushed by.

Three days before Christmas Christy woke with a tickle in the back of her throat. She loaded up on vitamin C and put some cold tablets in her purse in case it got worse while she was at work. By ten o'clock she had taken the antihistamine, which helped to clear her sinuses. For lunch she went to a café down the street and ordered soup. She went straight home at five o'clock and took a long, hot bath, using bath salts she had bought at the spa. Christy took some nighttime cold medication before she went to bed and hoped it would help her to sleep.

By the next morning, she knew she should admit that she had succumbed to the flu bug that had been going around. Determined not to let a nasty virus get the best of her, she took her cold pills, gargled with salt water, used a nasal spray she found in the medicine cabinet, and prepared a Thermos of hot herbal tea to take with her to work.

In spite of her heroic efforts, Christy finally let Todd convince her to stay home. She had entered the phase of the virus in which her eyes were red and her voice was raspy.

"The last thing anyone needs to see when they arrive for their day of soothing spa treatments is a hostess who is contagious," he said.

She heeded his counsel and returned to bed where she slept deeply. She woke sometime later to a loud pounding on her bedroom door. Pushing up on her elbow she turned to the door as it opened, and Doug's anxious face appeared.

"Her water broke! I'm taking her now. Can you watch Daniel?"

It took Christy half a second to focus and realize what Doug had just said. "Yes. Oh, yes, of course. Go!" Christy swung her feet over the side of the bed and felt dizzy from the cold medication. She held the railing as she went downstairs and found Daniel watching a DVD as if nothing unusual was happening in his little life.

"Hey, buddy. Have you had lunch yet?"

He didn't answer. He was fixated on the animated cartoon truck characters that were in a race. It was his favorite DVD, and she knew he would be tuned in for the next half hour at least.

Christy heated up some chicken broth and called Todd. He had received a text from Doug and was already on his way to meet them at the hospital.

"Keep me updated."

"I will. How are you feeling?"

"About the same. I hope I didn't give this to you."

"I'm feeling all right. You just take care of yourself."

"I am." Christy carried her soup and a plate of crackers into the living room and sat on the love seat with a blanket wrapped around her legs.

Daniel came over to her like a pigeon, checking to see if she would toss any crumbs his way. "I put some crackers on the coffee table for you, Daniel."

He reached for a cracker and stood unmoving with it in his hand, locked in on the movie.

The soup felt good on Christy's throat. She prayed for Tracy, watched the DVD with Daniel, and continued to check her phone. They were down to the last few minutes of the movie when Todd came home.

"How's Tracy?"

"She's in labor."

"Do you know if everything is all right? It's nearly two more weeks till her due date."

"I don't know. I wasn't able to see either of them. But Doug texted me that he called her mom, and Lynn is going to catch a flight down here tomorrow so she can help to take care of Tracy."

Christy was surprised. "We never talked about her parents coming. Where are they going to stay?"

The movie ended, and the theme music played as the credits rolled. Daniel, who hadn't even looked up when Todd came in, picked up the remote control and pushed the replay button. He sat down on the couch with her cracker and started to watch it again from the beginning.

"I'm sure Tracy's parents will make arrangements to stay somewhere. I don't think we should have them stay here. Especially since you've come down with the flu. How are you feeling?"

"A little better. Thank you for taking care of me." Christy's voice was raspy, and her ears were ringing. "I hope you don't get this bug. It hit me so hard all of a sudden."

"You've been going full speed for a long time." Todd rubbed her shoulders. Christy let her head fall so he could rub her neck as well. "Why don't you take a bath or go back to bed? I'll watch the little guy."

Christy liked that idea a lot. "Come and tell me as soon as you hear any updates, okay?"

"I will. Let me know if you want me to bring you anything."

"Okay. Thanks."

Christy inched her way back upstairs and took a hot shower. The steam helped her sinuses but started a coughing jag.

I hate being sick.

Finding her most comfortable pajamas, she crawled into bed where she slept soundly for some time. When she woke, she could tell the fever had broken. She turned to the window and saw that the evening cloak of ocean mist and darkness had closed in. She could hear Todd talking to someone downstairs.

Christy ventured downstairs wearing her cozy slippers and her big, fluffy robe. She looked into the living room and saw that Daniel was asleep on the couch with his stuffed toy tiger under his arm.

Todd had just ended a phone call when she shuffled into the kitchen.

"You must be feeling better."

"A little. What's the news?"

"Doug called about ten minutes ago. They had to do a C-section." Todd's expression was serious, and his voice was low. Christy bit her lower lip, expecting the worst.

"They are all doing fine. The babies are being run through some tests, but Doug said they were bigger than they thought, and that's going to be an advantage. I guess the doctor was concerned about their lungs being fully developed or something."

Christy had read enough and had talked about developmental stages with Tracy enough to know this was good news when it came to preemies. "How big were they?"

"I wrote it down because I knew you would want to know." He reached for the notepad on the counter by the blender. "Annie Lynn was five pounds exactly and fourteen and a half inches long. Samuel Dwight was five pounds two ounces and sixteen inches long."

"Wait. Did you say Samuel?"

"Yeah, Samuel Dwight. I think Doug said that was his grandfather's name. When the baby came out, they looked at him, and Doug thought he looked like his grandfather. Something like that."

"Wow, I'm surprised." Christy smiled at Todd. She felt as if someone had just placed another birthday cake in front of her, and she could make one more wish for a baby boy named Cole.

"I never thought Doug or Tracy would change their minds about the name choice," Todd said. "Did you?"

"No."

He gave Christy a smile. It was a great smile. She knew that he was ready to wish again along with her.

Christy went to the refrigerator.

"You want something to drink or eat?" Todd asked. "Let me get it for you."

"It's okay. I can manage."

"No, sit down. You serve everyone else all the time. Don't rob me of the chance to serve you for once."

Christy returned to the stool at the counter and let Todd wait on her. He gave her some juice and a bowl of applesauce with cinnamon sprinkled on top, the way he had seen Christy prepare it for Daniel.

"I had an idea," Todd said. "What if I call Bob and Marti in Maui and ask if you and I can stay at their house in the guestroom while they're gone? That way Tracy's mom and dad can stay here."

Christy thought Todd's idea was brilliant.

"It will give us a break. We can bring meals over and help out. But at least at night we'll be able to get some sleep."

"It sounds like the perfect solution, if Bob and Marti will let us stay there."

"Only one way to find out." Todd made the call to Bob's cell. He explained the situation and asked about them using the guestroom. His relieved expression and vigorous nodding let Christy know that Bob and Marti had said yes.

"Your aunt said we should stay as long as we want and not to worry about cleaning up because she'll ask her maid to come in every Tuesday."

"What did my uncle say?"

"He said that he wanted us to make ourselves at home because the only reason God blesses us is so we can be a blessing to others. He said he likes having a chance to bless us."

"Did he really say that?" Christy asked.

"Yeah, he did. Remember when Eli's dad said that when we were in Kenya?"

"I do. I thought then it was a good motto for how we

should live."

"If you're up to it, let's move in tomorrow."

They put the plan into motion and moved into Bob and Marti's the next day. She reluctantly let Todd do all the organizing, cleaning, packing, and moving in order to get them set up as guests in her aunt and uncle's home. He drove her over to the house in her pajamas and her Rancho Corona University sweatshirt that she wore with the hood up.

Christy lumbered into the family room and made up a bed on the sofa with a sheet over the nice upholstery and a cozy blanket and pillow. She flopped onto the couch as if she had just completed a hundred-mile journey to get there. Christy was grateful that Todd had made arrangements for Lindee to watch Daniel while he readied the house for Tracy and the twins as well as Tracy's parents.

At first it felt odd to Christy to be alone in Bob and Marti's cavernous home while relinquishing her much loved house. Especially at Christmas. But it was like her uncle said, the only reason God had blessed them was so they could be a blessing to others.

In some ways it felt as if they were living out the true focus of Christmas in that they were giving to their friends without expecting anything in return.

That night Todd arrived at Bob and Marti's with a bag of groceries and calling out, "Ho, ho, ho! Merry Christmas Eve!"

Christy got up from where she had stretched out in the family room watching Uncle Bob's ultra wide-screen TV. She had spent the day with a box of tissues, watching every heart-tugging Christmas movie she could find, one after the other.

Her favorite was one on the Hallmark Channel. She wanted to watch it again and again, even though she knew she would cry every time when it reached the heartwarming ending.

"How's this for creating a Christmas memory?" Todd

pulled a bunch of cans out of the grocery bag.

Christy was starving and had hoped he would have bought a pizza. Some pizza place somewhere had to be open on Christmas Eve.

"I'm going to make us some Christmas chili. I'm starting a new tradition."

Christy blew her nose and plugged in the electric teakettle to make another cup of herbal tea. She was wary of what Todd would create but didn't want to whine after all the poor guy had done already that day.

"So, Tracy's parents arrived okay?"

"Yep. I picked them up at the airport. They were super grateful that we turned our place over to them. I made sure our room looked like a hotel room, like you asked."

"Thanks, Todd."

"No problem. They brought some presents for Daniel, so he was having a great time when I left. Doug said that Tracy is doing well. The twins are doing well. It's all good." He pulled out a big frying pan and tossed in a block of frozen hamburger.

Christy usually defrosted all meat before cooking it. She sat back and watched Todd. This appeared to be something he was excited to do, and she didn't want to spoil the fun for him by directing his cooking.

He chopped up an onion and added it to the frying pan. The heat was too high so the meat on the outside of the frozen block was burning and bits of onion flew out of the pan. Undaunted, Todd used a knife to break up the hamburger. He drained the fat after the meat had cooked and dumped it into a big pot. He added two cans of black beans, two cans of kidney beans, and an entire jumbo-sized tub of salsa.

Christy coughed and covered her mouth as he added a guy-sized dash of spices from Bob's extensive spice rack and gave the concoction a good stir. So far, Christy deemed it would be edible. Unlike a few of Todd's other inventions in years past. At least he had gotten off his kick of buying frozen bean burritos and calling that dinner.

"We'll let it all simmer for a bit and have some hot apple cider while we wait. How does that sound?" He pulled a glass container of apple cider from the grocery bag and held up a tiny canister that held cinnamon sticks.

"You thought of everything." Christy loved watching Todd pour the cider into a pan and pop in a couple of cinnamon sticks.

"I have to say that having Doug around all these months has rubbed off on me. He's a pretty good cook."

"Tracy is an excellent cook," Christy added. "I've learned so much from her. Who would have thought this year would turn out the way it did and that you and I would spend Christmas Eve like this?"

"Do you have any regrets?" Todd asked.

"Regrets about coming down with the flu? Yes, plenty."

"No, I mean opening our home to Doug and Tracy."

Christy shook her head. "Do you?"

"No, not at all." He gave Christy a serious look. She realized this was the first time in months that the two of them could talk openly in the middle of a house without the possibility of anyone overhearing them. "You've been amazing through all of this, Christy. You're such a good wife."

Her heart felt all mushy, the way it had while she was watching the Christmas movies. "And you're such a great husband." She coughed again and felt her ribs ache as the rattling cough kept going, along with another round of throat tickling. In a raspy voice she said, "I'm sorry."

"No apology needed. Here, try some of the apple cider."

The first sip worked like a charm, soothing her throat and giving her rumbling stomach something to gnaw on. The cider was good, but the chili was great. Christy ate a large bowl and felt ready for bed.

She returned to her sofa bed so Todd could have the upstairs guest bed to himself, undisturbed by Christy's hacking cough.

She spent Christmas Day on the couch watching movies with Todd and sleeping off and on. She topped off the grand recovery day with a long bath in Marti's jetted whirlpool tub and went right back downstairs to sleep some more.

The day after Christmas Tracy was dismissed from the hospital, but the twins had to stay another day until they both passed all the necessary tests. Doug sent Christy lots of photos of the two little ones in their plastic incubator cocoons. They looked so small and pink. It felt strange to have been so connected during most of the pregnancy but to only be able to look at photos on her phone now that the twins had arrived.

In spite of their best efforts not to share the flu, Todd was hit with it two days after Christmas. He went down hard and fast. Now it was Christy's turn to carry the tray of orange juice and oatmeal to Todd.

She returned to work at the spa even though she still had a few coughing jags. She worked until noon on New Year's Eve and brought home a big pizza and a box of fruit juice Popsicles. When she arrived at Bob and Marti's, Todd was stretched out on the sofa in the family room watching some sort of 1950s army movie. A flurry of wadded-up tissues gathered at the base of the small wastebasket Christy had put beside the couch. A half-dozen emptied glasses decorated the coffee table. Todd's eyes were red, and he was grumpy.

"I feel for you," Christy said. "What can I bring you?"

"You can bring me a stick of dynamite I can put up my nose to clear my sinuses."

"Have you taken any medicine?"

"Yeah."

"What did you take?"

"I don't know. Whatever you left on the counter in the kitchen by the vitamins."

"Those are to be taken every four hours. When did you take the first one?"

"When you left this morning."

"So, what is it now? Almost one thirty? I'll go get you another one." Christy thought it was funny that Todd had been so organized and efficient in taking care of her when she was sick. Yet, now that it was his turn to do whatever needed to be done to get better, he seemed to have forgotten how to do that.

They watched another movie as they ate the pizza. Christy was tired of TV. She was tired of hearing Todd cough. She was tired of the two of them sleeping in separate beds.

Christy made sure he was comfortable on the downstairs sofa and had everything he needed. Blowing him a kiss from across the room, she headed upstairs to spend the night alone again.

The long days of isolation and illness ended on January 1. Todd had progressed to the feeling-fine-but-still-occasionally-coughing-like-a-chain-smoker stage. Christy was back to normal and felt more rested than she had for months. Doug and Tracy had brought the twins home, and the chilly, foggy weather of the last two weeks gave way to a bright, sunny, clear New Year's Day with temperatures in the midseventies.

The year ahead seemed to once more brim with possibilities. Christy felt as if she had every reason to make another wish.

twenty

$\mathcal{I}$t seemed only right to get out into the gloriously fresh New Year's Day and enjoy the sunshine. Todd and Christy pulled Bob's slightly rusted tandem bike out of the garage and pedaled over to their house.

Dozens of other Newport Beach residents and visitors had the same impulse to enjoy the beautiful day. The beach-front sidewalk was crowded with bikes, strollers, roller skaters, and leashed dogs of seemingly every breed. Everyone was in a friendly, cheery mood.

Christy couldn't help but think what a strange overlapping this was of the familiar past mixed with their haphazard present. She remembered the time she and Todd had biked to Balboa Island for Balboa Bars on this same bike almost twelve years ago. It was their first unofficial date and had been marked by her nervous adolescent awkwardness. Now, here they were, married and heading down a familiar cement walkway to their home, the same house Todd had grown up in. Even the way they pedaled together now was more in sync.

The years have taught us what the days and hours never could.

Christy wasn't sure where she had heard that saying before, but it fit their lives at the moment. She thought about how timid and worried she had been in her earlier years with Todd. If she could go back now and change anything in their relationship, it would be her anxious insecurities and her stretches of indecision.

Aunt Marti had remarked once that the only reason Christy had dated Doug in her late teens was because of her inability to make a decision. The words had stung at the time, and Christy inwardly disagreed with her aunt. Now she saw the truth in them. The casual, friendship-based dating she had with Doug included his insistence that they not kiss. Doug had saved his first kiss for the altar when he and Tracy married.

The choice seemed extreme to Christy and others during their teen years. Now she was grateful that she didn't carry any memories of what it was like to kiss Doug. He was her friend then; he was her friend now. The discipline at the beginning of that friendship was part of what had made it possible for the two couples to live in the same house all these months and maintain their closeness all these years.

Todd and Christy pulled the tandem bike around to the side of the house. Like most of the closely stacked beach houses in this part of the neighborhood, they didn't have a fence or even a yard. With so many people coming and going down their street to the beach, leaving anything valuable unlocked or out in the open was a risk.

Todd bent over to lock the bike to the thick pipe of the outdoor shower. When he stood up, he started to cough. The coughing spell lasted several seconds, and his face turned red.

"Are you okay?"

"I better keep my distance from everyone when I go in there."

"I don't think you're still contagious."

"Better to not take any chances. You know what? I'll hang out on the deck. You go on in."

Christy and Todd walked around to the other side of the house and took the side steps up to the deck. The sliding windows were closed. With the bright sunlight reflecting against the glass, Christy couldn't tell if anyone was in the living room.

"Do you think we should ring the doorbell?" Christy asked. "It's weird not knowing how to enter your own home."

The sliding door opened, and Doug came out with a finger to his lips. He looked exhausted. "Glad you came over. Both of them are sleeping right now. It's a minor miracle. Tracy's folks took Daniel with them to pick up some groceries, and Tracy just laid down for a nap. Come on in and meet the dynamic duo."

"Dynamic duo, huh?" Todd said in a whisper. "Do they have superpowers?"

"Yes. They have the amazing ability to wake up at the sound of a sneeze."

"That's another good reason for me to stay out here," Todd said. "I still have a cough."

Doug nodded his agreement with Todd's decision. "We've all stayed healthy around here, which is another minor miracle." He looked at Christy. "You good to come in?"

She nodded. "I'll wash my hands right away."

Doug stepped aside to let her pass. Christy took one step into the living room and paused for a moment. She hadn't prepared herself for what the house might look like with all the life going on under its roof. The furniture had been rearranged, two collapsible cribs were set up by the window, large boxes of diapers and toys were strewn across the floor, and unfolded laundry was mounded up on the love seat. The sofa had been turned into a bed, and the coffee table was cluttered with dishes, glasses, baby blankets, and more toddler toys.

The kitchen was in the same chaotic condition, if not worse. Christy tried to close her eyes to the mess. She turned on the water in the kitchen sink and pumped a tiny puddle of antibacterial soap into the palm of her hands. Running her hands under the warm water, she washed thoroughly and dried off with a paper towel.

Without any apologies for the disaster zone that Todd and Christy's home had become, Doug proudly motioned for Christy to come over to the cribs that were being warmed by the filtered sunlight coming through the closed window. She peered into the first crib. It was empty. Both babies were swaddled and lying beside each other in the second crib. Their tiny pink faces were all that was visible, and they were the sweetest, most delicate little faces Christy thought she had ever seen. They looked like two peas in their own pods.

The baby on the right was clearly Samuel. He was slightly longer and larger and had a broader nose and fuller lips. Annie resembled Tracy with her rosebud lips and narrow chin. Both of them looked like cherubs from an Italian Renaissance painting.

Christy gave Doug's arm a squeeze. "They're beautiful," she whispered.

He beamed with daddy pride. "Do you want to hold them?"

"Won't they wake up?"

He shook his head.

With slow motions, Christy gingerly reached into the crib and slid her hands under Annie's tiny frame. The baby barely stirred. Christy lifted her and tucked the precious treasure into her arms. For a few seconds it seemed as if she had picked up the whole universe and was balancing it precariously in her arms. Tiny breaths flowed in and out of Annie's slightly opened mouth. Her eyelids remained closed. She appeared to be dreaming sweet dreams.

Doug lifted Samuel and carefully placed him in her other arm. Christy balanced the two little cherubs and marveled at the wonder of new life. Doug motioned for Christy to sit in the glider rocking chair that he had pulled from their belongings that were stored in the garage. She lowered herself carefully, all the while memorizing the faces of the two tiny miracles that had no idea yet that she existed.

All her mothering instincts rose to the surface and, with the overwhelming emotions, came a swell of tears. She swallowed and tried to blink them away. The happy tears refused to obey and came tumbling down her face.

What she didn't try to halt were her bubbling-over thoughts and prayers. She silently thanked God for the gift of these two little lives. She asked His blessing on both of them, and she asked, humbly, if God would remember her and Todd and bless them with a baby, too.

The time Christy spent rocking Annie and Samuel and praying a blessing over them was not long as minutes were measured. But she felt as if she took an invisible journey forward in time, just as she had felt that the ride over here had been a strange trip into the past and present simultaneously. Christy felt, really felt, as if one day she would sit in a rocking chair like this one, and she would be holding another baby— her baby.

The clarity of the moment stirred her heart. She recalled the same sense of deep awe when, months earlier, the Holy Spirit had ruffled her spirit and had told her to trust God more than she trusted Todd. Again, the clear impression that rumbled inside was *Trust Me*.

Christy tried to explain those thoughts to Todd many days later when they were walking on the beach at sunset. It was the second Sunday in January, and Bob and Marti were due to return from Maui that week.

"This feeling that's growing in me is tenacious. That's the only way I can describe it," she said. "It's not going to go away."

"I feel the same longing. I'm sure what I feel is different from the way you feel it, but I'm hoping God will bless us with a baby soon." Todd buried his bare feet into the cold sand as if burrowing down deeper for warmth. "I checked on some health-fact stuff on the Internet."

"Oh, there's a source of reliable information," Christy said.

He ignored her teasing comment. "The sites all said the same thing. If you're being intentional for a year and don't get pregnant, you should see a doctor."

"We've definitely not hit a year yet. Although it feels a lot longer than what it's actually been."

Todd stopped walking and spread out the heavy blanket he had been carrying. "This a good place?"

"Sure." Christy sat beside Todd and cuddled up to him. She tucked her hair into the back of her sweatshirt and pulled the hood over her head. He strung his arm over her shoulder. Together they gazed at the layers of ivory clouds stacked on top of the pale-blue horizon of the ocean like cream cheese frosting on a fancy birthday cake.

"While you were looking up medical information, I've been reading about a woman in the Bible who deeply wanted a child."

"Which one?" Todd asked.

"Hannah."

"The mother of Samuel," Todd said.

"Yes." Christy knew she wouldn't be able to keep up with Todd when it came to particulars from the Bible. He had an exceptional ability to remember details and verses. Christy mostly remembered the stories.

"You probably already know the story. Hannah was so distraught about not having a baby that she couldn't eat. She cried out to God, and she begged Him for a child. Just one baby."

"And God gave her Samuel," Todd said.

"Yes, He did. But what I saw in her story is how difficult and painful she found it to wait for God to answer her prayers. Waiting on God to have a baby when you're sure you're ready is painful for women, no matter what generation they live in."

Todd wrapped both of his arms around her, and she

leaned into him, resting her head on his chest. They sat quietly watching the watercolor shades of pink that tinted the clouds on the far horizon.

"What else did you see in Hannah's story?" Todd asked.

"She promised God that if He gave her a son, she would give him back to God and that the boy would be raised in the temple so he could serve God all of his life. And that's what happened. She kept her promise."

"Even when it hurt," Todd added.

"I'm not like Hannah. I don't think I could make a promise like that. If God blessed us with a baby, I would want to be the one to raise him. She gave Samuel over as soon as he was weaned. How awful to give up your only son like that."

Todd added in a solemn voice, "Which is exactly what God did when He gave His only Son for us."

Christy felt a familiar feeling of respectful awe at the way Todd could see the bigger eternal picture of God's plan in almost any situation. She loved that about him.

But that quality also drove her crazy and always had. Her focus at the moment was on the present—right here, right now. Her immediate wish was for a baby. Not for deeper understanding of God's sacrificial love for her.

"Did you read the part in chapter 2 of 1 Samuel about how God was gracious to Hannah?" Todd asked.

"No. But I read the poem Hannah wrote in chapter 2. I wondered if when she wrote it, she ever guessed that the words of her poem would be in print for thousands of years and that millions of people would read them. That's pretty cool when you think about it."

Todd rested his chin on the top of her head. "I love the way you think."

Christy let his compliment sink in and held it fast. He was the one with the ability to hold the attention of everyone in the room when he taught. He was the one who remembered the references for verses and knew about the history and the culture at the time the different books of the Bible were written. She just thought about the people in the Bible. They were real people, and they had the same problems then that she struggled with now. She wanted to meet Hannah one day.

"So you didn't read all of chapter 2 of 1 Samuel, then."

"No, I don't think so."

Todd shifted so he could pull his phone out of the pouch of his hoodie. Christy sat up as he scrolled through his Bible app until he found what he was looking for.

"Here. Verse 21 of 1 Samuel 2. This is the best part of Hannah's story. You should read it." He enlarged the words on the screen and held it in front of Christy so she wouldn't have to take her cold hands out of her pouch pocket to hold the phone.

"'And the LORD was gracious to Hannah; she gave birth to three sons and two daughters. Meanwhile, the boy Samuel grew up in the presence of the LORD.'"

Todd put away his phone but was still grinning. "That's how gracious God is. Hannah only asked God for one baby. Just one."

"And God gave her six." Christy finished the thought and felt her heart melting. She knew God was extravagant like that. In her life she had seen Him give her so much more than she had ever asked.

"That's beautiful," Christy said. "So beautiful. God gave Hannah six babies, and she only asked Him for one. Although I don't know that I want six kids."

"I wouldn't mind."

Christy ignored his enthusiasm. "But I do believe that God can bless us like that, too."

"I believe He can, too. Let's ask Him to do that."

She reached both her hands for Todd's, and he grasped them with a firm grip. She could see the faint, white scars that remained from the car accident he had been in the year before they were married. God had protected and provided for them in so many ways. Her heart responded to every word Todd prayed as he humbly asked God for the privilege of being a father one day.

Christy prayed next. She thought of Hannah's prayer poem and started, as Hannah had, with words of praise to God, declaring how great and victorious He was in every situation. "You are the Lord of my life," she prayed. "I wait for You. My whole being waits. In Your Word I have placed all my hope. We ask You, together, Father, to please bless us with a baby."

Todd ended the prayer as he often did, with a portion of the Lord's Prayer. "'Your kingdom come, your will be done, on earth as it is in heaven.' Amen."

Todd kissed her, and she kissed him back. They rested their foreheads together with their eyes closed and drew in the scent of each other.

Christy smiled, knowing she would always remember this moment.

"We have a couple of things we need to talk about," Todd said.

"I know. Bob and Marti are coming home this week. We need to figure out what's happening with Tracy's parents and see when we can get back in our house."

As much as Christy had loved the peace and quiet and luxurious space she and Todd had enjoyed while they were at Bob and Marti's, she knew it could turn tense quickly if they stayed on as houseguests. She was eager to get back to their home and the beautiful chaos that awaited them there.

"Let's make the calls and see what will work out for everybody," Todd suggested. "I'll talk to Doug first and find out what's happening with Tracy's parents."

They lingered on the beach for another half an hour enjoying the unhurried sunset and the chilly ocean breeze.

"You know what I've like the most about the past few weeks?" Todd asked.

"No. What?"

"I've liked that we've been able to spend time together

like this."

Christy didn't remember many walks on the beach or leisurely conversations over the last few weeks. Her memories
were still tainted by the flu they'd shared and the many movies
they'd watched together. She didn't recollect a lot of heart to
heart talks or focused prayer times like they'd just had.

"Do you think you feel that way because we've had more
privacy at Bob and Marti's than we had at our own home ever
since Doug and Tracy moved in last fall?"

Todd rose to his feet and offered Christy a hand as she got
up. "Yeah. I guess that's it. It's been good to be just us again."

They started heading back to Bob and Marti's house with
Todd carrying the blanket. Christy slid her arm through
Todd's free arm and held tight with both her arms.

"I love what you said about how it's good to be just us
again. I feel that way, too."

Todd stopped walking and leaned in to give her a deep
kiss. When he pulled away slowly he said, "No matter how
old we get and no matter how many children we have, let's
never stop making time to be just us."

"Agreed." Christy contentedly leaned her head on his
shoulder.

They picked up their walking pace in tandem and hurried
to brush the sand off their feet before entering Bob and Marti's home. Christy had a pretty good idea that Todd had started thinking what she was thinking after his voracious kiss.

She was right.

twenty-one

*I*t took until the last week of January before Christy felt
as if her life returned to something that felt slightly normal.
She and Todd bunked at Bob and Marti's until Tracy's parents returned to Oregon on January 23. The month that Tracy's parents had spent helping out with the twins and Daniel
seemed to be the best thing that could have happened to their
splintered relationship with Tracy and Doug. Christy hadn't
been there to see how the healing and changes were enacted,
but she could see how differently Doug felt about his in-laws.
Tracy said her mom treated her differently and that the two
of them had figured out how to move on into the next season
of their relationship.

Fortunately Marti was more gracious and hospitable
during this stay than she had been when Christy and Todd
had come to them out of near desperation three years ago
when they were both without jobs.

Christy and Katie had set up a time to talk on the last
Friday in January as soon as Christy finished work at the spa.
Eva didn't mind that Christy hid away in one of the unused

massage rooms to make the private call. Christy couldn't wait to talk to Katie. She missed her so much.

Katie started the call by putting her bright-green eye up to the camera on her phone and saying to Christy, "Preggers?"

"No. You?"

"No."

"Sorry."

"Me, too. Okay. Well, we got that out of the way." Katie settled back in the chair at her kitchen table. "So, tell me, vagabond girl, where are you living this week?"

"We're home, in our own bed. It feels so good to be back."

"Does that mean Doug and Tracy found a place?"

"No. They're still here but only for a few more weeks."

Katie gave Christy a skeptical look. "Did they find a place?"

Christy drew in a deep breath. What she was about to tell Katie was so new she hadn't quite processed it herself. "Doug found a new job."

"Where?"

"In Oregon."

"Seriously?"

Christy nodded. "It still hasn't hit me. They just told Todd and me late last night. They're moving up there to be near Tracy's parents and her aunt and uncle."

"They couldn't find a place to live in all of Orange County?"

"That wasn't the issue. Tracy is overwhelmed. She really is. The twins need constant attention, as I know very well." Christy felt her expression soften. "They are so cute, Katie. I'll have to send you some more pictures. Annie is the most demure little baby. When she cries she sounds like a kitten. Samuel weighs seven pounds already. He's going to be all boy, just like Daniel. They really are sweet."

"I wouldn't expect Tracy's kids to be anything but sweet."

"She's just not the most organized, firm sort of mother. And having the twins has really taken a toll on her body. The reality is that she needs a lot of help. A lot more than I can give her as a friend who is working all the time. A lot more than Doug can give. He's exhausted, too. It's been really hard. I don't know how any of us would have done it if her parents hadn't both come down and spent that first month with them."

"Nice the way it turned out for you and Todd to sneak away to Marti's beach villa during the first month that the twins were home." Katie was eating breakfast while she was talking to Christy. It appeared that she had taken a spoonful of ugali, a local staple that Christy had tried when they were in Kenya. She thought it looked like Cream of Wheat that her mom used to make for breakfast when Christy was growing up on the farm in Wisconsin. Ugali didn't taste much like Cream of Wheat. Katie had come up with her own version with cinnamon, honey, nuts, raisins, and even a few drops of vanilla extract if she had it.

"You're right. It was a lifesaver staying at Bob and Marti's, especially while they were on Maui, and we had the place to ourselves. After I got over my cold, though, I spent every spare minute at our house holding the twins, changing a thousand diapers, and to be honest, cleaning."

"You said before that the house was trashed."

"All for good reason. Tracy had no energy. Especially not to clean the house. Her mom was on twin duty all day and many times at night. Doug had some time off work, but he's not a mop-the-floor kind of guy. Neither is Todd."

"Eli is. I scored in the husband department, just in case you didn't know that already. He is way more organized than I am. He's the one who does most of the house stuff like that around here. It's a good thing, or maybe I should say it's a God-thing, because you know what a slob I can be."

Christy had a flashback to their college-roommate days and teasingly nodded vigorously.

Katie laughed and a tiny fleck of ugali flew onto her phone. She wiped off the camera lens with her thumb, and for a moment all Christy saw was a rosy screen turning to black. She thought of how God definitely knew that Katie needed to marry someone who was on the tidy side because, as Katie herself had said many times, that gene was missing in her chromosomal makeup.

Once Katie managed to clean the lens by going a second round and using her shirt's hem, Christy returned to the topic. "I never thought I was a picky person or OCD about being clean, but maybe I am. I like things to be put away and not strewn all over the place. I like it when the counter in the kitchen is cleared and the beds are made. Is that not normal?"

"Yes!" Came a shout from the other room. Christy recognized Eli's voice.

"Hey," Katie called over her shoulder. "Private conversation going on here, Lorenzo. If you don't mind."

Christy laughed.

Katie returned her attention to Christy. "As I was about to say, for you, it's totally normal. You're orderly and tidy. And you have good hygiene, too."

"Good hygiene, huh?"

"I've always appreciated that about you." Katie said it in a funny voice, and Christy laughed again.

"So, I take it that it's been hard on you to see your home looking like a pigsty every time you went over there."

"It was never a pigsty." Christy quickly defended Tracy and Doug. "None of the many people who were living there were able to keep things the way I prefer to keep them."

"That's gracious of you to put it that way."

"You would have to have been there to see why I really couldn't get mad at anybody. The twins consumed everyone's full attention day and night. And Tracy's dad isn't in good health. I found out that's why he took early retirement and they pursued their long-delayed dream of living where it was green all year round in the Northwest."

"And now Doug and Tracy are going to trade in the beach for the evergreens," Katie said. "How do you think they'll like it?"

Christy shrugged. "It's taken them a long time to make the decision. Todd said they were seriously thinking about it when they went to see her parents on vacation last fall, but they couldn't come to a conclusion then. The reality is they need help with their little family, and what they need, they can find in Glenbrooke."

"Is that where they're going to be living? In Glenbrooke?"

"Yes. Tracy said it's a small town not far from the Oregon coast. Have you heard of it?"

"I don't know. It sounds familiar, but I don't know why."

"I thought the same thing. I think Tracy mentioned it last summer before her parents made the big move."

"When are Doug and Tracy moving?"

"They're saying they want to drive up on February 8."

"That's soon. Won't that be hard since the twins are so tiny?"

"That's what I thought. Tracy doesn't want to fly, or maybe she said the babies can't fly yet. I don't remember. Driving seemed the only way to go. They'll rent a moving truck and tow their car behind."

"Can Tracy and the kids all fit in the cab of the moving truck? No offense, but this isn't sounding like a very good plan. I mean, we see crazy amounts of people packed into cars and trucks here, but I can't picture this being a possibility on a thousand-mile trek up the California coast."

"This is where the plans get kind of squiggly."

"Squiggly?"

Christy gave Katie a flustered grin. "I don't know the word that fits the situation. Todd volunteered to help them make the move. He wants to drive Gussie or maybe have Doug drive Gussie with Tracy and the kids, and he'll drive the moving truck."

"How is that squiggly?"

"The squiggly part is that they're all talking as if I'm part of the big caravan, but I'm not sure I can go."

"Seems like that would be a significant fact to mention, Christy."

"I know. The problem is that I was so sick at Christmas that I used all my sick time, and I don't want to jeopardize my job at the spa. It's a great job."

Katie squinted as if she was trying to scrutinize Christy's expression. "You don't want to go, do you?"

Christy bit her lower lip and shook her head like a child who was afraid she might be in trouble.

"Christy, you don't have to go with the traveling circus. You've given to them over and above for months. If they have enough help with just Todd, let him go. He would love the road trip. You know he would."

"I know. Things have been going great for him at Zane's. He's worked so many extra hours over the past few months, he can take the time off. He's really excited about it, and that's another reason I guess I'm feeling guilty about not jumping in and making the sacrifices I'd need to make to go."

"You don't have to go." Katie said it a second time, firmly, as if she had the authority to absolve Christy of all guilt over this conundrum. "You don't have to go."

Christy let out a long breath and let Katie's words sink in.

Katie took one last spoonful of ugali. She stood and carried the phone over to their small sofa. Christy's view was a jiggled collage of color. When Katie stopped, Christy could see Eli in the background. He was sitting at the small desk with a laptop.

"*Jambo*, Eli." she called out.

"*Jambo*, Christy." He came over and put his head next to Katie's. "For what it's worth, I agree with Katie."

Katie made an exaggerated happy face. "You heard it heard first, folks. My husband agrees with me! He interrupts my private conversations, but at least when he does, he affirms my wise counsel."

Eli appeared unflapped by his wife's humor. Christy noticed that he'd grown his goatee again and his wavy brown hair was longer than he usually wore it. He kissed Katie on the top of the head, and as he walked away, Eli lifted his arm in the air with his finger pointed as if he were making a sermon point like an old-time preacher. "'They also serve who only stand and wait.'"

"What did he say?" Christy asked.

"It's one of his favorite quotes from a guy who lived a couple of hundred years ago."

"John Milton," Eli called from the desk. "It's from his poem, 'On His Blindness.'"

"Did you hear that?" Katie asked.

Christy nodded. She wasn't familiar with John Milton, nor did she know the poem. But she knew that Eli loved classic British literature and had an impressive collection of old books.

"Here's the thing." Katie gave Christy a firm, sisterly look. "When your gifting is the kind that means you enjoy making sure everyone else has what they need, you have to also make sure you have what you need."

Eli had left the view of the phone camera, but he popped his head back in. "I agree with my wife."

Katie made another cute, comical face. "Did you hear that? Twice in one day! It's a new world's record."

Their call ended with lots of smiles and wishes that they could be together on the same side of the planet one of these days. Christy went home fortified with exactly what she needed to tell Todd as well as Doug and Tracy.

To her surprise, they all understood and agreed that she was making the right choice. The relief Christy felt gave her the energy to jump in and go over and above in helping with all the work to pack them up and get them on the road.

The great race to hit the trail to Oregon began on Wednesday night when the guys loaded the moving van. Fortunately they started early because, even though Doug and Tracy didn't have a lot of furniture, they had accumulated a lot of stuff that was scattered throughout the house. The packing boxes kept increasing. Christy picked up and packed toys on Thursday night as soon as Daniel had gone to bed. He had wailed uncontrollably when Tracy tried to pack them earlier that day.

Everything that the twins and Daniel needed for the two-day trek had been packed into Gussie along with the car seats. Christy was surprised that Tracy didn't try to convince her to change her mind. At first she had a twang of hurt, thinking that Doug and Tracy should have been more insistent about her going.

But then she realized this wasn't a vacation. This was a long-term displaced family on a mission to reach their new abode as quickly as they could, and all their thoughts were on the logistics, not on the travel companions. Christy was relieved to stay home, and she was glad that Katie, along with Eli and his Medieval-sounding quote, had helped her to make the decision that was best for her.

On Friday night the Gathering met at their new location in the empty garage of Trevor's home. His parents had become supporters of Todd and appreciated how much time he had spent with their son by taking him surfing. They had a large beach house and a big garage. The teens brought low beach chairs and filled the garage to overflowing. Christy pulled together a farewell party for Doug and Tracy and went directly to the garage after work.

Lindee was there early to help Christy set up the folding tables, open the bags of chips, and put out the platter of warmed taquitos. Christy carried in the large sheet cake from the grocery store bakery and showed Lindee how to line up the napkins in a festive way. Tracy came with the twins for the first half hour and was rightfully protective of them. She held Samuel and let Christy hold Annie and show her little face to the teens who were interested enough to gather around. Lindee kept Daniel under control, as she had come to do so well.

For one last time, Doug and Todd played their best worship songs while the teens sang along. Christy and Tracy stood close in the back of the garage, each cradling an infant, both casting glances at each other with teary eyes.

"It's the end of an era," Tracy said.

Christy wanted to cry or say something meaningful or at least mark this moment with more than a sheet cake in a garage. But it was what it was, and everything was moving at such a fast pace she found it difficult for her sentimental thoughts to catch up.

The moment Christy had hoped for came late that night, after everyone else had gone to sleep. She crept downstairs and found Tracy on the sofa, holding one of the babies. Sitting next to her, Christy whispered, "I'm going to miss you more than I can even put into words."

"I know." Tracy was crying. "I'm going to miss you, Christy. I'm going to miss you so much. You have been the sweetest, kindest, most supportive friend I've ever had."

Christy reached over and stroked the forehead of the infant in Tracy's arms. She knew it was Annie. Christy had spent hours holding both the twins over the past six weeks. She had changed them, burped them, and fed them countless bottles. Even though she knew she would never say it aloud, Annie was her favorite. She was a miniature Tracy and would be forever endeared to Christy's heart.

"I'm going to miss these little ones and Daniel something awful. I know Todd will slip into sadness the next time he sits down to play guitar on Friday night and Doug isn't there with him. It's going to be brutal."

"I know," Tracy said. "We had it pretty good, didn't we?"

"Yes, we did." Christy took sleeping Annie from Tracy one more time and held her close enough to feel her tiny breath against her neck. She closed her eyes and memorized the feeling, the scent, the softness of Annie's skin and her feathery down hair against Christy's lips.

Tracy wiped the silent tears that wouldn't stop racing down her cheeks. "I wish we didn't have to leave."

"It's like you guys said when you told us you finally had made the decision to move to Oregon. This is the next season for you as a family. There are five of you to think of now. You are making this move for all the right reasons."

"I know." Tracy's voice was faint, and her words were tender. "Thank you again, Christy, for letting us stay here. A thousand thank-yous."

"A thousand you're-welcomes." Christy grinned. "You would have done the same for Todd and me if we had been in the place you guys were."

"We may have opened our home to you, but I don't think we would have done it with as much grace as you guys showed us. We completely took over your home, your life, and every waking hour that you weren't at work. Thank you for loving us so well."

Christy felt twinges of regret over the many times she was angry with Doug or Tracy, and the times she had grumbled under her breath or wanted to donate Daniel to a traveling circus and label him the world's smallest human-destructo unit.

In the very beginning Todd had emphasized that they were doing this for a season. And it had been a season. Just a rather long season. Christy was grateful for the time, though, and grateful that things were ending well between all of them. Having this final midnight time with Tracy and Annie was God's gift.

Christy felt compelled to do something that Todd had done many times for her and for others. He probably would have done it for Tracy at some point, but now Christy's turn to duplicate the gift had come. She held little Annie close and placed her free hand on Tracy's face, cupping Tracy's heart-shaped jawline in her palm.

"Tracy, may the Lord bless you and keep you. The Lord make his face to shine upon you and give you His peace. And may you and your husband and your children always love Jesus more than anything else. Amen."

"Amen," Tracy repeated solemnly. She drew in a staccato breath. "I know it's not good-bye forever. It just feels like it."

Christy placed Annie back in Tracy's arms and gave Tracy a hug and a kiss on the cheek. She stood before her emotions got the best of her. With a crack in her voice she said, "You and your little family are welcome in our home any time. And I know you know this, but I hold you in my heart, Trace. I always have, and I always will."

Tracy couldn't reply. She didn't need to. The two friends had said all that needed to be said. All the tense moments that had unfolded in the house over the past six months blew away like ashes rising into the night sky from a warm beach campfire.

One More Wish

twenty-two

*C*hristy awoke on the morning of February 9 to a strange sensation.

She was alone.

No babies were crying, no toddler was jumping on the end of her bed saying, "Come play cars with me." No one was in the kitchen rattling frying pans or making coffee. The TV in the living room wasn't turned to the morning surf report. She had the entire house to herself, and it was Sunday—a day of rest.

Christy rolled over in bed and stared out the window, remembering all the intense moments of the past few weeks. The reruns in her thoughts ended the way an old-time movie reel ended—the light flickered, and the tail of the reel made a flapping sound as it stopped spinning. Christy felt as if the weeks and months of spinning all around her had stopped as well. She breathed in and out in time to the sound of the ocean outside her open window.

Since it was too late for her to go to church, Christy decided to take a bath. A long bath. She lingered in the warm water and lavender-scented bubbles for a long time. Part of her wanted to make some tea and toast and curl up on the couch to watch all the Jane Austen movies she had been wanting to marathon-watch for ages. Another part of her knew she wouldn't relax completely until her home was clean again. Scrubbing up her nest would take at least three hours. It might be empty now, but it was marked by dirty floors, dusty blinds, messy bathrooms, and lots of hidden clusters of nasty dust bunnies that would plan an attack if she didn't rout them.

Letting her favorite Jane Austen characters wait, Christy put on a pair of shorts, an oversized T-shirt, and wound her hair up into a bun on top of her head. After a swig of orange juice from a fresh bottle in the nearly empty fridge, she went to work. It wasn't the first time she had done a deep cleaning of her home, but it was the first time she had been so excited about doing it. She knew how she would feel once everything was shipshape.

With the music turned up, Christy hummed along as she went room to room. It felt as if she were performing a cleansing ceremony the way she and Todd had when he renovated the house after a stretch of horrible renters. She prayed in each room, thanking God for the time they had had with Doug and Tracy and praying for their new beginnings.

Christy found three toy trucks, one of Doug's nice shoes, two of Tracy's earrings, and a half-eaten granola bar that thankfully hadn't been discovered by ants yet. Tracy's mom had helped a lot while she was here to keep things tidy upstairs so the master bedroom and bath required the least amount of cleaning.

When Christy opened the door to the small upstairs room that had been Daniel's bedroom, she noticed a teddy bear in the center of the room with a white envelope balanced between his outstretched paws. Christy's name was written on the outside. She recognized the handwriting as Tracy's. Inside was a short note and a check for almost a month of what

Christy made at her job.

Christy,

I knew that if we handed this to you or Todd, you would have tried to give it back. It's our gift to you, and since it's bad manners to return a gift, I'm confident you'll keep it. Doug says to consider it our last month's rent check that should be kept to cover damages and incidentals. However you want to look at it, this is a gift from us.

The teddy bear is for you, too. He comes with a small wish from my heart to yours that the next time I see you, you'll have your own little one in your arms. I hope he or she will adore this teddy and know that it is from Auntie Tracy and Uncle Doug with much, much love.

Your Forever Friend, Tracy

P.S. May your heart be made even more lovely and tender as you wait on the Lord in this next season of life. "Those who wait for Me shall not be put to shame." Isaiah 49:23b

Christy stood for a long moment, holding the letter in one hand and the teddy bear in the other. She probably would have teared up or gone into a deep place of contemplation if it hadn't been for the sounding of the doorbell. She clamored down the stairs, turned down the music, and found Aunt Marti on her doorstep holding a large take-out tray covered in foil.

"Are they gone?" Marti peered past Christy into the living room.

"Yes. The caravan headed out yesterday."

"Are you sick?"

"No. I miss them, but I'm not sick about them leaving."

Marti bustled past Christy and headed for the kitchen. "I meant are you fighting a cold or some other illness. I called you twice and sent at least four text messages. When you didn't pick up, I thought you must be ill. I brought some comfort food. Chicken, mashed potatoes, green beans. I know you like the less complex and more rustic foods."

"Thanks, Aunt Marti. That was really nice of you." Christy followed Marti into the kitchen and watched her aunt scrutinize the remaining contents in her refrigerator as she slid the take-out food inside.

After turning to take in the condition of the rest of the kitchen, Marti gave Christy a look of surprise. "Have you been cleaning?"

"Yes. I'm almost done. One more room to go upstairs."

"You certainly are a whirling dervish when it comes to tidying up the place."

"What is a whirling dervish?"

Marti looked taken aback by Christy's question. "Something fast. I don't know. Ask your uncle." Christy guessed that the agitation in Marti's voice and the birdlike movements of her head as she looked right and left and up and down must be because she had come by to assess whether there had been any permanent damages done to "her" house over the past six months.

Christy cut to the chase. "Would you like to look around?"

"Look around at what?"

"I thought you might have come by to check on the house."

"I came to check on you. I realize you've been cleaning, but it wouldn't hurt to keep your phone nearby."

"You're right. I should have had it with me. It's upstairs. I'll get it now." Christy felt like stomping her feet up the first few stairs to show her aunt a little passive-aggressive behavior to match Aunt Marti's. Instead she quietly retrieved her phone from where she had left it plugged in beside her bed and saw that she had two text messages from her aunt, not four. Marti had called once, not twice.

She wondered if her aunt realized that you couldn't make up the number of times you called or texted someone because her phone would reveal the truth.

Christy also noticed that she had one text from Todd. He said that everything was rolling along smoothly so far, but traveling with so many young ones was a lot slower going than he had thought it would be.

Christy texted him back and added I MISS YOU in all caps.

Christy returned to the kitchen and placed her phone on the clean kitchen counter, making sure the ringer was turned up all the way so she would hear Todd's text if he replied right away. She noticed that Marti had pulled out a tray and placed Christy's china teapot and teacups on it.

"Are we having a tea party?" Christy asked.

"I thought we could finish the one we started quite some time ago. Would you mind making some tea for us?"

"Do you remember that tea party I brought to you last fall?"

"Last fall? No. I was referring to the one you and I went to at the hotel in Laguna, and they said they lost my reservation."

Christy remembered the awkward event. It had been more than two years since that embarrassing incident. Until this moment, Christy had forgotten about it. Oddly, her aunt had not.

"I'm afraid I don't have any fancy macaroons." Christy started the kettle. "And I'm not exactly dressed for an occasion."

"We don't need anything with sugar in it. Just tea will be fine. You can change, if you like, while the water boils." Marti had a look of determination, but around the corner of her eyes Christy noticed a vulnerable sadness she had rarely seen. All of this made Christy even more curious as to what was going on.

She hurried upstairs and slipped into a loose-fitting summery dress with a warm, flowing sweater on top. She let her hair down with a shake and gave it a quick brushing. Returning to the kitchen, she found Marti waiting patiently right where Christy had left her.

"Would you like to have a seat in the living room?" Christy went along with the moment and felt gratified that she had cleaned the living room. She already had lit a coconut-mango-scented candle in a big jar, which was sitting on the clean coffee table. The candle had been a gift for Christy that Marti had brought back from Maui, and it filled the whole downstairs with a tropical fragrance that made Christy happy.

What didn't make Christy happy was the way her aunt sat rigidly on the love seat facing Christy at an angle and looking as if her thoughts were far away. Marti finished her cup of tea before their sparse chitchat ended, and she finally revealed her intentions.

"I've been wanting to discuss something with you for some time, but I wasn't sure how to approach the topic."

"Okay." Christy had a feeling her aunt was going to announce that she was raising the rent to something way beyond what Christy and Todd could pay. Her heart pounded.

I don't want to move. Please don't tell me that we have to leave this house.

"I know this is a delicate subject, but I'm concerned and felt the only way to clear the air was to speak with you about this openly."

"Okay." Christy waited.

"Would you be comfortable sharing with me what your thoughts are on having a baby?"

Christy blinked. It wasn't an announcement about higher rent. It was Marti's attempt at a personal, woman-to-woman conversation. Clearly, this kind of heart-to-heart was difficult for her to initiate.

"Todd and I have talked about it a lot."

"And what have you decided?"

"We've decided that we're ready, and we've been praying

about it."

Marti didn't seem to think that was a satisfactory or medically sound answer.

"I know of a specialist." Marti reached into her purse and pulled out a business card. "He doesn't usually take new patients right away, but in your case, if you chose to go to him, he would agree to see you within two months of when you call for an appointment."

Christy looked at the card. Marti's specialist was a fertility doctor.

"I don't think we're at the point yet where I need to see him." She handed the card back. "But thank you for being concerned."

"I am concerned." Marti held the card out again. "At least keep his contact information."

"Okay. Thank you."

Marti cleared her throat and put her cup and saucer on the coffee table. "As you know, Christina, not every woman can conceive simply because she decides she's ready and has prayed about it."

"Yes, I understand." Christy wished she had opted for the Jane Austen marathon after all. She wished she hadn't opened the door to her aunt and instead was watching *Pride & Prejudice* right now instead of being grilled by the personification of that movie's title who was sitting across from her. If Christy narrowed her eyes and looked at Aunt Marti through the steam rising from her freshly poured second cup of tea, she could almost see Marti with one of those nineteenth-century funny little bonnets on her head and the lace ruffles framing her face. She was the well-meaning neighbor who had come to express her disapproval in the most amiable sort of way, over a cup of tea.

"I know it's not for me to interfere," Marti said. "And believe me, I'm not trying to. But if it were up to me, I see no reason you shouldn't make an appointment with the specialist and at least begin the testing process to make sure there are no hindrances. It could be there's a problem with Todd."

Christy definitely didn't want to continue this discussion if they were going to talk about her husband. Marti was approaching this as if they were closest friends and yet for Christy, there would always be a boundary that kept Marti in the "aunt" category and Christy in the "niece" category. What she talked about with Marti would never be the same as what she talked about with Katie.

"I think Todd and I would like to let everything settle for us around here over the next few weeks and then see how we feel about setting up an appointment with the doctor."

"That's reasonable."

"I appreciate your concern, Aunt Marti. I really do."

"And I appreciate that you're willing to listen." Marti finished out their tea party with some small talk about her book club and a new Cuban cuisine restaurant she and Bob were going to try for lunch that week. She gave Christy advice on how to trim the wicks on the coconut-mango candle and reminded her about the home-style meal waiting for her in the refrigerator.

With all her bases covered, Marti rose and made a straight path to the front door. "I'm pleased to see the house looking in as good of shape as it is." She looked around. "Whenever I come inside I think of the night we all came over and wrote verses on the floor before the carpet was installed."

"The house blessing has endured." Christy remembered how Marti had written the verse with the three simple words "God is love" in the center of the floor.

Christy initiated the brief cheekbone-to-cheekbone hug and air kiss with Marti at the front door. "Once Todd returns, we would like to have you guys over for dinner."

"That would be lovely. We'll look forward to it." Marti didn't have shoes that she needed to slip back on at the doorstep the way most of Christy's guests did. That was because Marti refused to take off her shoes when she entered the house. Usually because they were an integral part of her outfit.

Christy put the music back up to a house-cleaning level of cheerfulness and washed the china cups and teapot. She warmed her chicken lunch and ate out on the deck, soaking up her vitamin D through the pale but welcome sunshine. It seemed the best way she could use the rest of the day was by doing two things that made her happy. First, she made a small pan of apple crisp with the six Granny Smith apples that were tumbling around in the crisper bin in the refrigerator. As it baked, filling the house with the comforting fragrance of cinnamon and brown sugar, Christy settled on the sofa and at long last started her Jane Austen marathon. She couldn't stop looking around at her clean home and noticing how quiet it was.

The next time Christy was on the sofa, alone, contemplating the quietness was on Thursday afternoon. She was eating the last of the apple crisp and thinking that she didn't want to taste another green apple for a long time. She and Todd had been texting all day, and they had set up a time to finally talk. He called right on time, and Christy answered immediately.

"I miss you, miss you, miss you," she said. "When are you coming home?"

"Hey, I miss you, too. I'm heading out early in the morning. I would have left today like I planned, but time got away from me while I was helping Doug set up stuff here in their new place."

"Is it cute? The pictures Tracy sent made it seem like their place is old and charming."

"It is. Especially the old part. Their landlord recently had the house rewired and updated some of the kitchen appliances so it's pretty nice. It's big. Four bedrooms."

"I know. That's what Tracy said. I'm sure they're loving that the rent is even less than what they paid here for their itty-bitty bungalow."

"Yeah, they're pretty stoked. It's the right place for them for now. Hey, I almost forgot. You will never guess who I saw at the grocery store here."

"You're right. I will never guess. Who did you see at the Glenbrooke grocery store?"

"Alissa."

Christy sat up on the couch. "You're kidding! You're talking about Alissa Benson, right?"

"Yeah. Only she's married now. I don't remember her last name. I met her husband, too. Brad. He's legit. They have two girls. Anyway, they wanted me to go over to their place tonight, so I'm heading over there now."

"I can't believe it. I have wondered about her so often. She's married. That makes me so happy. And did you say they have two daughters?"

"Yeah. They adopted them from Romania. Or maybe it was Bulgaria. One of those places. I'll find out when I'm over there."

"Todd, that is incredible. Tell her hi, and I'd love to catch up with her sometime, too. I always felt bad that we lost track of each other."

"She was saying the same thing."

"I wish I was there with you."

"I wish you were here, too. You would like it here, Christy. Glenbrooke is sort of a storybook town. It's small, and everybody knows each other. Doug took me to breakfast this morning at a café that Tracy's parents like a lot, the Wildflowers Café. They had a lot of different kinds of tea on the menu, and I thought about you. You would have liked it."

"Maybe we can go up there and visit this summer. It would be fun to plan to go for my birthday." Christy tried to calculate how old the twins would be by then.

"It's a long drive," Todd said.

"Maybe we could fly."

"Or take our time going up the coast and stop and camp along the way."

"Sure." Christy was open to anything at the moment. She liked the idea of having a vacation plan to look forward to.

"We could stay at Refugio State Beach again. That was a fun weekend."

"I wish you were here now and doing the drive home with me tomorrow," Todd said.

"I wish I was there, too," Christy said. "Believe it or not, I'm all caught up here. The house is clean. We have groceries. I had the day off today, and I set up the sewing machine and finished a couple of covers for some throw pillows. I wanted to send something to Doug and Tracy as a housewarming gift."

"They'll like that. Has Lindee been coming over?" Todd asked.

"No. Not since you guys left. I'll probably see her Friday night, though. Why do you ask?"

"Doug and Tracy called her yesterday and asked if she wanted to come to Glenbrooke to spend the summer with them."

"You're kidding."

"No, they miss her. She was becoming a significant part of their family. Daniel keeps asking for her. I thought maybe she would come by to tell you."

"No, she hasn't come by. It's interesting though, isn't it? Lindee wanted to live with us, but instead Doug and Tracy moved in. Then Lindee came over to help with Daniel, and now Lindee has the second family she was looking for."

"God's way of doing things is always good. The household of believers, man. It's a crazy bunch, connected in crazy ways. I still can't believe I saw Alissa this afternoon. Katie would have called it a God-thing."

"Did Alissa recognize you, or did you recognize her? It's been a long time since you guys have seen each other."

"She looks different, but the same, I guess. I don't know. Her husband said her name when they were in front of me in the checkout line. When I heard her voice, I knew it was her. I said something, and she turned around and recognized me. We kind of made a scene. I don't think her husband knew what was going on."

"What did you say to her?"

"I don't know. Something like, 'Have you ever been to Newport Beach?'"

Christy could see her husband trying to be cool, and beautiful, blonde Alissa being effusive like Christy had seen her at parties when they were teenagers. But once they made the connection, Christy was sure there were a lot of hugs and probably some tears.

"I hope you can ask her tonight about what happened with Shawna. I'm dying to know if they ended up staying in contact."

"I was thinking the same thing. I want to be sensitive to her husband and daughters because I don't know how much any of them know," Todd said. "I better get going. I'll call you tomorrow after you get off work."

"Okay. I love you. Be safe on the road tomorrow. Come home to me soon."

"I'll be there by Friday night, Lord willing. I love you, Kilikina."

Christy sat for a long while after hanging up the phone. She was thinking about the conversation she and Todd had on the way home from their camping trip. They had talked about being open to adopting a child the way that Alissa's daughter, Shawna, had been adopted by an eager, loving family.

She also thought about her conversation with Marti and her recommendation that Christy consider going to the specialist.

Then a new thought flitted past her like a butterfly. What if it wasn't either conceive on their own or adopt a child? What if it was both? What if they had enough love and enough home and enough affirmation from God to adopt and have a child naturally?

Christy looked around her clean, quiet, unruffled house. It reminded her of how she had felt sitting in Marti's pristine, barely breathing living room at Christmas. This home was meant to be filled with life. She didn't know yet how God would do that, but these walls needed to reverberate with the echo of infant cries and toddler squeals. These floors needed to wear jewelry made from Cheerios and toy trucks.

As much as she had enjoyed her brief respite in her own private, tidy nunnery, Christy knew that when Todd had renovated this house three years ago, it was to fill it with life.

What life do You want to bring to this home, Lord? You are the Giver of all good gifts. What do You want to give us?

Once again, the only heartstring that played in response to Christy's prayer was simply the word, *Wait.*

This time, however, another clear, piercing thought came to her. *What if all this time the issue hasn't been about me waiting for God? What if God has been waiting for me?*

The thought humbled her. God hadn't changed. He never changes.

But she had changed.

That was the final question on the test. She had known the answer all along.

Wait. Trust God. Let Him do His transforming work in His way and in His time.

And be thankful no matter what.

twenty-three

*O*n Friday Christy hurried home from work. She had an hour and a half before she had to take snacks to the Friday Night Gathering. For Valentine's Day, she had made heart-shaped sugar cookies for the group.

Todd wasn't back from Oregon yet, so two of the guys in the group led worship. They were the two who had always hung out with Todd and Doug and played guitars on the deck after the Friday Night Gatherings.

An older guy who surfed with Todd gave a short talk. He seemed nervous, but the group responded well to him, and they loved the sugar cookies.

Christy was one of the first to leave. She missed having the group at their house on Fridays, but the garage setup was better all the way around. They could fit more students in, and the parking was much better than at Todd and Christy's. Tonight she realized another advantage was that she didn't have to stick around and clean up. She could slip out to go home.

When she pulled into their driveway, she pressed the button to open the automatic garage door so she could pull inside. Not having to park blocks away was something she was beginning to enjoy again.

However, when the garage door went up, Christy let out a squeal. Gussie was parked in the garage. Todd was home!

She dashed inside and saw the kitchen counter was covered with his stuff. She had never seen a more beautiful sight.

"Todd, where are you?"

Christy could hear the water running upstairs. She rushed up to their bedroom and found Todd in the shower, singing one of the songs he and Doug had written years ago.

"You're home!" Christy was so thrilled to see him that she opened the shower door and stepped inside to kiss him good. Her hair and her clothes were soon soaked, but she didn't care.

Todd laughed. "Did you miss me or something?"

"You have no idea! Stop talking and kiss me. It's Valentine's Day, you know."

Christy and Todd gladly exchanged their happy Valentine's Day wishes for each other in a spontaneous, laughter-filled way. She was sure that both of them would remember this happy night for a long time.

They fell asleep in each other's arms and enjoyed the added luxury of sleeping in late Saturday morning. When they finally woke up, Todd suggested they go shopping.

Christy stopped in the middle of dressing and stared at him. "Did you say shopping?"

"Yeah."

"Wait. Who are you, and what did you do with my husband?"

Todd grinned. "I want to see how our benches look at the shopping center in Huntington Beach. I figured we could eat out for breakfast, I could check out the benches, and you could do some shopping."

"Okay, so it's about the benches and not the shopping. You had me confused there for a minute."

They took Christy's car instead of Gussie and stopped for breakfast at Julie Ann's. She found that being there with Todd didn't have the same feeling as being there with Tracy. Christy sipped her tea latte while Todd sat across from her, scrolling through his phone. Memories of all the times she had been here with Tracy came back and wrapped her in a sweet and sad melancholy. Christy knew she was going to miss Tracy more than she first imagined.

Once the food arrived, Christy had Todd's attention back. She posed all the questions she had been most eager to ask about his time with Alissa and her family. Todd already had said that her husband was a great guy. He played bongo drums and had a dry sense of humor. Todd said their two girls were both shy and really sweet. Alissa worked from home for a global travel agency that sold tour and cruise packages.

"Did you have a chance to ask Alissa about Shawna? Or would that have been too awkward?"

"No, it wasn't awkward at all. She was the one who brought it up. It was an open adoption, so Shawna and Alissa have seen each other a couple of times."

"Really?"

"Yeah. Shawna and her parents live in the Seattle area. A couple of years ago Shawna started asking questions. Her mom and dad decided it was time for her to read the letter Alissa wrote her, and after that it's gone well. They have regular contact. Alissa says that Shawna's adoptive parents get the credit for that."

"That's amazing. Did you see any pictures? Does Shawna look like Alissa?"

"I saw a bunch of pictures. She's blonde. I think she has Shawn's eyes." Todd finished off his bagel. "She gave Shawna my letter, too."

"Who? Alissa?"

"No, Shawna's mom. I don't remember her name."

"Wait. What letter?"

"I wrote a letter to Shawna when she was born. Or actually, I think I wrote it before she was born. I told her about Shawn so she would have a piece of a memory of her birth dad."

Christy felt deeply touched. "You wrote Shawna a letter before she was born? I didn't know that." She wondered if she should tell Todd that she had written a couple of letters to their not-yet-conceived child. It seemed best to wait, she decided.

"Shawna read my letter and said she wanted to meet me like she met Alissa. Alissa didn't know how to get a hold of me since I'm not on any social media. I told her to go ahead and give Shawna's parents our contact info. I wouldn't be surprised if we hear from her. Cool, huh?"

"Yes. Wow. I didn't think we would ever know what happened to her. How old is she now? Eleven?"

"Yeah. Or almost eleven. She was born in the spring. April, I think."

"That sounds about right. She'll be eleven in a couple of months. I'm dying to see pictures of her."

"Give Alissa a call sometime. All her info is in my phone. I guess she and Brad used to live in Pasadena. They were saying that they haven't been back to Southern California for a long time, so they might have to come down for spring break. I told them they would be welcome to stay with us." He paused, holding his coffee mug in midair. "That's okay with you, isn't it? I mean, now that the guestroom is available."

"Yes, of course. I'd love to have Alissa and her family stay here."

"Like I said, give her a call sometime. She would love to hear from you."

They left Julie Ann's Café walking hand in hand. The February morning was chilly, with a light rain falling. Christy cuddled up to Todd and loved feeling the warmth of his closeness.

"I missed you so much."

"I missed you, too."

They climbed into the car, but instead of heading for Huntington Beach, Todd turned, as if they were going home.

"Did you forget something?" Christy asked.

"No." He kept a straight face and kept driving. The earlier drizzle became rain, and Todd turned on his windshield wipers.

They came to a stoplight. The light was red. Todd put the car in Park and opened his door and got out.

"Todd, what are you doing?" Christy looked at him out the windshield. He was standing in front of their car grinning and motioning for her to come.

That's when she realized where they were. This was *their* intersection. This was where he had kissed her for the first time the summer she was fifteen.

Christy bounded out of the car. Laughing and shaking her head at her crazy husband, she kissed him vigorously in the rain.

They ran back and settled into the car just as the light turned green. Todd said, "Okay, now we can go to Huntington Beach."

"Or we could go home and change out of these wet clothes."

Todd glanced at Christy and grinned. He turned on the blinker, and they headed home.

Over the next few weeks Christy and Todd enjoyed a quiet, steady routine between work and the reclaimed haven of their home.

They repainted the living room that had taken a bruising from Daniel's toys and the months of having so many high schoolers packed into that space. When they painted the room together before they first moved in, Christy had selected a yellow color called "Tuscan Sunday." It was the same shade Marti had chosen for her bedroom, and Christy loved how it made the room feel sunny.

This time, Christy selected a color that Todd called "gray," but she called "pale silver blue." The neutral color brought out the beachy feel of her attempt to work toward a decorating theme for their home. All her months at the gift shop had influenced her tastes. She had begun to collect more seashells, starfish, and sea glass and to incorporate more ivory candles inside large glass vases, which was a decorative feature at the spa.

The end result was soothing and made their home feel more like a beach house than it had with the Mediterranean colors.

"Now I need to make some new pillow covers," Christy said when she and Todd had moved the furniture back in place. "And we should replace that floor lamp in the corner. It's been knocked over a dozen times. The shade is taped together. I'm surprised it hasn't started to crumble into pieces."

"Let's buy a new one," Todd said.

Christy folded her arms across her stomach and scrutinized the room one more time. It felt so good to know they had enough money to buy things like new lamps and fabric for pillow covers. So many wonderful, sacred, as well as painful moments had taken place in this space. Christy closed her eyes and prayed that God would bless them and this home with more. More life, more friends, more joy.

Todd put his arm around her and kissed her on the side of her head. Christy slipped her arm around his middle and rested her head on his shoulder.

"You happy?" he asked.

Christy knew he was asking if she was happy with the results of the new paint. Her answer of "Yes, very" carried more meaning than just paint. She was content. Content and ready for whatever God had next for them.

Christy's phone chimed from the kitchen counter, and she went to see who was calling her in the middle of this quiet Saturday afternoon. She read the name on the screen and immediately felt intimidated.

"It's Alissa," she called out to Todd.

"Oh, good. You guys have been trying to connect for a

while now."

"I don't know what to say." Christy held out the phone, indicating that Todd should answer the call. She suddenly felt like a teenager, showing up on the beach and being wowed like everyone else at the slender, blonde, stunning Alissa, who sauntered through the sand as if she were doing a modeling shoot.

Todd didn't seem to understand her sudden insecurities. "Aren't you going to answer it?"

Christy pressed the Accept button. "Hello?"

"Christy?"

"Yes?"

"It's Alissa. How are you? I'm so pleased that we've finally connected."

Christy felt her apprehension melt away. She took the phone out to the front deck and lowered herself into one of the beach chairs, then stretched her legs out in the sun. "I feel like we have so much to catch up on. Tell me about you. Todd said his visit with you last month was really great."

"It was. Christy, I'm so glad to have this chance for us to be back in each other's lives. If it weren't for you and Todd, I don't know where I'd be right now. The two of you have made more of a lasting impact on my life than you will ever know."

Christy wasn't sure how to respond. "I'm glad we've reconnected, too. Todd said you might be able to head this way for a vacation sometime. We would love to have you stay with us, if you would like."

"We would love that. We haven't formulated our plans for this summer yet, but Newport Beach is definitely at the top of my list. I'm sure the girls would love it, too."

They went on to talk about how Doug and Tracy were fitting in with Brad and Alissa and their circle of friends in Glenbrooke. Alissa told Christy about Shawna and their visits. She talked about adopting their two girls and a little about how she and Brad met.

Their call lasted more an hour. By the time they hung up,

Christy felt as if she had no reason to feel insecure around Alissa ever again. They were two Forever Friends, and the next time they connected, they would effortlessly pick up where they had left off.

Christy went inside and found Todd sitting at the kitchen counter working on his laptop. She gushed about how great it was to catch up with Alissa and then asked what he was working on.

Todd looked as if he had been caught with a cookie before dinner. "I wanted to wait until Jordan's guy got back to me with the final version before I told you. It's taking longer than I thought so I guess I should tell you."

"Tell me what?" Christy looked at the laptop screen and saw what looked like an article or blog posting with a photo of Bones in his early days, standing next to one of his vintage long boards.

"You know how I recorded everything Bones said when we were at his place last fall?"

"Yes."

"Well, I've been transcribing the recording and working on a story about him."

"You mean, like a book? You've been writing a book about Bones?"

"No," Todd said quickly. "Not a book. I could never write a book. It's just an article. A summary of his life. I told Jordan about it when they were here at Thanksgiving. He pitched it to a couple of editors he works with at a surfing magazine he sells photos to. The editors were interested, so I finished the piece and collected some photos from Bones. It looks like it's going to run in the August edition. Pretty cool, huh?"

"Todd, that's awesome!" She threw her arms around his neck and hugged him back and forth.

"Did you just say 'awesome'?" Todd pulled back and gave Christy a teasing look.

"Yes, I did. If Doug and Daniel aren't here anymore to fill this house with shouts of 'awesome,' then somebody needs to.

Todd, this is amazing and wonderful and so, so cool."

"Best part is, they're going to pay me."

Christy hugged him again. "We should celebrate. Let's go out to dinner somewhere."

"You won't get any resistance from me on that idea. Where do you want to go?" His expression turned playfully cloudy. "Please don't say Julie Ann's."

"Where do you want to go? Crab Cooker? Ruby's? Hansen's Parlor?"

"You're pulling out all the oldies but goodies. I was thinking Mexican food sounds good."

"You always think Mexican food sounds good." Christy kissed Todd on his scruffy cheek. "I don't care where we go. You pick the place. I'll get ready."

Christy scurried upstairs. She decided to take a quick shower. When she pulled a clean towel out of the crowded cupboard, a small box fell onto the bathroom floor. Christy picked it up and was about to jam it back into the cupboard.

She stopped. Holding the box and feeling her heart grow still, Christy waited. Thoughts of all the other times she had taken pregnancy tests crowded her mind. She remembered each time and places she had been when she had held the wand. The result was always the same. A single line that indicated a negative sign, or the words NOT PREGNANT.

Christy didn't understand why she felt compelled to take another test or why she had any reason to believe it wouldn't reveal the same result all the other tests had. The room was silent as she weighed what to do next.

The Teacher is always silent during the test. Just take the test.

Christy tore open the box and went through the steps that were now as familiar as brushing her teeth. She stood by the sink in front of the mirror with the wand in her hand. Closing her eyes, Christy made one more wish.

She counted to ten and opened her eyes.

A feathery glimmer of hope rose in her spirit. She bit her lower lip and felt her eyes fill with tears.

"Todd! Todd!" Christy caught her breath. "Todd, come here! Quick!"

She heard his footsteps bounding up the stairs. Christy looked at the wand again.

In a moment her husband would come rushing through the open bedroom door. When he did, Christy would need no words. The tears in her eyes would tell him everything.

Their lives were about to be changed forever.

Here is where it all began

Christy Miller Collection

Vol 1: Books 1-3
Vol 2: Books 4-6
Vol 3: Books 7-9
Vol 4: Books 10-12

Follow Christy and her Forever Friends on an unforgettable journey through the ups and downs of high school.

The Friendship Continues

Sierra Jensen Collection

Vol 1: Books 1-3
Vol 2: Books 4-6
Vol 3: Books 7-9
Vol 4: Books 10-12

Christy and Sierra meet in England and the adventures pick up speed in the Sierra Jensen Series.

Sierra's Story Continues in:

Love Finds You in
Sunset Beach, Hawaii

Katie Weldon Series

#1 Peculiar Treasures
#2 On a Whim
#3 Coming Attractions
#4 Finally & Forever

Katie Weldon

Join Christy's best friend, Katie, as she takes the world by storm during her final year of college.

ROBINGUNN.COM

Christy & Todd
The Married Years

For information on more books about Christy and Todd visit Robin's website at **www.robingunn.com**.

Be sure to sign up for the Robin's Nest Newsletter and you'll be the first to receive updates on future stories.

Forever With You   **Home of our Hearts**